Red Masquerade

Red Masquerade Duology

Book One

Shaye Madison

Red Masquerade

SHAYE MADISON

*To my partner, for supporting me through everything.
I love you forever.*

I am not I: thou art not he or she
    they are not they

— EVELYN WAUGH

Author's Note

Red Masquerade is a dark, gothic and erotic *The Great Gatsby*-inspired romance.

Content warnings include: misogyny and sexism, mentions of war (WWI), gore and blood, explicit sexual content, physical harm and verbal abuse by a family member (brother), sacrilegious use of an altar/church.

For a complete list, my website has all updated content notes.

shayemadisonbooks.com

Part One
Nouveau Riche

ONE

It began in a dark corner of an illegal bar, with a stranger holding my hand to his lips, smoke wafting between us and gin humming in my veins, and a fogginess in my head that I didn't mind as the stranger peeked up at me with a crooked grin. The dim lamplight cast a sickly green glow across his face, my own skin the color of absinthe, the shadows of the room rippling and mingling with the living, as the large clock upon the wall watched over us all, silent and unmoving.

"Another drink?" he asked.

I shrugged, though the smart answer would have been *No*. My blood was warm: heat in my cheeks, my legs like jelly, even though I sat lazily upon a velvet bench.

He raised his hand to get the attention of one of the bartenders, who quickly made his way over with two fresh glasses of spirits.

Though illicit, the small bar was crowded with patrons.

Couples huddled at the bar, men moving animatedly as they laughed, women in their beaded dresses fluttering their lashes. Cigarettes burned cherry-red between their painted lips as shouts cut through the carousing.

My stranger pushed one of the new glasses over to me.

"You have not yet told me your name." My fingers found the etchings in the crystal, condensation collecting on my skin.

"Brancato." He leaned back on his side of the booth. "Marcel Brancato."

There was a lilt to his words, a sort of foreign accent I couldn't place. Maybe I vaguely recognized the name—my father must have mentioned it long ago when speaking of one business deal or another. Business I cared nothing for, especially once Lucas took over.

"And I know who you are," he said, eyes shimmering.

"Oh?"

"Helena Quintrell." Saying my name on smirking lips like it was proof. Like he had won a game.

"I hope it's not a *bad* thing you recognize me." I laughed.

"Quite the opposite." Those dark eyes pierced through mine, a lock of his brown hair falling across his forehead. "I have been wanting to meet you."

He was not unattractive, and when he had first approached me, I thought that perhaps he was rather good-looking. He was clean-shaven, hair styled back and waved, his jacket unwrinkled and smart. He leaned against his chair with a casualness many of these men seemed to exude, an easiness and confidence that came only from knowing you could command the room, if only you wanted.

But already I was finding he was like every other man, his gaze dipping down to my bodice, the exposed skin of my chest, lower, thinking about how I would look on his arm, what I could do for him.

"And why is that?" I asked, sneaking a glance around the room, wondering where Flora had run off to. I knew she was somewhere with Lord Dixon, her usual beau.

It normally went this way: we would arrive to the club or bar of the evening, and shortly after, Dixon would arrive, and as though parting the Red Sea, she would run right to his arms, and I would be alone for the rest of the evening, forgotten and left to entertain whoever bought me a drink. Most often, my companions for the evening were charming, fun enough to make the night worth it. Though, every so often, a darkness lingered there in their eyes that spoke of their hunger for flesh.

We were all playing with fire, every one of us in the bar, ignoring the possibility of arrest, were the cops to find this place. Though, many cops made their way to these things after their shift. The risk added a dazzling attractiveness to everyone in the room: men who were simply average before seemed daring, women even more ethereal. "I've seen you before," Brancato said, pulling my gaze back to him. "I had to introduce myself. You really are quite beautiful."

"So you wanted to speak to me, only because I am beautiful?"

He raised a brow, that amused smile still pulling at his lips. "Can a beautiful face not precede a worthwhile conversation?"

"Hmm." I lifted my glass, though I did not take another sip. My previous drinks were already working their way through me, and the night was too young to lose my wits. "And what is it you want to speak of?"

"How you found yourself in a place like this."

"'A place like this?'"

He didn't answer, waiting for me to continue.

"Well, what brings you here?"

For a moment, I did not think he would answer, those dark eyes unnerving. A man hadn't made me so flustered with his attention in quite some time. But after a breath, he adjusted in his seat. "I'm new to the city. Wanted to see all that New York has to offer."

I tilted the glass, deciding to hell with it, adding more fuel to the fire in my belly, the liquor burning my throat.

"Funny, isn't it, fate?"

I couldn't stop the unladylike snort that came out of me. "What?"

He shrugged. "You and I, in the same place at the same time. Feels like fate, to me."

"Is it?" His image once more wavered, green and smoky under the lamplight. I blinked, feeling the telltale warmth in my chest, my legs. "How many girls have you seduced with that one?"

"Would you believe me if I said I did not flirt with girls at bars often?"

"Sure. Because men who *don't* frequent bars would know how to find a speakeasy."

He smirked. "I have my ways."

And there was that darkness, a directness in his stare that set warning bells ringing in my ears. He crossed his arms, leaning his elbows on the table with no regard for propriety, lifting his own glass and letting his wrist dangle. The amber liquid swirled.

I hummed again, letting my eyes wander once more across the sea of people. *Where was Flora?*

Brancato was the kind of man who had a name to hide behind, and no doubt his father's checkbook, too. An inheritance. And though Lucas left cash for Mother and me, paid our staff and covered our tabs at dressers and salons, I was mostly left in the dark. I had an *allowance*.

Marcel, I knew by the way he gazed across the table at me, had *money*.

Freedom.

"We should meet again. Though, perhaps, elsewhere."

The table next to us exploded in laughter, the woman reaching over to the man across from her, flinging over her drink in the action. Frizzy, over-processed blonde hair in a near-halo around her head, wire-thin brows drawn on in a dark line. A cacophony of giggled apologies. Some of the splash hit the tops of my feet.

Brancato grimaced, lips pulling back in a hint of disgust. "Somewhere less... loud."

"And where would you take me?" I asked, dabbing at the spill on my skin.

"To dinner. I am staying in Midtown and have been told of a few nearby spots that I *must* try. I'd prefer to do it with you."

I imagined another evening with this man, with his glancing eyes, his haughtiness. I *could* entertain him. At the very least, I'd get dinner, some time away from the house, perhaps even a whirlwind romance over the course of a few hours.

That's what we were all after, wasn't it? Chasing the pleasure we could draw from each other in the shortest amount of time possible, before we went on in the daylight like nothing happened.

But with him—no, something about him was unsettling, like he was looking for something, after *more*.

"No?" he asked. I hadn't realized I'd shaken my head at the thought.

Dark brows furrowed, but after a moment, the corner of his lips lifted. Some girls played hard to get, and some men liked it. I was not one of those girls, but he seemed to think so.

"I—that's not what I meant." My cheeks warmed, though whether from the alcohol or from my nonsense, I didn't know. "I think—"

"Great," he said. "Should I fetch you tomorrow evening?"

"Oh." I blinked. "You misunderstand."

He laughed, white teeth shining, his skin pale and sickly, a trick of the light. "Come now," he said. "Just one night, and we'll see where it goes."

"We had tonight to get to know each other," I said, firming my voice as much as possible. "But maybe we'll run into each other again?" I made to stand.

"Oh, *I* see," he said, leaning back further into his seat. "You're one of *those* girls?"

"And what does that mean?"

His gaze wandered around me again, eyeing my neckline, my chest. "Come on, we can be honest with each other. You came here, wanting certain things, and I came here, wanting the same. And here we are, together."

The chair beneath me screeched as I stood, but the bar was so loud, it hardly disturbed the scene. The blonde and her men next to us were still caught up in their conversation, one of them with their face buried in her neck.

"Don't presume, Mr. Brancato," I said.

"You don't have to pretend with me, Helena." And I saw the darkness in his eyes spread.

Shivers ran down my back at the way he said my name.

I turned on my heel. "Thanks for the drinks."

It felt all made-up, then, how we happened to run into each other, Marcel and I, complete strangers not thirty minutes prior. A bump of shoulders. A charming smile and an offer for company, a glass of gin that never emptied.

"Helena!"

A sudden grip on my arm, long nails lightly digging into my flesh, as Flora emerged from the smoke, Dixon in tow. My eyes met his brown ones immediately, and though I said nothing, with one glance at my evening partner, he seemed to understand my wariness. He scowled at the man before slinging an arm over Flora's shoulders.

Flora, bubbly and drunk, didn't notice a thing.

"We lost track of time." She beamed at me, her cheeks flushed. "We have to go now if we don't want to be too late."

"Go?"

She giggled. "You know," she said, slipping away from Dixon and wrapping her arms around me. Her lavender perfume surrounded us like a cloud. "That one party—the house on Long Island!"

She'd mentioned it earlier, on the way to the bar. One of the new-money men on the island threw parties—and we *had* to go.

Anything to get away from the dark stare I felt boring into my spine.

"Who is he?" she asked, shouting in a whisper, one hand covering her mouth as though to conceal it.

"Marcel Brancato." I rolled my eyes as we disappeared into the crowd of revelers.

A woman, dancing, jolted into me, but quickly spun away, knocking into other people as she went, laughing open-mouthed, her hand in a man's. I inhaled a deep lungful of smoke, my throat dry, coughing, my head spinning. We passed a man holding a cigar, his face heavenward, exhaling through his nostrils and lips like a beast, the smoke curling toward the ceiling like another dancer.

There was another man, one I had flirted with previously, that held my eyes as we neared the door to the joint, sipping on his own drink, a spark of jealousy in his eyes. I couldn't remember his name. For only a moment, I wondered if he had seen me with Marcel, but then dismissed the thought, because why would it matter?

I hadn't chosen *either* of them.

Looking away, I still felt his stare searing into me, too; too many stares, too many eyes following me.

Starving eyes, demanding.

"It appears we saved you just in time," Flora said, her lips brushing my ear, the teasing lilt of music in her voice.

I nodded absently. "Yes."

"Don't worry." Her hand on my arm was comforting and familiar, grounding me. "Tonight is about having *fun*. I will not let anyone ruin your fun, doll."

"The night isn't ruined." I gave her my best smile.

"Perfect!" Her hand tightened on mine before she spun

around. "And now to make it even better, we'll dance until our legs fall off and drink until we're flying!"

With that, she whisked me onto the street, away from the insatiable hunger and excess of the speakeasy, away from the wandering, insistent stares, and into the open night.

Two

As though our spirits were not tied to our bodies, there was a sense of weightlessness on the lawn of the grand house. Champagne—real champagne—flowed, glasses towered into pyramids atop golden tables, liquid shining like the ichor of the gods.

We certainly believed that if we drank more, we were that much closer to divinity.

Dixon, Flora, and I had arrived on the teeming lawn minutes to midnight, arms linked, stumbling out of his Duesenberg, which he parked expertly amongst a row of similarly gleaming and polished vehicles.

The man was forgotten as soon as the cool night air hit our skin.

It was strange, the combination of stares, of curious attention, and the sense of anonymity.

As we made our way to the house, my heels sinking, the soft grass caressing my ankles, I thought perhaps we had stepped onto some sort of stage set.

"Helena! Look!" Flora clutched me tighter when the house finally erupted from the trees.

Every window lit, dazzling against the black of the midnight sky. The white columns of the house appeared as bright as though it were midday, gas lamps illuminating the porch, strings of lights hung over the lawn, their bulbs mingling with the stars, flickering, glowing softly, glimmering like fireflies. Crafted from stone, spires reached upward, stabbing through low-hanging clouds.

Though, it was not simply a house.

"It's a church." Flora's voice was steeped in wonder.

"Who wants to live in an old church?" I said, my eyes swimming. "What if there are ghosts—"

My toe caught on a stone step, and I was falling—but Dixon was there immediately, grabbing my arm. He held on firmly until I got my feet under me.

"Thanks." I laughed.

He lifted a brow and sighed, steering us down the path toward the front of the house—*church*—before answering my question. "Vince Thornton, that's who."

"Vince Thornton?"

"Of course you know him." Flora rolled her eyes.

"I don't *know* him," Dixon said. "He—his name is *persistent* in our circles."

Vince Thornton. Odd and commanding on my tongue as I repeated the words. "Who is he?"

"No one."

"Well, that's not true," Flora said. She gestured to the party surrounding us on the lawn—no doubt spilled out from the real revelry inside. "It's not just '*no one*' who can manage this."

At that moment a server swooped by, light on his feet, somehow carrying a tray of impossibly full glasses and never spilling a drop. He stopped momentarily to offer us a drink.

Dixon, gentleman that he was, grabbed two of the glasses and promptly handed them to Flora and me without taking one for himself, before ushering us on.

Heaven burst on my tongue. A heady warmth traveled down my throat, across my shoulders, settling in my bones. Easing my tension, carrying away the strange feelings left behind by my conversation with Brancato.

"Trust me," Dixon said. "It's not worth thinking about Thornton for a second."

"Kind of hard not to," Flora said, linking her arm with his. "Look at this place!"

The speakeasy couldn't hold a candle to the party at this mansion.

I'd lived in the city my whole life and never knew of this place. We had attended many parties in the area, but it was as if this particular house had sprouted from the ground, growing like the forest of trees around it. Lost to time until its new benefactor brought the mansion back to life.

The exterior glowed like a palace from the heavens. Everyone on the lawns was dressed in their best—flapper girls with short skirts, straight hems, and strings of beads flying around them; other women and men in their evening dresses and suits, pressed and steamed and ironed as though they'd jumped right off an Arrow Collar ad. Gelled and wavy hair, cigarettes on long holders, deep rouge on the cheeks of the girls, indistinguishable from liquor-flushed skin.

Many times, I almost lost Flora and Dixon, having fallen

behind, unable to look away from the behemoth we approached.

As we entered the house, my neck ached with the urge to look upward, to gaze at the painted ceiling of the foyer. Cherubim, devils, angels, gods, all twined together, an image perhaps a century old but seemingly so fresh I could reach up and smear the paint. The figures watched as we entered, devils with complexions gray bordering on pitch black, figures with horns and tails and bat-like wings. Their roped muscles were splattered with blood, crimson and bright against their dark flesh. They grabbed at the angels with feathered wings, snatched them right out of the sky, dragged them downward. I could not look away from these hellish beings with fangs and claws, snarling with delight, while the beneficent gods watched in deadly apathy.

"Helena!"

I was pulled from my stupor as Flora grabbed the bones of my wrist and scolded me like a child. "Don't get lost! I'll never be able to find you again."

And she was right—the place was so large, hundreds of people crowded in, she could lose me in the blink of an eye.

The ballroom before us was an explosion of light and laughter. "Ballroom" wasn't the right word—because it was perhaps the congregation room, yet was so expansive it was impossible that we were in a house, and that a man lived here on his own. A massive chandelier hanging from the ceiling glittered with electric bulbs, red ribbons streaming down and across to the banisters of the grand staircase that crawled up each wall and met on the far side of the room. Each step was packed with people, women clinging to their man's arms, the men shouting above the noise to hear each other, drinks in hand.

Flora easily slipped her grip from me, back to Dixon's elbow again, sending me a wink.

I envied them.

Dixon was a viscount, come from England for "business ventures"—that is, taking advantage of the money there was to gain in American prohibition. Flora, no higher in class than I, had somehow snared him at a party a few months prior, and now, as soon as they were in the same room, they were inseparable. Of course, this did not stop her from entertaining other men in the meantime.

I longed for the consistency of a companion such as Dixon, of the advantages of falling in with a British man with a title—someone who could whisk me away from the city, from my mother, from Lucas.

I used to joke with them that perhaps Dixon could set me up with one of his business partners, or anyone, really, from across the sea. None of these men, not Marcel nor the other dozen I had given the time of day could even compare. We were all the same—new money, wealth acquired that had not yet gone very far, families masquerading as the effortlessly rich names we heard often from overseas.

We were all wearing masks, playing as people we were not.

The room was packed from wall to wall, men smoking, some women even, the smoke curling and dancing like the girls peppering the floor. The faint sound of stringed instruments and a horn, a trumpet, hidden somewhere out of my sight. Girls moving so quickly, their feet never seemed to touch the floor. Men slinging them around, twirling them into other partygoers, bouncing off each other like Dodgems.

The center of the room held all the revelers, the people lost to the bliss of it all—and along the walls were those who seemed entirely too sober. A more grim party seemed to take place at the edges of the room: appraising eyes, watching those spin with ecstasy in the center, sipping their glasses calmly, whispering amongst each other. Observers. A few snickering, amused, smiling at the stray girl whirling with her man and shrieking in delight.

I plucked a marzipan sweet off a server's tray as they passed, never looking at who they were serving, only where they were going next, a dullness to their eyes, their faces plain, empty. Perhaps exhaustion. I had heard these parties happened weekly, and some weeks, even nightly. Throughout the summer, slowly waning in the deep winter, picking up again in the new year, with spring right around the corner.

How had we not attended one of these extravaganzas before?

Everyone was talking about it this year: the mansion up on the hill, the mansion that used to be a church, of all things, and the man that lived within, throwing lavish parties where you could be anyone, meet anyone, and get drunk doing it.

Lucas would hate it here. He would hate that *I* was here.

Smiling into my glass, I let the bubbly champagne simmer, almost burning, for a moment before popping the sweet on my tongue.

Yes, Lucas would hate this.

All the more reason to do it.

"Oh, Dixon, look!" Flora pointed from behind me.

A woman, dressed in nothing but wide ribbons wrapped around her breasts and the widest part of her waist, streaming down her legs, stood atop a table in the center of the room. Her hair was wrapped up on her head, the blood-red ribbons laced throughout, brown locks twisted and knotted atop her skull. Her lips were painted the same dark, bleeding red, her brows lined, a streak of kohl like wings at her eyes.

My champagne-addled brain thought for a moment she seemed to turn to one of the winged devils.

Men whistled, women gawked. Outstretched hands reached for her, wanting to touch the nearly naked woman above the crowd. She drew all eyes in the room, gazing upon the crowd below, the corner of her mouth lifted in a smirk. Moving elegantly, limbs gliding from one position to the next, her hips slithered from side to side like a serpent, red ribbons threatening to expose her to the room.

She motioned to the band, who had quieted amongst the ruckus, and who then began to play a cabaret tune.

Glancing back to my friends, I saw Flora entranced, eyes wide and gleaming. Her mouth hung open, hand still clutching Dixon's arm, as though she feared she'd fall over in her hypnosis.

Dixon met my eyes briefly, unreadable.

"What, are you scandalized?" I teased.

But he didn't laugh with me, and I realized why a second later. He wasn't looking at the beauty standing atop the table; his gaze went past her, tracking the movements of a line of people, cloaked in the same blood-red color, making their way up the stairs, behind the revelers gawking at the banisters.

"What—"

A few of the observers at the edges of the room followed behind, and I realized they too wore the deep red cloaks, until each and every one had faded into the crowd, disappearing around the bend of the landing above.

Stranger things had happened at these kinds of parties, I supposed.

I brought my glass to my lips again, about to turn to Dixon, when once more my attention was stolen.

The carousing continued, shouts directed at the near-naked woman towering above the crowd. She moved sinuously to the band, though the music was nearly swallowed up again by the noise of the partygoers. She writhed, hands wandering on her body, coy and demure as she made sure every man around her had her attention.

I had the distant thought that perhaps it was intentional, her arrival and the sneaking of the cloaked people behind the crowd.

But I was entranced by a different figure.

High above it all, a man, easy to miss, standing upon the balcony. Hands splayed out on the banister, his head turned, so I saw only his profile. I could not see his features, just that his hair was long and dark, and there was a sobering look about him as he gazed down upon his revelers. A true king of his court, feeding the masses, giving them their bread and circuses.

Vince Thornton.

And somehow, like there was no one else in the room, his eyes found mine. I could feel it, deep inside me, like he had shot an arrow straight at me. His eyes cut through me, dissected me.

I gasped.

A harsh grab to my arm. Dixon pulled me out of the reverie. "We should leave."

"Leave?" Flora gasped. "It's not even that late! We just got here!"

I opened my mouth to retort, but it died on my tongue.

Dixon dragged us off immediately.

I felt entirely like I had just seen a ghost.

Felt it in my bones that I had looked up at a dead man.

No, it couldn't be—

And when I peeked over my shoulder once more, that man was gone. Eaten up by the crowd, as though he were a wraith and had never existed at all.

THREE
SIX YEARS AGO

We collided on a street corner.

I was waiting for my family's driver to pick me up. He was walking home from work. And we collided like two suns on that sidewalk, forever trapped in each other's orbit.

I did not know then that it would become what they call a whirlwind romance. I didn't know how he'd worm his way into my heart.

He was disheveled. A smear of dirt on his cheek, a tiredness to his eyes that only darkened to disdain when he saw how nicely I was dressed, how clean I was. Derision for the purse at my wrist, the crisp dress I wore, the short heels.

But I only laughed and watched as confusion, then relief, fell upon him, when I did not shout.

I could see how attractive he was, even under his hard exterior. His hair was a dark brown that shone red in the sunlight, and there were creases at the corners of his light hazel eyes when he tentatively returned my smile. He took off his cap, strands of his hair falling in his eyes.

"Apologies."

"Don't apologize!" I insisted. "I should have been watching where I was going."

I wasn't sure what it was about him; he was perhaps ordinary in every way, except for that we'd run into each other.

His eyes roved over me, taking note of my dress, my shawl, my curled hair. The white gloves covering my fingers.

A man of his station would be expected to defer to me. To take the blame, to take the verbal lashing I should throw at him. He expected it.

But I would never; I wasn't Lucas, and I wasn't my mother.

"Both a bit caught up in our heads, then, yes?" he said. His accent was rounder, curling around my neck and my ears as he spoke. His fingers were stained in black—grease? Ink? —with smudges on his trousers about where his hands would reach, as though he wiped his fingers as he worked.

Of course he worked.

And then I had the mortifying thought—what if he was employed in one of our factories?

My cheeks reddened with a peculiar embarrassment. What if he already knew who I was?

"What do you do?"

I only ever saw Lucas with his starched suits and clean hands.

His eyes widened in surprise. "I'm an apprentice," he said, glancing down at his dirty hands, as if he was only then realizing his skin was stained. "For a printer."

"A printer? Like newspapers and such?"

He nodded skeptically. "Books, too. Pamphlets sometimes."

"So, you must read a lot." I smiled.

And then he smiled back, a dimple appearing at one cheek that sent my heart fluttering. "I do."

Completely oblivious to the bustle of the street, we stood there as cars and carriages passed, mothers with their children, working men in the same state as the young man before me, tired and hobbling home. But he, this man before me, still had a vigor that straightened his shoulders, brightened his eyes.

I sighed and looked out on the street. The scent of roasted coffee wafted toward us from a cafe across the street. A stand with candies and fresh cakes and pastries was stationed nearby, gathering school children on their way home. A florist stood with a wooden cart full of their blooming bouquets out of the way of traffic.

"I used to read," I said. "I haven't found the time recently."

It wasn't entirely true. I had not read much since my tutoring was completed, but I remembered what I did read fondly: some books recommended by my dashing tutor Samson, and many others I had to hide from Mother. Literature she thought would only lead me to debauchery—Ethan Frome, Dubliners—but they were fascinating to me all the same.

Perhaps, if I had not been so caught up with the society parties, with seeing Flora and spending our days out and about, I would've read more.

"That's a shame," the young man said simply, his voice soft.

I thought he would offer to bring me some recommendations, if only to see me again—it played out quite romantically in my head.

"You never told me your name." I turned back to him.

That easy smile still pulled at his lips. "You didn't tell me yours.".

I held out my hand after slipping off a glove. "Helena Quintrell."

"Adam Vering."

Hesitantly, his eyes widening at my bare hand, his rough palm encased mine softly, like he thought me fragile. The moment our fingers touched, a shiver trailed down my spine. Like I was doing something scandalous, something I wasn't supposed to do. I didn't care if the ink stained my own skin. It would be a story to tell Mother: how I'd met a working man on the street and shook his hand.

He didn't let go at first, and a part of me didn't want him to.

We stood like that for a moment, hand in hand. Could he read me like a book? Did he know everything about me just by looking at me? By touching me?

A blush bloomed across his cheeks, the dimple appearing and disappearing, and he glanced at the ground, pulling his hand away and shoving them into the pockets of his trousers.

My hand came away clean, the ink on his flesh having dried long ago.

"Adam Vering." I tried the name out, letting it roll off my tongue.

"Helena..." My own sounded like golden, hot caramel from his lips. Indulgent cream and berries.

My last name dropped. *Quintrell.*

My father's name, and his father's, and so on. Not wholly mine.

But I was wholly me, completely Helena.

"Do you make a habit of running into girls on the street?" I asked.

Calculation behind those hazel eyes. "Not normally, but perhaps I should."

"You'd run into any woman?"

"Not any woman."

He looked at me directly, intensely, through his lashes. But he didn't move closer, his hands rooted in his pockets.

In the span of a few seconds, I imagined what he was like at home. I imagined what we could become before I scolded myself—he was just a boy on the street, and I had met plenty of boys before. None that Lucas liked, or let me speak to, but even still. My mind went wandering, conjuring up a future that would likely never be.

Oh, Flora would want to hear about this on the telephone later. We had a new shiny receiver that Lucas had bought, so I didn't have to wait until the next day to speak to Flora anymore.

Mistaking my silence for disinterest, Adam's smile faltered. He glanced past me at the crowd across the street, as though in that mass of people were directions for his next move. "I fear I've kept you," he said, replacing his cap. "Miss Quintrell."

"No!" I reached out to grab his arm, but froze at the look on his face. As soon as he walked away, that would be that, and he'd be gone forever. I'd never find him in this big city. "You haven't kept me."

I floundered over my words, feeling like a little girl all over again. But I couldn't help it, not under his gaze like that.

He exhaled a laugh, and I felt ridiculous.

"You—do you work near here?" I asked.

He nodded, lifting a thumb over his shoulder. "On Exbury Street. We're the only printer there."

"Okay," I said, committing it to memory.

"Why, you want to come watch us work?"

"I—Can I?" The thought of him caught up in his work, smearing ink on his face absentmindedly, the strength in those arms, putting all his weight against the press, those fingers on delicate paper. I blushed.

"I don't see why not." He swallowed. "I can... I can save one of the books we're printing for you. That is, if you want me to—"

I nodded, not realizing how close I'd drifted to him. But the way those hazel eyes flickered to mine—I didn't think he minded.

"How far is your house?" he asked, forcing casualness into his voice. "I can walk you. It seems your driver is taking a while."

I'd hear all about it later. How irresponsible it was of me to walk home with a strange boy; how rude of me to leave while the driver was on the way, and how he wouldn't have known I'd taken an alternative route home.

I didn't care.

Grinning, I told him our address and let him lead the way. At the next street corner, he looked left and right, giving me an opportunity to study the strong profile of his nose, straight, like a Roman god, cheekbones striking under the tan skin of his face. An angular jaw with the dusting of a shadow. His auburn hair curled under the edges of his hat, messy after a day of moving around.

God, if Mother knew I was even thinking of a boy, she'd lock me in the house.

He caught me staring and grinned, offering me his arm. "Do I have something on my face?"

I shook my head, averting my gaze to the ground. "No, not at all." Tucking my hand into his elbow, he stepped down into the street and led me around the traffic, stopping when cars seemed not to slow down for us.

The streets of the city used to terrify me as a child, but as I grew older, Lucas made fun of me for it, going so far as to push me out in front of a carriage. I had enough time to move out of the way, but it only put me further in the street, and at that point I'd been shouted at so many times, I could do nothing but cross and cry once I got to the pavement across from our house. Lucas only laughed, and when Mother asked why I refused to move, he said I must have wandered off. When she sent him to fetch me, his fingers had dug into my arm, leaving little purple bruises.

Adam's hold on me was gentle, his hand sitting atop mine. "Let's hope no one recognizes us."

"And why not?"

He leaned in just slightly, so he could lower his voice. "Because you're holding on to me like I'm your lover."

I gasped, nearly pulling away, because he was right—the way our fingers nearly intertwined, anyone would think we were familiar with each other. And here I was, in my crisp day dress, and he in his work clothes.

But I didn't pull away. "Well, it's none of their business."

"Do you have a boyfriend?" Adam asked, turning onto a different block. We were nearing my street, and the passersby began staring at us more, gazes lingering.

"No." I kept my eyes forward, refusing to look at any of them. Maybe they wouldn't notice me, wouldn't spread any talk that would make its way to Mother.

Adam hummed. "Then no one is calling on you."

I bit my lip to keep from smiling. "Why, do *you* want to call on me?" Nervousness nearly had me covering my face with my gloved hand. "Mother would never let you."

He paused, a crease forming between his brows. "No, I suppose not," he said, acknowledging the fundamental differences between him and I. The differences that every other person on that sidewalk noticed as they sneered at him, at our joined hands. "Though I *suppose* I could do it, anyway."

His words sent a thrill through me. No boys I'd spoken to at those seasonal functions ever spoke this way—there was a way to do it, rules we had to follow. Calling on each other under the guidance of our mothers and fathers, and if we liked each other enough, perhaps they'd let us go to the next dance together. A stilted politeness, a script we all followed, ensured the utmost propriety.

Maybe Adam didn't know the rules. Maybe he was used to falling in with girls.

"But—have you had any girlfriends?"

He glanced at me and laughed. "Would it bother you if I had?"

"No, of course not. I just met you."

The mirth didn't leave his eyes. He let go of my arm, only to keep holding my hand as he came to a stop in front of me. We were face to face, inches apart, and he loomed over me, a good few inches taller than me. I hadn't realized it, but we'd walked blocks and were outside the short gate to the walk up my family's townhouse.

Mother or Lucas could be watching through a window.

But all thoughts left me as he lifted my hand to his lips, and I finally got to feel that stubble against my skin. I couldn't move as he pressed a kiss to the tops of my fingers, never shutting his eyes, never looking away from me. I almost melted there on the pavement.

"I hope to see you again, Helena," he said, gently dropping my hand.

The absence of his touch felt like ice water down my back.

"You will," I whispered, and those eyes lingered on me before he turned and strolled back down the street, like he'd never been there to begin with.

FOUR

One moment, I'm soaring—red ribbons, the taste of wine, the feeling of someone holding me, all reeling through my mind—and in the next, all pretense of dreams were ripped away with the shoving of curtains, the expulsion of darkness from my bedroom. I was abruptly awakened by the maid, rousing me from sleep with the sudden light filling the room. My eyes snapped open to a blinding brightness that sent spears of pain through my head.

"*God*—" Hands flying to my face, shielding myself from the shooting pain, I pressed my fingers into my eyes.

"Good morning, Miss Helena," the maid said, setting a tray of coffee on my vanity. The ceramic rattled. "Long evening?"

"What time is it?"

"Oh, only half past eleven. Your mother is waiting for you in the sitting room."

I groaned. "Of course."

"You're lucky she let you sleep this late."

I scowled at the maid, a young girl, not much younger than myself, who had only been in the house a couple of months. Due to the nearness of our ages, she seemed to think she could speak so casually to me. And I didn't correct her, because someone who was willing to speak plainly was refreshing nowadays.

Her dress was ironed so there were no wrinkles, the black fabric starched, the apron over her skirts unstained. Her dark, curly hair was braided into a knot at the base of her neck. She shrugged at my sour expression. "I only speak the truth, Miss."

"I know," I sighed, feeling the ache in my muscles. I didn't remember returning home. My memories of the last evening were foggy—no doubt thanks to the gin and champagne—but I knew I danced with a man—almost did *more*. Brancato, was it?—and eventually, Flora and Dixon had corralled me back into the Duesenberg. A line of red, a snake, a dancing woman. Writhing bodies, moving together in tandem, and shouts, and spilt liquor, and a red substance that stained the floor and moved under my shoes, flooding inch by inch until it crawled up the walls.

The whole evening played in my mind over the course of a few seconds. I remembered spinning, the shattering of glass, raucous laughter. The smell of cigars tickled my nose, like I was still there in that grand foyer. The feeling of Brancato's stare. Frustration.

And the gaze of one of those demons on the ceiling—or, not a demon, a stranger—his stare intense even across the crowd.

I could not distinguish between what was real and what was a dream.

Soon overpowered by the pounding of my skull, I covered my face with a silk pillow to drown out the sunlight. "Tell Mother I'll be down in twenty minutes," I told the maid. I didn't hear a response, but in a few moments, the door clicked, and I was alone.

We sat in tense silence, the sitting room's air thick enough to sever with one of the serving knives.

I had managed to make myself up, to brush through my hair and pinch some color into my cheeks, before coming down the stairs. My head still pounded, the light still too bright for my poor eyes.

"What's wrong with you?" Mother sat across from me, gaze piercing and critical. Her voice was loud and cutting, shrill to my ears.

I forced a smile. "Nothing's wrong."

"You look ill."

"I'm alright." Though I would've gladly continued to sleep the day away.

She scoffed and shook her head to herself. "Where were you last night?"

"At a dinner club." The lie came smoothly, as it always did, slipping easily off my tongue. "With Flora and Lord Dixon."

"Until the early hours?"

I fought an incriminating blush. Mother always went to bed not long after dusk, since Father had passed and Lucas had left, so I never thought to worry about how much she noticed about my comings and goings.

My fingers found a loose thread at my skirt's hem. "We lost track of time."

Mother sat embroidering, weaving the needle back and forth. Though her gaze was on her task, I knew it was just to look anywhere else but at me. To avoid looking at her daughter. A small voice within me told me she could sense every lie, as though my mind were wide open, hers to read.

I picked at the cucumber sandwiches before us, as though trying to pick just the right one, when really my stomach rolled.

I will never drink again.

"Young women should not be out that late," she said. "*Polite* young women."

I plucked a sandwich from the platter. "Everybody goes out at night, Mother. I don't think anyone would look down upon—"

"I assure you, people speak." Her hands moved furiously at her cloth, her brow furrowed in concentration. She had some stray grays that escaped her braid, frizzy and framing her face.

"Why, has someone said something about me?"

Skimming through memories for each salacious, indulgent evening—surely she wouldn't know about *those*. The time I'd let that one particular charmer take me into a dark corner and had to wear scarves for the next week. The one party we'd gone to at a rooftop pool and everyone jumped in with nothing but their underthings.

There couldn't be that many eyes around the city. Not trained on *me*, of all people, waiting to report back to Mother, or, worse, Lucas. Ready to spread the latest rumors about the sister to *Lucas Quintrell, heir extraordinaire.*

Mother glanced up at me, gray stare pointed and direct. Fingers paused at their task. "No."

My shoulders relaxed. "Well, then, why worry?"

My teeth ached. The room nearly spun, the sunlight streaming in the windows still just too bright.

Why worry, indeed.

"*Because*, Helena, no respectable man would choose a wife who could not control her whims. Who was the topic of much... *debate*." Her fingers began once again, picking up speed, moving deftly along the thread.

Lord Dixon would. He chose Flora. At least, for now. He did not seem too concerned about marriage, and neither did she. She hadn't mentioned as much to me, but I couldn't say she would refuse if he offered, not with those deep coffers.

"Mother, you worry too much."

"I do not worry *enough*."

I often wondered if Mother thought we were still in the nineteenth century, if Victoria was still queen across the sea, and our biggest problems were trains and smog and how long it would take for a letter to be delivered. A life that lived with the sunlight, dying with the darkness.

The same era in which she met Father. I did not know much about their romance, or lack thereof. Only that he courted her, the "proper" way, and that they had Lucas not long after their wedding, then me, a few years later. And from that point on, they never slept in the same room again.

Is that what she wanted for me? A loveless consummation, children born into a house with love most definitely lost, a male patriarch who found affection elsewhere?

She would never admit it, but the years before Father's

death, their disdain for each other was no longer kept to their private chambers. We saw him less and less, especially in the evenings, and when he passed, Mother wouldn't tell me where he'd been found.

The next morning, the papers read—*Quintrell Family Business To Pass On To Heir*. Then the rumors began.

And here Mother was, stuck at home with her frivolous daughter, spending her days embroidering away, having ladies over for tea, waiting with bated breath for any word from her dearest son, the heir of that company now. Her star-child.

"It's the twentieth century, now, Mother," I said, taking the tiniest sip of tea. I winced again. *Not* Earl Grey.

"You can flout all you want about being *modern*, but I'm telling you," her hands moved the thread and needle furiously, "it *matters*."

A sigh brushed past my lips again.

"I never had to worry about Lucas," she muttered.

I lowered my teacup, watching her fingers move. Deftly, they wove over and under in a complicated dance.

Red thread, ribbons, a pale limb.

His *face*.

My breath caught. The sudden tightening of my throat, the pinch at the corners of my eyes.

It had to have been a gin-induced dream. A memory come to haunt me. It was a face I hadn't looked upon in years, one I'd tried hard not to forget, but to set aside for later. For when I was ready to think about it again, to think on all the good I'd once had.

It was impossible that he was there last night. It was a trick of my mind. A champagne hallucination.

"Are you listening to me?"

Setting down my teacup, the ceramic tinkling against its saucer, I forced my lips back into a smile. "Of course."

"No one's going to want a wife who can't listen, either, Helena."

"Well, then, perhaps I won't marry." The words nearly snapped out of me, despite knowing better.

"Don't be ridiculous. Of course you'll marry."

We'd had this conversation so many times, I may as well have read from a script.

"Every respectable woman marries."

"Can I not be respectable *and* stay unmarried?"

Mother looked exasperated. "*No*, Helena." She set her fabric down on the table and stared at me for a moment. I couldn't read her—couldn't read anything in the furrow of her dark brow, the dullness of her gray eyes, other than a deep tiredness that had become a disease. A tiredness for not only me, but *everything*.

The woman she was, the woman she wanted me to be, was killing her with exhaustion.

"What is it you want?" she demanded.

I blinked. "What?"

She scowled even further, if that was possible. "You always refuse. No matter what I say, you have to fight it."

"Perhaps we're just different people," I said gently.

She shook her head, and I didn't know if it was a refusal of my answer or further exasperation. "You must have some goal, then. What is it?"

"A goal?"

"Yes. To be so... *contrary*."

"You think I'm contrary?"

"Yes," she said again. "You've always been this way."

I crossed my arms, feeling a sudden chill in the room, the window open just a crack. The breeze from outside raced down my arms, lifting a curl off my cheek. I stood, making my way over to the window so I could look at anything other than her.

If I've always been this way, then why do you try to change me?

"I'm sorry we cannot be in agreement, then," I said, but I wanted to take the words back almost immediately, because no, I *wasn't* sorry. I wasn't sorry that I liked to spend my evenings with Flora and Dixon, and whoever else we found. I wasn't sorry that I wanted to experience what the night had to offer. I *liked* flirting, grabbing a man's attention for the night, making him so absolutely mad with his want for me that he'd think about me for days. I *liked* when my feet ached because I couldn't stop dancing the night before. I liked coming home at all hours, because when the sky turned just a slightly lighter shade of indigo, the night coming to its end, *that* was when it was most quiet, *that* was when a person was the most honest they could ever be.

I was just sorry that she wanted me to change.

"It doesn't matter," she said, her voice a little more resigned.

"It doesn't?" I turned toward her. She was again focusing on her fingers, her brow arched in concentration.

"No. Your brother will remedy this situation"

I wanted to laugh. "Lucas?"

"He is coming at the end of the week." *To straighten* you *out,* she left unsaid.

My stomach instantly dropped, the breath sucked out of me. "But—surely he's busy. He doesn't need to come—"

"He will be staying with us for the next few weeks, and in the meantime, I expect you to remain at home." Her focus broke from her task, so the glare turned on me, pinning me with those eyes, nailing my feet to the floor. "*With your family.*"

Blood rushed to my ears, and a chasm opened up within me. The emptiness in my chest I tried so hard to disguise, to hide. "You cannot expect me to just never leave the house." I almost laughed because it was so ridiculous. Like I was a criminal. Untamable.

"That is exactly what I expect."

My hands curled into fists, my nails digging into the flesh of my palm, the biting pain anchoring me. My vision blurred. "So you summon him because you feel you can't control me?"

"That is *exactly* why I summoned him. I did something right with him, and as the head of the family, he needs to know you cannot be left to your own devices."

I laughed drily, wishing my fingers were claws that could puncture my skin, bring blood to the surface.

Red thread, ribbons, his *eyes. He was there, he found you, he found you.*

He found *you.*

"If we do not figure you out, Helena, what future do you have?"

I didn't want to hear it anymore. I left the room without a reply, heart pounding against my ribcage, my eyes burning, teeth nearly biting through my lip, and I could not catch my breath.

FIVE

It became difficult to control the path of my thoughts. Flora had invited me to a small dinner party that she and Dixon were attending that evening, as their plus one. I immediately said yes, because I did not think I could stay in that house for one more second, knowing my mother stewed in her rooms, eagerly awaiting the arrival of her son, and I could do nothing but sit in *my* room and glare at the reflection in the mirror.

I'd grown older, I noticed, and tried to push the thought away.

I didn't want to remember.

Six years older, in fact.

I sat at my vanity, and the clock on my wall chimed at the hour, its incessant *tick, tick, tick*ing reminding me of every further second that passed.

Flora and Dixon would arrive in half an hour.

The woman staring back at me was not the girl I once was, six years ago. My hair had been longer, still the same ebony color, but twisted into braids and knots at my neck. My eyes used to be brighter—

He always said they reminded him of decadent chocolate from overseas; dark, rich, amber honey.

But now they dulled, and there were shadows under my eyes I hadn't noticed before. A symptom of too much drink the night before?

I had chopped all my hair off so that it sat in curls, brushing my ears, my jaw. The day I'd done it, Mother nearly wept.

I had spent my allowance on a new wardrobe, increasingly more revealing, extravagant, up with the times. My dress for this evening hung from my wardrobe's door. It was a scintillant silver, a color I'd not even consider wearing six years ago. Mother would place me under permanent house arrest if she saw how it hardly reached my knees.

What would he *think if he saw you in that number?*

I shook my head, shut my eyes, before a flash of anger overwhelmed me.

When I glared at myself in the mirror once more, the frustration was plain on my face, and I schooled my features, a skill I'd learned over the past few years. No one would approach a scowling girl at a bar.

And that's what I needed. I needed the drink, the men, the dances and the parties—to be able to forget, if even for a second. To distract, to remind myself there were good things in life; that I *could* still enjoy it.

I twisted the cap off my lipstick, rounding out my lips in a deep red. *Floozy red*, I thought to myself. The movements that were almost second nature, lining my eyes and brows with a pencil. Flora had found a new mascara a couple of weeks ago that made my lashes positively dark. She told me I couldn't leave the house without it, and who was I to disobey?

The me of six years ago wouldn't have felt the need. Why cover your face, like you're hiding behind a mask? Why not show the world who you are?

I almost laughed at the notion.

Standing, I brushed loose strands of hair behind my ear. I wondered absently what Flora would be wearing. She seemed to have a new dress every night, and I had a suspicion it was Dixon funding her shopping habit. But I didn't think he minded—he certainly had the money for it.

I didn't know how deep—or not—*our* coffers were. When Father was alive, I'd sometimes join him in his study, probably bothering him more than anything, but he let me do it. I'd ask him questions, though I'd never really understand the answers. We got our money from munitions factories, and we'd done alright before the war. Did even better during and after.

It never felt right, even as a young girl, knowing our money came from weaponry. Of course, I didn't understand when I was really young, but in adolescence it became clear to me that our staff at the house, our out-of-season fruit, our expensive electric chandelier, was all paid for in death.

We had blood on our hands.

It was on my hands then, as I applied my lipstick, as I donned the sparkling, decadent dress.

As though the weight of all those souls sat on my shoulders.

If *I* felt it, Father and Lucas *had* to feel it. But only once did I ever suggest investing our money in other sources to

Lucas—after Father's death, after the rumors circulating that he was found dead on the front lawn of some lady's house, a lady we'd never met before, bawling her eyes out, like she knew him—and it was met with laughter. How could *I*, a woman, know what to do with our money? I didn't know how the business was run. I didn't know what our money was tied up in.

Lucas continued Father's legacy and was happy to do it.

That blood stained Lucas, must have dripped from his fingers everywhere he went, leaving a trail in his wake, like a creeping vine, invasive, spreading until it touched everything, stained *everything* with which he came into contact.

A small part of me wished Father was still alive, if only to save me from them—my mother and Lucas. He'd at least understand what it took to get me to be agreeable. He was good at that, at talking me down, at being placating, a mediator. Were he alive, he'd screen suitors, know what they *really* wanted—did they actually have an interest in me or our money? And despite his faults, he wouldn't chain me to someone who couldn't stand me.

Perhaps because he'd done it to himself.

I faced the full-length mirror leaning in the corner, brushing my hands down my hips. The beading was rough under my fingers, the dress itself smooth like water, rippling as I moved. I slipped my feet into black heels, and my sore feet twinged, the straps pinching my skin and my heel bruised from the night before.

But once I had some liquor, I wouldn't even care.

I shut my eyes for a moment, just to feel it. To feel the ache. I had to remind myself, often it seemed, that the pain, the aches, the bruises—they all meant I was alive. A racing heart, pounding against my rib cage; the drowsiness of drunkenness; the tears that came from remembering, the stolen breaths, the crushing weight pushing me down.

They all meant I was *alive*.

I leaned back over my vanity, reaching for a pair of golden earrings, when there was an abrupt knock on the door.

"Come in." It couldn't be Mother. She never left her boudoir after dusk.

I clasped one earring as my maid pushed open the door, carrying a tray with tea. She latched the door behind her, but didn't walk any further once she saw my getup.

"You're leaving?" Her brow furrowed, and she added a hasty, "Miss."

"I am."

She nodded and moved into the room to set the tray down at my bedside table. Her dress was still immaculate, not a wisp of hair out of place.

"Apologies for wasting your time making tea," I said, clasping the other earring. I shot her a quick smile. "Are you going to tell Mother?"

She seemed to consider, but there was a flash in her mahogany eyes. "No."

"Hmm."

"Though it would be in my best interest to."

"It would," I agreed, pulling a long golden chain necklace over my head. The charm rested just between my breasts, a weight swinging right against the spot of my heart. "She'd favor you more."

"Alas."

"Alas," I echoed. I straightened and gave her another

clipped smile, reaching for the small purse I brought with me every night. "It seems she's made an enemy of both of us."

"Miss?" In the low light, her eyes gleamed, and a small part of me wondered if perhaps she had indulged in a drink or two herself. But she was steady on her feet, the ceramic teacup never rattling when she came into the room.

I had noticed, in the months she'd been with us, she was light on her feet. Quiet. Polite. It was an old house, at least a century or so, and I never heard her come up the staircase, when Mother's presence would've been announced at the first step. She was agreeable, mostly, except when I saw her professional exterior slip—never around Mother. Only around me, it seemed. A girlishness that drew me in.

There was no one else in this house to save appearances for, except the cook and Mother's own maid, I supposed.

"You cannot tell me you *like* my mother," I laugh, my voice perhaps too loud.

"This feels incriminating," she mused. "I cannot speak ill of my employer."

"You wouldn't be," I said, my hand finding the door-knob. "If anything, *I* am your employer." I hadn't meant it to be, but it felt like a pointed reminder.

"I am still obligated to her, no?"

"Perhaps not for long. She intends to marry me off, and if so, *I* intend to take you with me." The words were bitter on my tongue, a sudden feeling rising in my throat, like they were poison, a lie, a curse.

I opened the door with a sigh. "Distract her for me, will you?" And I slipped down the back staircase and into the garden to make my escape for the evening.

Six

The elevator doors opened onto the suite of the top floor, the gazes of at least a dozen people in the foyer turned toward us, inspecting our hair, how well-dressed we were, our manners—were we worth entertaining?—and deeming us acceptable guests, all in the space of a second.

The car ride wouldn't have been long if not for the traffic. Everyone in the city seemed to be out and about, and half of them must have ended up here, at one of the tallest apartment buildings in Manhattan.

Flora squealed in delight and began hugging women as soon as we entered the room, touching cheeks with pursed red-painted lips. Dixon shook the hands of a few men, whose eyes all seemed to mostly skip over me.

My dress was perhaps a bit superfluous for the evening, but the rest of the guests seemed to get the same memo: they dressed as though attending a club, a high-scale party of sorts, rather than a bash in someone's apartments.

Flora grabbed my arm and led me around, bubbly as ever, in her element.

"We need to find you a guy," she said, her blonde curls brushing my cheek.

"That is always your plan."

"Somebody to erase the stench of—what was his name? —*Brancato* off of you."

I rolled my eyes. "He won't be here, will he?"

"God, no," she laughed, pulling me further into the apartment. Dixon had found a group to chat with, though I felt his eyes tracking our movements the whole time. His hand had lingered on Flora's waist before they parted—a reluctance to let us wander out of his sight.

She and I entered the back room, another parlor of sorts, with a few men lounging, all but one smoking.

Flora ground to a halt. "Sorry!" she said, adding a bit of her usual bubbliness to her voice.

No other women were present, and the way the men were all facing each other on the couches made it clear they were deep in discussion.

The man who reclined closest to us waved his hand. "No, come on in." He wore a black suit that matched his dark hair, combed neatly back, his bronze face clean-shaven, cheeks sucking in as he pulled on his cigarette. "We need some more *personable* company in here, anyway."

Flora raised a brow at me, so I led her in, the group silent as I sat myself on the arm of the chair of the man who spoke. Lifting his fingers, he proffered his cigarette.

I hardly smoked, but the burn brought a lightheaded-ness I welcomed. A teaser of what was to come once we got our hands on some gin.

He watched me with cool eyes that then fell to my lips wrapped around the white burning paper. His irises were a bright amber, a golden brown, sparkling with intrigue, which then fell to the column of my throat.

I exhaled, sending the smoke outward. Handed him back the cigarette. "Thanks."

Our fingers brushed.

"No problem." Those golden eyes zeroed in on mine again.

"Hope we weren't interrupting anything," Flora said, sitting at the only other available spot on one of the cushioned chairs.

"Nothing that can't be discussed later." A man with amber-colored hair smiled, his arms braced along the back of the couch. His suit jacket had been discarded somewhere, his sleeves rolled up to his elbows, showing off the tight muscle of his forearm.

There were only four of them, all well-dressed, gelled, the smoke creating a haze in the room between all of us.

"How do you know the host?" my companion asked, nodding once at Flora. Like he knew I was the third wheeler, the plus-one.

"Oh, *I* don't." Her hand found her chest, and she beamed at him, teeth pearly. "But my man does."

"Your man? Do I know him?"

"Do you?" She leaned forward. "Dixon."

"Lloyd Dixon?" An incredulous laugh.

Lord Lloyd Dixon.

The hand with the cigarette fell to his knee, two fingers angling the burning paper away from his tailored trousers.

An affronted scoff from one of the other men.

"Yeah," she said. "We came with him."

"What are two beautiful ladies like you doing with *him*?" He laughed again.

"Careful, he's just in the other room." The mumble came from the amber-haired man, glancing over his shoulder.

"Why don't you stay with us tonight?"

Flora grinned. "Maybe we can be persuaded."

She couldn't be, not when Dixon was in town. But they didn't know that, and I was by myself, *looking for a man*, after all.

Music wafted through the haze, a jovial little tune from a fancy radio receiver in the corner, crackling and buzzing but unmistakable.

Flora stood and held a hand out to the amber-haired man. "Dance with me?"

He laughed but obliged, his hand finding the same spot Dixon's had rested on. She braced her own on his shoulders and they did a slower number, swaying with both feet on the ground.

"Are you going to introduce yourself?" I turned to my companion.

There was a weight present in the small creases at the corners of his eyes. He wasn't much older than me, it seemed, but centuries could have lingered behind those eyes, and I wondered just what he had lived through to make his soul feel so old.

He offered his hand. "Alexander Sinclair."

"Helena," I said, placing my fingers in his, which he brought to his lips, never taking his eyes off of me.

"Pleasure to make your acquaintance."

"Likewise," I grinned, crossing my legs, causing our knees to brush. I leaned in conspiratorially. "I do hope we weren't interrupting anything."

Sinclair sat forward to tap his cigarette against an ashtray before bringing it to his lips again. "Just... investments and other such boring things." He winked at me, dismissing the topic. "So, *she* came with Dixon," he said, glancing at Flora. "Who did *you* come with?"

I suspected he knew the answer. "With them. I'm terribly single."

"Yes, how terrible." He exhaled a laugh.

"Are you single, Mr. Sinclair?"

He shrugged a shoulder noncommittally, a sparkle to his eye, as he studied me for a second—and not in the way most men did it, inspecting my looks, deciding what their favorite part was. Cigarette at his lips, but not breathing in the smoke. A flash—and then he was jamming the butt into the ash tray. "Would you like a drink, Miss Helena?"

Sliding my fingers into his. "I thought you'd never ask."

Across the small room, behind the couches, was a cart with a few decanters of various colors, clean glasses, and a tin of ice. "Absinthe?"

"Oh—sure." I had only tried the drink once, at a party when I was already five gins deep.

He poured a finger of the greenish liquor, setting a spoon over the glass with a sugar cube. I watched, silent, as he prepared the drink, pouring chilled water from one of the decanters over the sugar. After a few moments, the drink was cloudy, swirling in the crystal.

Our fingers brushed again as he handed me the glass.

I brought it to my lips. But he waited, eyes lingering, as if waiting for me to taste.

"Nothing for you?" I asked.

He shook his head. "I've had plenty this evening," he said, but he looked entirely sober to me.

It was good, and it gave me a warm rush, but it didn't even begin to compare to the champagne and gin of the other evening. I couldn't stop thinking about it, about the ornate house, lit up and sparkling along the Sound. It was a beacon of light, probably a nuisance to the neighbors, even if they were a mile or so away. The fresco-like paintings on the walls, on the ceilings, as though once you stepped within, you were indeed in another realm of sorts, one with conniving devils and trickster faeries and fallen angels.

Flora faltered in her steps as a loud cheer erupted from the other room. She smiled at her partner before leaving his arms and coming over to me, her lavender perfume following in her wake. She leaned in, whispering in my ear, "I'm gonna go find Dixon."

Sinclair, though he couldn't possibly hear her, watched her exit.

"Can I ask you a question?" I turned back to Sinclair, lifting the cool glass to my lips.

He tilted his head in the affirmative.

"Vince Thornton? Have you heard of him?"

A twitch to the muscle in his jaw. "I have."

"Well, we were just there last night. At his house. He throws these huge parties—Have you been?"

His brow arched, the ghost of a smile dusting his features. "Many times."

"We just went for the first time. I can't say it's like anything I've seen before."

Amusement curled his lips. He leaned boyishly on the window frame; the panes speckled with the lights from the scraper across the street, little yellow dots sparkling in the late evening darkness. "It is truly spectacular, isn't it?"

Had he been there last night? There was no way we could've run into each other, not with a crowd that large. Would he be so charming in a space like that? Would I have stopped to give him my attention? We hadn't stayed long—not after I thought I saw—

"Were you planning on returning?"

"Oh." I lifted a shoulder, unsure. "I don't see why not."

"Next weekend. You should find me."

"That's an impossible thing for you to ask of me," I laughed.

"Is it?"

"Maybe you didn't see the same mob of people I saw."

"I'm an easy person to track down when I want to be." He shot me a dazzling grin, his white teeth glinting in the dim electric lights of the room.

"Hmm." I felt my cheeks warm, though from the absinthe or his charm, I wasn't sure. I decided I liked him, this maybe-bachelor and his worldliness and old soul. He gave me the impression he knew of everyone, had been everywhere.

"Tell me more about him?"

He knew who I meant. "Asking me about another man while I'm trying to win you over?" he teased. "Well, what do you want to know?"

"I don't know, anything—everything? He's a bit mysterious, is he not?"

Vince Thornton.

Lucas had never mentioned the name. And Dixon seemed to know *something*, but getting the viscount to crack would be a feat.

Sinclair glanced away from me. "He's just a new face in this city full of old money."

"Sure, but where'd he come from? He seems to have just appeared one day and now everyone *has* to go to his parties." The more I thought on it, the odder it seemed that Lucas *hadn't* mentioned Vince Thornton.

Sinclair shook his head noncommittally. "He makes his money the way your family does. The way I do, the way we *all* do, I suspect."

"And how do you make money, Mr. Alexander Sinclair?" I leaned closer and gazed at him through my lashes.

My companion grinned. "Wouldn't you like to know."

The effects of the liquor warmed my limbs, my thighs, settling deep, after only a few sips.

"His parties last the weekend," Sinclair continued. "He's thrown them for the better part of a year, and each one draws more and more in."

And I believed him. I wouldn't want to miss a chance to get real champagne, either.

My eyes were growing tired. I downed the rest of the absinthe, wrinkling my nose against the burn. In my fuzziness, I could have sworn Sinclair turned wary, eyeing my lips where the absinthe had disappeared.

"You like it, don't you?" he asked. "The champagne, the flirting, the extravagance."

"Who wouldn't?"

He smirked. "We can give you something more."

We?

Sinclair leaned in, so he stood right before me, his hand on my arm to steady me. I must have been swaying.

"You saw them, didn't you? You seem like an observant woman."

My eyes were closed, and when I opened them, we were alone in the room, the radio still playing its dinky little tune to a missing crowd. We were alone, and Sinclair was so close to me, and my vision was turning fuzzy, green around the edges, my thoughts moving on their own.

Red robes, ribbons of crimson, writhing bodies—

"Pleasure—it's what we're all after, isn't it? The permission to let go." Sinclair was at my ear, his voice mesmerizing. "You never made it to the top floor, did you? At Vince's house? Meet me there. Next weekend. You'll know."

He pulled back enough to make sure our gazes met, so serious and dark. I swear it was desire written across his brow when those dark eyes fell to my neck—and then it was gone.

He steadied me once more before smiling at me. "Don't forget, Helena." And in a moment, he slung his suit jacket over his arm and was gone, returning to the main party without me. In the haze of my mind, loose and swimming, I couldn't find him in the crowds of the apartment. And then Flora was grabbing my arm and bringing me into the smoky front room, placing another glass in my hand.

Don't forget, forget, forget, don't—replaying in my head like a mantra.

SEVEN

SIX YEARS AGO

It was a lucky thing I spotted him outside through my window, standing at the street corner, looking up at the house. Lucas was out, and if he came home while Adam was outside... I didn't want to think about what would happen.

It was also a lucky thing that I was nearly ready to go, so all I had to do was grab my purse before racing down the stairs.

Mother hardly even glanced up as I flew by.

"Going out with Flora for a bit!" I called over my shoulder, doing my best not to slam the door behind me.

Adam was waiting at our gate, just at the end of the little walk to our front door. He wore his nicest clothes—untattered trousers, a jacket over his linen shirt, shoes shining—and in his hand was a single flower, a deep red rose.

When he saw me, he softened, his lips curling into a smile.

"You can't be here," I whispered, voice low to keep from drawing the attention of Mother and our servants.

A crease formed between his brows as I led him away, his smile faltering. "I can't?"

I hadn't realized he remembered where I lived. We were supposed to meet a few blocks away, outside a cafe. Seeing him out my window had been a shock, in which my heart soared for two entirely different reasons all at once.

"My *brother*—" I pulled him down the sidewalk, our arms linked. "We can't be seen."

Adam peered at me with narrowed eyes. "You don't want your brother to see us?"

"I—He's a bit... overprotective." The lie burned on my tongue. The truth was that I'd be locked inside.

Adam frowned, but he let me lead him away. A few people strolled by, only glancing briefly at us out of the corners of their eyes. We were not of the same status, and being seen together could have harmed my reputation. He knew this, I knew this; we'd said as much that first time we'd spoken to each other. Any passersby could report me to my mother, who would inevitably tell Lucas, too.

"I'm sure his attention is elsewhere today," Adam said.

"You're so confident?"

The look he gave me was strange. A shrug, a small smile. "Just a feeling."

A few blocks away after some hurried walking, I pulled him to a stop, my heart still quick in my chest, both from the young man next to me and from the prospective trouble we'd avoided. Boyishly, a strand of hair hung down in front of his eyes as he gazed down at me. His fingers free of ink, his hazel-gray eyes bright in the late afternoon sun.

"I managed to get the afternoon off." A dimple appeared

in his cheek. "For you." Reaching up and tucking the rose right behind my ear.

"Thank you," I whispered.

And he leaned down, our faces so close, I thought my heart stopped. No time to think before he pressed a soft kiss to my cheek, lips feather-light, melting me like chocolate.

A twinge of pink turned his cheeks, too.

"I was looking forward to this all day," I said, unable to make my voice any louder than a whisper, for fear I would shout. "I don't want you to think—"

"It's okay," Adam smiled.

Maybe he understood my fear of being found out, then. In order to prolong this curiosity, this desire, as long as I could. I didn't want to mess this up. I didn't want my fear to push him away, or worse, make him think I was ashamed.

Any boy I fancied would draw Lucas' temper—it wasn't Adam's fault.

There was something about him, something in his eyes, a dark sheen, an intensity I hadn't seen in any other of the boys my age, that drew me in.

He felt *real*.

And the way he looked at me now, with those gleaming eyes—there was a hunger there that sparked a flame inside me.

My cheeks were positively red as he offered me his arm again. "Shall we?"

We began down the street, but not before he glanced over his shoulder. Perhaps my paranoia was rubbing off on him.

Then his eyes met mine again, that small smile pulling at his lips. "You never came to visit me."

"I don't think your boss would appreciate some girl hanging around."

"No," he admitted. "Especially one so distracting. But that doesn't mean I don't watch out the windows every day."

I blinked. "You watch for me?"

"Of course," he said, like it was obvious. "But it seems I just needed to come retrieve you myself."

The way he said it, low and teasing and laced with want, the same want that burned my own veins, fluttered in my own heart—my face heated at the lilting promise.

An envelope was left for me in the mail, which my mother swore she hadn't seen when she brought it in, with just my name on the outside in a stilted script. When I opened it in the privacy of my bedroom, I found it was from him. A letter, proposing a date. And without any return address, the only thing left to do was make sure I was ready when the time came.

I just hadn't expected to see him outside our gate. Brazenly, unabashedly, out in the open.

We strolled on in silence, a confident smirk pulling at his lips as blocks of houses and other pedestrians passed behind us. He didn't pay them one mind, but I caught the eye of a few passersby, saw the way their upper lip hitched, the way the spot between their brows wrinkled.

Eventually, we made it to the cafe, and he ordered for the both of us, before we found a table and he pulled the wicker chair out for me. In a few minutes, a waiter was bringing us our drinks, as well as a few flaky pastries I hadn't expected. A steaming black coffee was placed before Adam, and for me, an amber-hued tea and a few cubes of sugar in a little cup.

My eyes shot to Adam. "Earl Grey?"

"Is it not your favorite?"

I blinked. "Yes."

A shrug. "You must have told me last time."

"Hmm." I dropped a few sugars into the hot tea and stirred.

He had taken his cap off and placed it in his lap. The late afternoon sun turned his hair a warm reddish hue, shining and illuminating his person, so that even his skin brightened. The other boys I'd spoken to, and the only one I'd ever had call on me, couldn't compare. When his dimple appeared, I wanted to touch him, to lean over and place my hand on his cheek, to pull him to me. To tangle my fingers in those red waves.

"What are you thinking about?" he asked me, pulling me from my silence. A few car horns honked somewhere on the street.

"Nothing." If only he knew.

He sipped from his cup. "Don't worry about your brother."

"I wasn't—" My face heated again. "That's not what I was thinking about." Though I wasn't sure I wanted to admit to the truth, either.

"He's taken over the company, yeah? There is plenty to preoccupy him." Another shrug, another sip. "From what I've read in the papers, he has his hands full. During the day —he's at the warehouse or his office, surely."

"Most of the time, yes."

"Then there is nothing to worry about. He didn't see us today, he won't see us next time." He studied me for a moment, reading my reaction. "That is, if you'd like there to be a next time."

I hid behind my teacup, his stare too intense. "Yes. Of course I do."

"Good." He grinned, leaning closer. "We've hardly gotten to know each other. I'm not done with you yet."

"Yet?"

Something flashed in his eyes. "Can I be honest, Helena?"

I nodded, drawn into his stare, so much so I realized I was leaning closer. "I much prefer honesty," I said. "I've found most boys tend to bend the truth."

"I'm not like the *boys* you've been forced to entertain."

How could words be so laced with desire?

Gently, he reached across the table, grabbing one of my hands in his. Rough, working fingers, so much larger than my own. Inwardly, I chastised myself for how nervous he made me—how girlish I was being, flustered over a simple touch.

"I know you feel it," he said. "This—connection between us. Maybe I'm speaking too soon, but it's gotta mean something."

It was like he read my mind, my thoughts and feelings on display.

"I think so," I said, barely a whisper. "I hope so." Perhaps it was foolish to admit it aloud.

"I–I *wonder* about you. I think about you." A laugh on an exhale, slight pinkening to the tips of his ears. "I watch for you out the window."

"Then, maybe I'll come by."

"You should," he said. Then a moment later, "You will."

I nodded. Because he was right.

This hold he had on me—

"Ever since we ran into each other," he continued, "I can't get you out of my head. Is it the same for you?"

Over the tiny cafe table, our faces were no more than two feet apart—close enough to whisper, entirely too intimate for our first outing. Too intimate for a young man and woman who were *not* courting. But the rest of the street fell away, all noises silencing, all wandering stares disappearing, until it was only the two of us, cocooned in this delicious tension drawing us together.

It was too much to admit—I hardly knew him.

"Yes," I whispered.

His eyes flicked down to my lips and back up. "What do you dream about?"

Our drinks were long forgotten. This close, I could see the little scar at his brow, the barely-there dusting of freckles under his eyes, how each strand of his auburn hair sparkled like gold under the sunlight.

"I dream of flying."

He laughed under his breath, smiling that charming smile. "Flying?"

"If I could fly, then I could go wherever I wanted, and nobody could catch me. I could do whatever I wanted. I'd be—"

"Free." He was staring at me, eyes hooded, that auburn hair curling around his ears. I could drown in those eyes, forever. "You want *freedom*."

You. I want you.

I'd never wanted something, *somebody,* so entirely.

"Or maybe it's just a *dream*," I said. "Can't I be content?"

"You're not." He shook his head. Like he knew how closely my mother still kept me. Like he knew how everything I did was met with scrutiny. Like he knew how they *monitored* me.

Embarrassment bloomed in my chest. "You presume to know me."

"I don't. But is that not what this date is for?" Adam studied me. "We're not so different, you and I."

Perhaps that was the cord between us that felt so tight.

"We both want *more*."

My breath hitched in my throat. He read me so plainly. Was I that transparent? Feeling as though I were at the precipice of a proposal, an offer to change my world, my *life*.

My hands in my lap clutched at my skirts, waiting for his next words.

"And I want to give it to you."

EIGHT

Not two days after the house party, I found myself at Flora's, lying on the settee in her tearoom, the curtains open and billowing. I watched as they fluttered in the currents of air, the window shutter pushed open, letting in the bustle of the street below.

I could not go home. If my mother cared at all for my unhappiness, she did not show it.

I had made my way to Flora's house sometime after lunch. I hadn't told anyone but the maid, whose eyes had sparkled like we were co-conspirators.

"Lucas is coming home." The curtains, carried on the breeze, light as a spider's web, fluttered through my fingers.

Flora paused, and out of the corner of my eye, I saw her hand still. She capped the lip gloss she was using. "What?"

I didn't repeat myself.

Once the words were out of my mouth, they did not feel like the truth. A lie, souring my tongue.

How I wished it was a lie. How much simpler it would be, if this were a story I'd concocted for her attention and concern.

He was always telling Mother how much of a busy man he was. He had a wife—Lucy—who was carrying their child, due in a couple months. The company—always so busy with the company, he'd say, with stocks and labor and profits and whatnot. Lunches and meetings to win investors over.

And he was interrupting it all to come home.

To find *me* a husband.

A lump had settled in my throat days ago, and hadn't faded.

"When?" Flora asked.

I shrugged, and suddenly my tongue felt like it was made of sandpaper. "A few days, I think."

Flora stood, aghast. "For how long?"

I shrugged again.

Some gin would do me some good, I thought. Or more absinthe, swirling with sugar and ice, the way Mr. Sinclair had made it for me.

Don't forget, don't forget.

The curtains fell, the breeze ceasing eerily. The air turned still, as if it too were surprised at the circumstances.

I didn't know how long my brother would stay. In the past, a week or two. Longer, if Mother could convince him. Maybe this time I had nothing to worry over—maybe his concern for Lucy would overshadow his need to oblige Mother.

"Why didn't you say anything the other night?"

Because I hadn't wanted to think about it.

"Mother says it is time for me to marry."

Flora scoffed. "Yes, she always says that, doesn't she?"

I turned to look at her, the cushion of the settee soft against my cheek. "She's serious this time."

"Helena, how many times has she threatened to sign you away?"

"*Lucas* is coming home."

"My parents are always saying the same thing, and here we are." She smiled, but it did not reach her eyes.

"Here we are," I echoed.

Her slim fingers were warm against my cheek. "Don't worry."

And I realized it was pity in her eyes. I knew she would never be forced into marriage, would never be forced to take a man's name, would never be forced to warm his bed. Her family hardly cared what we got up to at night. Dixon had dropped her off with his shiny Duesenberg on more than one occasion.

Her blonde hair was curled so perfectly, framing her small ears, her headband holding the waves away from her eyes. Her skin glowed. *She* glowed. She always did. It was how she had gotten Dixon's attention. How she kept it.

I envied her.

"Would it be so bad?"

"Would *what* be so bad?"

"Marriage."

"Flora—my *brother* is returning home." I willed my voice not to shake. "To *pick out* my husband."

She thought for a moment, a crease forming between her perfectly manicured brows. "Maybe I can have Dixon do something."

How could she possibly understand?

I shook my head. "He can't do anything."

"He is a *viscount*. That has to mean something to your mother."

Another thing I wished were true. But if Lucas was on his way, her mind was made up. "Dixon can do nothing. He could bring a duke, a *prince*, to my mother, and she still wouldn't agree unless Lucas said so."

"Then let's make him say so."

The curtain swayed once more over our heads. My sigh was swallowed by the wind, which whistled as a chill seeped into the room.

"Perhaps you can refuse," Flora broke the silence.

I propped myself up on my elbows. "Yeah, right."

"Why not?"

Because I will be flayed. Because Lucas would not let *me refuse.* "I could be cut off," I said instead.

"Then you can stay here. Oh, what if you just moved in?"

"I'm sure that'll go well with your parents." I reached up once more to feel the gossamer against my fingertips. I had known her parents as long as I had known her. Friends since childhood, some of my earliest memories were of us playing in the small garden behind her house, running up and down the stairs, sneaking into the pantry with their cook, who gave us extra tarts and candies; her parents always giving me closed-mouth smiles, tolerating the girl who seemed never to want to go home.

"Flora, you cannot solve this for me." Plastering on a smile, but it wobbled, my cheeks already aching with the effort. "There is no solving this."

"But—" She loosed a frustrated sigh. "It is just not *fair*."

"I know you want to help," I said, linking our fingers together.

"Of course I want to help. Lucas has been getting his paws all caught up in your business for *years*."

"Is it not what brothers do?" But the words brought a sour taste to my tongue.

"No, Helena. *No.*" Her fingers squeezed mine. "I know you want to move past it, that you *have* moved on. And I know how difficult this will be—having Lucas around again, after... after what he did. But that does not mean you must forgive him, just because it is in the past."

Had I moved on?

She wrapped her arms around me, and even though I had tried so hard to forget, images rushed back to me, memories of years ago, the face of a boy I had loved, Lucas and his sneering anger, his threats. The lump in my throat nearly choking me, I sucked in a breath, willed myself to calm.

I will not cry. I had already cried so many tears.

I had not wept about it since I had received the letter from his parents. Hadn't let myself feel that rage, that grief again. Had locked it away inside me somewhere, and threw away the key, because it was the only way to go on.

"Don't ever forgive him," Flora said, her words low. "Don't you ever."

I wouldn't, I *couldn't*. I knew that if I ever forgave Lucas, then I had given up on that younger version of myself, that girl in love, who still felt hope for the world. Who still thought she had *choice*, who still thought the world was hers for the taking.

There was a shout outside the window. The breeze picked up again, a caress on my warm skin, fingers of a lost lover of years gone.

Don't forget, don't forget.

At night I dreamt that I soared over the city, the sparkling lights of the buildings scraping the sky, feeling like feather-soft touches to my belly, the wind holding me up, carrying me away, and there was a hand in mine.

A strong, familiar hand.

Fingers laced through mine, skin warm and worn.

Coney Island sparkled in the distance. Bright, colorful, twinkling lights against a backdrop of dark cerulean, scintil-lating indigo, the stars winking in and out. The black specks of ships, like shadows on the water. The screams of elation on the roller coasters echoing in my ears.

A laugh bubbled up through my own lips.

He laughed with me.

The wind should have been frigid against my skin. We were high above all, flying, free as we could be, before we swooped down, touched the antennas on the buildings, danced along rooftops. He twirled me around amidst the skyline, our feet barely even touching down on the gravel tops, the iron and steel.

His hand never left mine.

What was his name?

I couldn't remember. Like a ghost on my tongue, dissolving, gone. But it didn't matter. I knew, deep down, a feeling in my chest, that his name and mine were the same.

I turned to look at him, to gaze upon my lover, my other half. But as I did, he disappeared, like smoke, drifting away in the breeze. Eurydice, back to the Underworld.

And then I fell.

NINE

I didn't tell Flora I was returning to the mansion, didn't tell Dixon.

Maybe I should have, maybe I shouldn't have gone alone, but I couldn't get Mr. Sinclair's words out of my head. *Meet me there. Next weekend. You'll know.*

The top floor. Where the people in robes convened.

Hundreds, maybe thousands of people trampling down the plush grass, spilling liquor and holding on to each other, lest they float away—and I was alone. Exposed. Without Flora at my elbow, without Dixon following us, I felt like I had arrived without a dress to cover me, shield me.

It was thrilling.

No one knew who I was. Just some brunette flouncing around on her own.

My throat itched for some gin. The servers whirled through the crowd just as they had the first evening I had visited this house.

I made my way toward the massive front door, the foyer,

and found the red ribbons from before had been taken down. This weekend, the decorations consisted of tinsel streamers hanging from wall sconces, shimmering under the chandelier. The lights had been dimmed, the sparkling highlights in the room even more eye-catching.

Many of the guests' wardrobe matched the scenery. Perhaps whoever took advantage of the parties every weekend knew what was coming next. Golden flappers, girls with shimmering kohl around their eyes, ruby lips, men with jackets both on and discarded, traces of gold along their cheeks and through their gelled hair.

But tonight I wore a deep emerald. I had painted on my makeup more sharply, dragging out the winged kohl around my eyes, exaggerating the curve of the bow of my lips with my rouge.

But no one noticed. Everyone glimmered in the lamplight, and the crowd writhed, couples spinning and moving together, limbs tangled in dances that bordered on indecency.

My mother would faint, but I just wanted to feel what they were feeling.

Perhaps that was why the parties were so popular; why they had grown in attendance so quickly, despite the house's owner being so enigmatic—on this lawn, in this repurposed cathedral, you could be anyone. Propriety didn't dictate you.

You could dance how you wanted.

Do what you want.

A heady freedom not felt outside these walls.

As though the air itself was laced with relaxing poison, a

giddiness settled in my belly, my tingling fingers. I'd walked through the door and forgotten all my worries.

A giggling woman passed me, her hand laced through another's, and her eyes caught mine. Auburn hair, cut so short it curled around her ears, a golden band across her brow. Her blue eyes glistened. She smiled as her hand trailed along my shoulder, an invitation to follow, before the crowd ate her up.

Don't forget.

I couldn't get distracted.

When a server appeared from nowhere and offered a glass, I didn't refuse, tipping my head back and downing it all at once.

The grand stairs were so crowded I feared I wouldn't be able to make it to the next level.

But I'd seen those robed figures go to the second floor, and I knew they must be related to whatever Sinclair wanted me to see.

I shoved my way through people, but upon the landing I paused, unsure where to go. Past the balcony, the hall split into two, left and right.

Making a guess, I went to the right. The music began to fade, the energy of the couples more subdued as I went on. Some leaned against the wall, chatting, smoking. Gilded sconces lit the way with bright electric bulbs against the velvety red wallpaper. Beneath my heels the marble floor shone like a mirror.

As I walked, the crowd lessened, until only a few milled around. But none wearing those dark robes. They stared at me all the same, observing with interested eyes. Smoke trailing from their lips, muffled conversations.

It was easy to forget the debauchery just below.

It was then I saw the slip of a robe around a corner, the same ruby hue of blood, gone in a blink.

The *clack* of my heels was stark against the silence. Cursing low, I stopped and nearly pulled them off, but— why should I sneak around?

Had I not been invited?

I straightened, took a breath.

We can give you something more.

When I turned the corner, the figure was gone, but a set of large wooden doors confronted me. No one lingered in the hall. Well and truly alone.

I swore I heard a whisper. A suggestion of a voice, right at my ear.

The feeling of a skeletal finger down my spine.

Carved into the wood of the door were twisting figures, calling to the painted scene in the foyer; demons and angels playing with the humans between them, their sneering faces more distinguishable as I approached. Decorated to the utmost, the doors could only be expected to draw my atten- tion, luring me closer, so that those thrashing figures could drag me into their dance.

The demons devoured, the angels wept, the mortals smiled.

I ran my hand along the wood, feeling the bite of the demons' teeth.

A soft, muffled sigh.

Then silence.

Then—I didn't imagine it: again, a moan. A panting sound, a chittering laugh. All behind the door.

As though whomever felt such ecstasy was inches away,

just on the other side. Another masculine grunt. A sharp inhale of breath and a low, drawn-out groan.

I pushed my weight against the heavy doors. Barely, just barely—enough to peek inside.

The mass of writhing bodies were starkly painted with blood.

Men, clearly aroused, with sharp glinting teeth. Women with the same teeth, fingers caressing themselves and others. Red streaking down their breasts, their limbs. The ruby robes were discarded, and every figure within bore themselves, unashamed.

The source of the soft sighs I'd heard—a couple on the floor, facing away from me. She straddled his lap, her back to his chest, his strong fist curled into her hair, gripping and pulling, her dainty hand reaching up to his skull, his face buried in her throat. Blood, staining like ink, running in rivulets down her breasts.

I couldn't stop the gasp that came from me. They were being *murdered*. No one could lose so much blood and survive.

The young woman suddenly cried out and became languid in the man's arms.

The merging of pain and pleasure, the blurring of those lines—I felt it there, in my flesh, like I was there with her. Like I *was* her.

But just as I turned to run, to shut the door and pretend I had not seen anything, the air rushed from my lungs, because amidst the debauchery, a familiar pair of eyes met mine.

Alexander Sinclair, set upon a couch with another man on one side and a woman on the other, his mouth stained with blood. It trailed down his chin and his bare chest, a woman latched onto the side of his neck, his hand tangled in her hair, and the other pushing down the head of the man whose face was in his lap.

And despite it all, his dilated pupils zeroed in on me.

Heart pounding, I fled down the hall.

We can give you something more.

I understood then what the look he gave me was. His peculiarity when I'd met him.

It was entirely predatory. *He was a predator.* A beast peering down at its prey. Amused by my curiosity, my *naivete.*

Around the corner, I leant to catch my breath. My fingers at my throat, as if to staunch a bite. I could feel it already—the piercing teeth, the pinprick of pain, the rush of adrenaline.

Would it hurt? Or would I, like that woman, cry out in ecstasy?

I should not have come here.

A hand roughly grabbed my arm, pinning me to the spot.

The shriek died in my throat before I could even breathe.

A man I'd never met before, flashing me a lecherous smile. "Going somewhere?"

I wrenched myself out of his grasp. "Yes. I'm leaving."

Though I was free of his hold, he leaned into me, cornering me against the wall. When I winced at his proximity, his grin only widened. "You're scared." He cocked his head. "Why?"

"I just want to leave," I repeated, forcing air into my lungs.

This man was a predator, too. And I'd been caught, all alone.

"Oh, come on," he cooed. "Why don't we return to the party together?"

He linked his arm through mine, pulling me back in the direction of those hellish doors.

I dug my heels into the floor. "I don't know who you think you are—"

His lip curled, brandishing a sharp tooth. A pointed canine, glinting razor-sharp and gleaming white against his blood-red lips.

That was the murder weapon. Those teeth—it was how they drew blood, how they *killed*.

"Calm down. We're just going to go have some fun."

His strength was otherworldly, his grip on my arm like a vise. The more I struggled, the harder his fingers dug into the flesh of my arm.

"*Stop.*"

We both froze.

The strong voice echoed down the polished hall.

My captor's eyes darkened, narrowing into a scowl. A rumble of frustration, animalistic and low, deep in his throat.

"What are you doing?" Sinclair asked. He wore his robe, swishing at his knees, tied loosely around his hips, as he approached us. He hadn't bothered to clean himself up, the blood painting his chin, his cheeks, along his neck, where two circular points had already healed to shiny skin.

"Just found another mortal to join us—"

Mortal?

"I think not." Sinclair's glare was sharp.

My captor's hold loosened just the slightest bit, his resolve faltering just enough I could wrench myself away.

"Come, Miss Helena." Sinclair held his bloodstained fingers out to me.

I shook my head, the words stopped in my throat.

"But—"

Sinclair turned once more to my attacker. "You're lucky I don't have you flayed," he hissed. "Find somewhere else to be."

His deference was clearly begrudging, but the man slunk down the hall, his hands in fists at his sides.

They were *murderers*.

"Come," he repeated.

My limbs wouldn't move. A lightness in my head, a buzz that I *knew* wasn't from the drink I'd had, expanding, overwhelming. The air turned sour in my lungs, my breath hitching in my throat, and I couldn't feel my fingers pressed against the wall.

"Really, Helena, there's nothing to worry about."

A laugh burst from my lips. "Nothing to worry about!"

"Relax."

He took a step closer, palms outward, as though I were some rabid animal he would placate. Covered in blood—his own, or another's—he did not seem to notice, and cared equally how I felt about it. It was all over him, all over his *mouth*.

They drank blood. They killed and then drank the blood.

"You're beginning to sound a lot like the guy you just scared away." A hysterical giggle stalled in my throat. "You want me to come with *you*? In there?"

"No, we'll talk elsewhere."

Of course. So he could have me to himself, no witnesses. *I hadn't told Flora where I was.*

I recoiled when he took another step closer. It wasn't lost on me, how he gazed at me predatorily, how his dilated pupils found a spot on my neck.

"I won't say anything." I swallowed. "Just let me leave."

"Christ, Helena, I'm not going to hurt you." He scoffed and lowered his hand. "Allow me to explain."

"Explain what?" I realized I had gripped my skirt with fists, the beading digging into my palms. "That you wanted me to walk into a den of monsters?" *So you could kill me?*

He rolled his eyes. "That's a little dramatic, don't you think?" The muscular planes of his chest were exposed to the air, unmarred yet lined in flaking blood. His hair was messy and tousled, like one of his lovers had run their fingers through it countless times.

"Then what *are* you?"

"I'll explain everything. Just, please, Helena." *Be smart.*

If I indulged him, perhaps I'd leave safe and sound. If I angered him, would I ruin my chances to escape?

Shakily, I nodded.

"I promise. Let me talk and you'll be on your way."

He turned to retreat down the hall. Expecting me to follow. And maybe he just knew I would, because even though my heart raced, I couldn't understand what I'd seen —what *he'd* been doing, what *any* of them had been doing —what manner of creature pierced flesh to draw forth the blood underneath?

One glass of champagne wasn't enough to dream this up.

He was truly naked under that robe, his bare feet silent

against the polished, unblemished marble. Heat flushed up my neck, across my face, as the adrenaline coursing through me died down.

I wasn't so naive to think that parties for any sexual appetite didn't happen. Especially here, where any vice could be supplied.

But to see their skin doused in so much blood, while they continued on, drinking and sucking and grinding—

Sinclair led me to a door and held it open for me, motioning me inside. I met his eyes—those amber eyes, flashing with restraint—as I passed him. He had said I wasn't being forced to stay, that I'd be let go.

But I couldn't calm my heart, because I knew what those teeth could do, how easily they could tear. He was wearing the evidence.

A study of sorts appeared from the door, a library, with bookcases reaching the ceiling. The shelves were full, over-flowing, yet the leaves of the books were still uncut. New novels, seemingly just arrived. A fire crackled in a huge fire-place across from the door.

And a man stood, waiting.

I froze mid-step.

I hadn't imagined him. The same man from my first time here, who had seen me across the crowd.

His dark red hair was combed neatly, not a hair out of place. He was dressed impeccably, in a stylish navy suit, but in his hand, he held a glass filled with a red inky liquid that I suspected matched the dried blood on Sinclair's face.

But his drink of choice was not what stopped me.

It was his face—

The face of a ghost.

I forgot all about the monster behind me.

Because the ghost smiled at me, dimpled cheeks sending my heart fluttering—and though his teeth were sharp and pointed, I couldn't fathom that *he* was standing in front of me.

Alive.

The floor was unsteady beneath my feet. "How…"

"Hello, my love." He set down his glass. Reaching toward me, those hands—*those hands*—I knew those hands. No ink, no blood.

Tears pricked at my eyes.

"You're not—You can't—"

I had to be losing my mind. This *was* a nightmare.

But when he touched me, it felt so real, so familiar I nearly sobbed.

"I'm here," he said. "I'm back."

My knees gave out, but he held me upright as though I weighed nothing.

Adam Vering, the boy to whom I'd given my heart and never seen again, had returned, and I'd found him at the center of a den of monsters.

TEN

Our reunion was not as I'd imagined it. I'd always hoped for his return, and in my waking dreams, I imagined his arms enfolding me, the warmth of his lips on mine, the ultimate bliss that was finding the owner of half my soul.

But in that moment I could not move, and the tears brimming my eyes were not born of elation.

"You can leave us now," my lost lover said, his gaze never leaving mine.

A moment later, the door *snick*ed shut with Sinclair's departure.

Adam had *survived*.

We'd all believed he'd died. But there he was, well and whole, not a blemish to his skin, his face as perfect as six years ago.

A face I couldn't forget, even if I tried.

Though... a preternatural darkness lingered in his eyes that hadn't been there before. A flash, and it was gone.

His hands steadied me, cupping my elbows, his fingers rough yet smooth at the same time.

"You're supposed to be dead."

The words came out hot, surprising even myself. Anger —that's what summoned my tears, that pushed me away from his grasp.

He blinked. "I'm not."

"I thought you were *dead*." I had been fooled. "It's been *six years*."

"I know—"

"You've let me believe for *six years* that you were dead."

His jaw clenched shut as I paced away, across the room.

"*What* is happening?" My voice cracked. "This is some cruel game I want *no* part of."

This was some joke, he was some imposter, it was *impossible*—

"Helena, breathe."

And there were *killers* here—

I couldn't get enough air in my lungs.

My grief had been buried deep, all these years, rotting into a putrid nothingness, melting into the fibers of my being, leaving behind a great, gaping hole that could never again be filled, not by men and their whispered promises, or liquor, or lavish dinners and expensive dresses and gold jewelry.

I didn't want to hate him, to scream at him. But I could do nothing else.

My chest heaved, fingers gouging my palms. Biting my lip, the pain was grounding, an iron tang spreading on my tongue.

And he just stood there, one hand fisted at his side,

unblinking, as if assessing my every move. He was completely unruffled, the creases still straight in his trousers, his jacket. Only the vague dusting of a shadow at his jaw.

He looked at me the same. Just as he used to.

His throat bobbed, gaze zeroing in on my lips.

It wasn't the expectant gaze of every other man I'd met these past few years. No, it was more like he was reacquainting himself with me, examining the makeup I'd applied, makeup I would never have worn before.

Maybe he hadn't changed much, but I had.

I'd *moved on*.

I took a shaky breath, stuttering out, "I need to leave."

When I made for the door, he stepped closer. "Helena, I understand this is a lot."

"I don't want to hear it." I shook my head. "I can't."

"Helena—"

"Adam, I *can't*." My hands trembled. I avoided his eyes, couldn't bear looking at him, couldn't bear the weight of his stare.

Lucas.

It was all his fault.

Adam never would have left if not for Lucas.

The silence between us burned. He nodded once, slowly. "Okay."

"Okay?"

"Just promise me—"

I shook my head. I had promised, years ago, to remember him as he crossed the sea to fight in something bigger than him. And I didn't know how, didn't know why, but he stood there before me again, and I wasn't sure if it was a miracle or a curse.

"Promise me you'll come back."

The soft pleading in his eyes cracked my resolve. But I couldn't, I *wouldn't*.

Without an answer, I grabbed the door's handle. He didn't stop me, didn't tell me to stay, didn't pull me further into his web.

And even after accepting every glass of champagne offered, even after rolling into bed as the sun peeked over the horizon, I could not shake the feeling of his hazel eyes peering right through me, following me home, tracking my every movement and wondering, *was I still his?*

ELEVEN

SIX YEARS AGO

"You're going to have to introduce us eventually."

Flora's arm was linked with mine as we strolled down the street, heading toward our luncheon. She knew about Adam—of course she did, who else would I talk to?—and never let me forget how much she wanted to meet him, my enigmatic suitor.

"I will," I said, lowering my voice.

The paranoia was still there, the worry that Lucas would find out. It had been a few months, but we'd managed to slip under his and Mother's notice.

"I want to know what he looks like," Flora gushed, squeezing my arm. "I need to know how handsome he is!"

My cheeks heated, as they always did when I thought of him. "He's quite handsome."

She grinned at me and leaned closer, her lips brushing my ear. "Have you kissed him yet?"

I should have expected the question from her, but I turned aflame all the same. "Flora!"

"What?" Her grin spread, painted lips glossy in the sunlight. "Don't act like you care about being proper now, doll."

"Quiet, or I'll never again leave the house unchaperoned."

Her eyes twinkled with mischief as she laughed. "You've done more, then?"

"Hush." I nearly covered her mouth with my palm. "Of course not."

In truth, we hadn't yet done much of *anything* past holding hands. He said such devilish things, sending me reeling, wishing for him to just claim my lips as his, making my toes curl—but nothing more. He held me, he pulled me to him, he caressed my face and brought me so close, but he never pressed his lips to mine, and I was beginning to wonder if he cared more for my honor than I did.

At night I tossed and turned, wondering if he did not crave me as much as I craved him?

He was pushing me away, holding me at arm's length, the rogue side of him melting away. He'd set me on my feet, make sure I returned home safe, but never would he press his lips to mine.

Flora sighed dreamily. "You're going to get married before me."

"I wouldn't be so sure."

"Do you think you will get married?" she asked as we neared the lunch club. "You and Adam?"

Adam Vering.

I didn't let myself imagine it. I knew what was allowed.

"I don't know." Because if I couldn't marry him, why let him worm his way into my heart? I did this all against my better judgment—I couldn't deny that thread between us, how every day it pulled taut, begging me to find him, wherever he was in the city. I *ached* every day for him.

"Well, I'll be your maid of honor, of course."

"I would have no one else." I gave her a smile. My worries were for the dark hours.

We crossed the street quickly, coming upon the hotel we frequented. The crowd was thicker here, carriages crowding the street and groups of people spilling out of the building. We managed to squeeze through, and the doorman let us in without a word, nodding as we passed. The lobby was just as boisterous, except voices bounced and echoed off the polished floor. Arms still linked, Flora and I passed the front desk, making our way to the club just past the grand staircase.

I never paid much attention to the crowds—in such a place, there were so many people, you could see thousands of faces in a day and return tomorrow to a whole new thousand. But I knew *his* face, *his* auburn hair.

As though I shouted his name in an empty room, he turned from where he stood. His eyes caught mine immediately.

A static charged the air between us.

"Helena." His lips mouthed the word—I had seen those lips say my name so many times now, had memorized the way they moved.

"Is that him?" Flora followed the direction of my stare.

He wasn't wearing the clothes he wore at the printer's. He was clean-shaven, no streaks of ink on his face, his hair clean under his cap. His jacket was the same as the one he'd worn on our first outing—clean, pressed, tidy.

"Helena." He stood before me, his cheek dimpling as he smiled.

"How—"

Flora stuck her hand out, as the men do. "I'm Florence Sanford. Nice to meet you."

"Adam Vering. A pleasure." He took her hand with no hesitation.

"Gosh, you're more handsome than she let on." Flora grinned, elbowing me in the arm. She turned to me. "You didn't tell me he would be joining us!"

"I didn't know," I managed to say.

"Well, why don't you?" She turned to him again, beaming.

There were already so many people looking at us—did they recognize me? Did they know who I was?

Adam's eyes were only on me, and though my heart warmed at his gaze, my fear took hold, its grip icy on my neck.

"Thank you, but I must be on my way," he replied.

I swallowed. I wanted so desperately to invite him in, to enjoy our time, but I couldn't jeopardize this. If word got back—

Flora pouted. "Well, when am I supposed to get to know you, then?"

He turned that charming smile on her then, holding out a hand. She placed her gloved fingers in his, and he brought them to his lips, his roguish smile as endearing as ever. "Someday soon, I expect," he said.

And then he turned those eyes back on me, and it took everything in me not to throw my arms around his neck and ruin my name. I wanted nothing more than to go out with him, as any normal couple would. The secrecy was eating away at me.

Turning to Flora, I patted her arm. "Go ahead and get our seats. I'll be there in a minute."

Her eyes flicked from him to me, smiling coyly, nodding slowly. "I'll give a shout if the food gets cold."

She slunk away, leaving us alone amidst a crowded lobby, where anyone could see.

"Why are you here?" I whirled on him.

His easy expression cracked just a bit. "What do you mean?"

"Don't you have to work?"

"I wanted to talk to you."

"But—we have plans. You'll see me in a few days."

Adam glanced around the room, peering over my shoulder at one of the many hallways leading away from the lobby. His fingers wrapped around my own, tugging me in one direction. "Follow me."

I let him pull me down one of the halls, leading probably to the many amenities for guests, and the crowd became considerably smaller. No one looked at us, caught up in their own conversations. And when he shoved through a door, we came out to an alleyway between this building and the next. It was immediately quieter, the sounds of the street muffled by the corner we were now hidden around. Brick walls on either side of us, a few trash receptacles, newspapers littering the ground. But no one else, save for an employee at the very end of the alleyway, smoking a cigarette and leaning against the wall, staring up at the sliver of sky between the two buildings.

The door fell shut with a loud *clank*, drawing the hotel

employee's attention, but he quickly looked away. He had probably snuck away without anyone knowing, for a breath of air, and I figured he wouldn't blab if we didn't.

I was suddenly whirled around, my back hitting the brick wall, knocking my breath from my lips. And Adam was suddenly caging me in, his broad shoulders blocking out the alley.

"Adam!"

His knee pressed between my legs, trapping me between him and the wall. My heart fluttered in my chest. "It was too loud in there," he said, leaning closer to me. His hands rested on the wall, one on each side of my head. And every time his eyes flicked down to my lips, I wanted to kiss him.

But if anyone saw us now, I'd be ruined.

My cheeks were aflame. "You wanted to talk—"

He brushed his nose along my cheek, sending shocks through me. My eyes shut, a gasp escaping me as my hands came up to his chest. His heart beat against my fingers, a rhythmic thud. "I want to do more than talk," he murmured, hooded eyes trailing along me, my body.

"But, how—" Another gasp was drawn from me when his hand came to rest on my jaw, thumb brushing against my cheekbone. "Flora—"

"Because once a week is not enough, Helena." His breath was hot against my lips. He was so close. So, so close. All it would take was a brush of our lips and I would truly be the harlot my mother feared. And the position he had me in now, the polite, sometimes devilish young man had made way for the part of him that desired me. Like he couldn't hold it back anymore.

And despite my best judgment, I wanted him to keep going.

"You are driving me wild," he said. "I can think of nothing else. Every waking moment is spent wondering where you are, what you're doing. And I hate that I can't be there." He dipped his head lower, nose lingering against my jaw, his breath fanning the sensitive flesh of my neck.

Another clank of the door signaled the absence of the employee, perhaps worried what he'd see if he stayed any longer.

My hand fisted in Adam's shirt. "You're going to get me into trouble," I whispered. My eyes were shut, every sensation of his touch lessening my worries. No man had ever pushed me up against a wall before. No man had been so wild with desire for me. The boys that I'd briefly courted—all polite conversation, supervised. Nothing like this.

It sent my body reeling, and all I knew was I wanted *more*.

"Is it bad that I don't care?" Adam said, placing a kiss on my neck.

Something in me tightened.

"I'm inclined to ruin you, Helena." Another kiss, closer to my ear. "To steal you away."

Every breath was ragged. My head spun. "I can't—"

"Why worry so much?" he murmured, leaning away just enough so he could look me in the eye. I saw the desire there, his pupils dilated. Felt how much he wanted me with every touch, with the way he pressed his body to mine.

I reached up, twining my hand around his neck, pulling him to me, our foreheads together. "Because," I said, tangling my fingers in his hair, "I don't want this to end."

TWELVE

For the next few days, I was bursting to tell Flora everything.

About how I had walked in on *something*—a scene which I increasingly could not believe, wondering if perhaps I'd made it all up: Mr. Sinclair's blood-stained chest and fingers, yet how he was absolutely *fine*. I hadn't heard that there were any deaths at the party, but I also supposed there were people powerful enough to cover up a story like that.

Sinclair had led me to *him*—to Adam, who appeared as though he had never left. As though he hadn't died in a field, in a land that wasn't his, with an entire ocean between us.

I was unable to leave the house, not because of Mother's demands, but because I didn't know how to face the world.

Wasting away in my bed, only leaving my room for meals. Mother seemed pleased that I would not take Flora's calls, that I did not go out in the evenings. After a few days, I lived only in my nightgown and robe. Dressing properly did not matter, I supposed, if I had no reason to leave.

I had to tell Flora. Had to get this festering truth out of me.

But would she think I was crazy?

People didn't drink blood, didn't... *consummate* while bathing in it.

An elaborate performance, maybe, meant to mystify unsuspecting guests? An utterly *immersive* staging of a horror novel.

Surely.

But Sinclair had blood staining his teeth. A woman at his side, sucking on his neck, and a man in his lap, unclothed. There was a shamelessness in that room that I hadn't seen before.

And Adam, amidst it all, totally unfazed by the crimson staining Sinclair's jaw.

No matter how I mulled it over, I could not make sense of it.

How was this Adam, *my* Adam? The same boy that ran into me on the street, the same one with ink-stained hands and a disdain for extravagance? And yet, there he was, in the most extravagant house in the whole city, the whole state, waiting for me to stumble upon him all over again.

My head ached, dwelling on these thoughts, and as I fell into a doze, there came a knock on my door.

And in walked Flora. Her lips were pursed as she entered the room, wearing a soft pink day dress, her brow furrowed as she saw me laying like a corpse in bed.

She shut the door softly behind her and came closer. "Why haven't I heard from you?"

"I've been... resting." I could only manage to bring myself up onto my elbows.

"For four days?"

I had days to come up with an excuse, but nothing even remotely convincing came to me, so all I could do was shrug.

"What happened?"

"Why did something *need* to happen?" I asked, knowing I was being difficult, but I was so overwhelmed, so tired.

My friend loosed a sigh. "Helena, you know you can talk to me. Hiding yourself away won't make you feel better."

Hiding.

From her, from Adam. From my brother, already on his way. From my mother.

And all that had replayed in my head, over and over, were the threats Lucas had thrown at Adam the last day we'd seen each other. The last day I'd seen him *alive*.

Or so I thought.

"It's just..." The words fled from me, stalled in my throat.

But she was patient.

Flora was my friend, my *best* friend, and had been my whole life. If I could tell anyone, it would be her.

"Adam isn't dead." My throat constricted, the dull ache there ever-present since I'd returned home, days ago.

"But he *is*." She blinked. "We had a funeral. His parents got a letter."

I remembered well. A letter from the government, issuing an apology that their son was missing, believed dead. Not even a pair of tags to show for it.

There was never a body.

Tears welled up in my lashes. "He's alive. I saw him."

"What *happened*?"

And how would I tell her? Any way I spun it in my head sounded like the ramblings of a madwoman. "I..." Choking on the words, I took a breath and willed the tears away. "The old church, the party—he was there."

"You went back?"

I should have brought her with me. I shouldn't have gone alone.

Nodding, I swallowed the lump in my throat. It all came rushing at me, everything I had tried to push down these last few days, few weeks—the same ache I never let myself feel when we'd heard the news six years ago.

"Mr. Sinclair invited me back, I suppose." I laced my fingers through hers. "I couldn't say no. And I went to a part of the house we'd not gone to the other night. Upstairs."

How not *to sound like I had been so completely drunk and hallucinating?*

"There was a... separate party, and I saw Mr. Sinclair there. And he led me away to a room, and there Adam was."

"He was just *there*?" She balked. "Waiting for you?"

"It seemed so."

He had been waiting for me, like he *knew* I would be there.

Did he wait every night?

And Sinclair had been the one to convince me to find the upstairs party. To lead me to Adam, who knew what was going on in that house, who knew Sinclair and was unfazed by the blood.

"I can't believe it, Helena." Flora pulled herself up further onto the bed, crossing her legs. "That's—this is crazy! So he just fooled everyone then? How long has he been back?"

"I don't know," I admitted.

"And when you say that he was at that house—"

"I believe it's *his* house."

It was the only thing that made sense. How he was so casually relaxing in that study. Well-to-do men like Sinclair at his bidding. That soft, confident smile, before I ran away.

"So Adam *is* Vince Thornton," she said, not sounding entirely convinced.

I had been chewing over everything for days, these thoughts that I had turned upside down and inside out, until they were no longer recognizable.

"And Dixon knows Vince Thornton." She sat up and scowled. "*That bastard*. And he didn't tell us!"

"Maybe he didn't know," I said.

Her cheeks began to flush, her ears turning red as she stewed. Perhaps she was learning then how us girls were just playthings to these men. "We should go back."

"What?" I paled.

"We should go back. To the mansion." She said it simply, but I saw a fire in her eyes that wasn't there before. "Just the two of us."

"But why?"

"*Because*. We need to talk to Vince—Adam. *I* would like to know what he's been up to. And Dixon would not allow it if we brought him along."

I fell back onto the bed, feeling entirely drained. "Flora, can we not?" My pulse was beginning to pound at my temples. I rubbed my eyes. I wasn't sure if I *ever* wanted to go back.

Promise me.

The thought of returning struck steel into my heart.

What did he want from me? And why *now*?

That blood—

I couldn't get it out of my head. Every time I shut my eyes to the light, a deep red marred my mind.

The bed dipped as Flora sat next to me, pulling me into her arms. "I just want the best for you. To figure this out for you."

"I know."

She leant her cheek on the top of my head, and we sat there for a moment. Like when we were little girls, hugging over simpler things.

If I could turn back the clock, I'd warn those little girls not to be fools.

"Do you want me to stay?" she asked, and my heart ached, because how could I not have trusted her? Why did I think she wouldn't be here for me, when she's never abandoned me? She was with me when I fell for Adam, with me when Lucas sent him away.

I shook my head. "You don't have to." *Mother would grow suspicious.*

She ran her fingers through my hair, brushing it away from my face. It was something I remember wishing my mother had done growing up.

"But I will," Flora offered. "I can't just go home knowing you are wasting away over here." A smile pulled at her lips, and it was infectious, my cheeks pulling tight for the first time in days.

"I'll be fine," I insisted. "I promise not to ignore your calls anymore."

"Good," she said, going to stand. She fixed her purse on

her shoulder, opened her mouth to speak, then paused. She bit her lip. "Is this about Lucas?"

When was it not?

No, I was upset because Adam *lied* to me.

I was mad, because how long had I been traipsing around the city, when he was right there under my nose?

Angry, because he never sought me out.

Broken, because I'd given up long ago, and for *nothing*.

"Maybe."

It was Lucas' fault we were here. Maybe Lucas already knew Adam was back and had threatened him again. Banned him from reaching out. It was the only thing I could fathom. But Lucas wouldn't pass up a chance to gloat, to dangle happiness over my head before swiftly taking it away again.

I rubbed my eyes again. "I don't know. Just—Can you come back tomorrow? I don't want to talk about it, but I need our teatime, even if Mother won't let me go out. I need everything to go back to normal."

When I opened my eyes, Flora nodded like she understood. "Same time as always?"

"Same time as always." I tried a smile.

She went to turn the knob.

"And don't bring it up with Dixon. Please. Not—not what happened." My past, Adam's past.

Flora glanced over her shoulder, raising a brow. "Anything for you, doll."

And then she was gone.

Thirteen

Lucas Quintrell arrived just before Mother and I were to leave for our luncheon two days later. Mother insisted on getting out of the house—though she never cared to ask why I was so quiet—and had the driver waiting for us outside. We had a noon reservation at a new spot, recommended by one of her ladies.

She was ushering me down the stairs of our townhome, after fussing at my hair for an hour, when our front door suddenly opened, and Lucas stepped in, a single suitcase in hand.

My mother gasped as though the air was stolen from her and rushed toward him, gathering him in her arms, like he was a child all over again. "Lucas!"

Halfway down the steps, my shoes were suddenly glued to the velvet runner.

Lucas was all smiles, his golden hair perfectly coiffed, his cheeks clean-shaven, grinning at her and her alone. Surveying the room, taking in all the paneled wood, the portraits of family members, racing across the electric wires connected to the small light fixture in the foyer. But those brown eyes darkened as soon as they landed on me.

"Oh, we're so happy you're home," my mother exclaimed, holding him tight to her.

He shrugged out of her grasp and set his suitcase down on the ground with a *thunk*. "Happy to make the trip." I could see right through that forced smile.

She nearly wept and wrapped her arms around him once more.

Forever her boy, even if he was the head of the family now.

Chills ran down my spine, my fingers digging into the wooden railing. I knew he was coming; Mother had warned me. But I thought we had another day or so—

All my wasting away in bed had made the days pass like a blur, time molten and rushing toward me all at once. I cursed inwardly that I spent the whole week wasting away, forgetting about his arrival. Not preparing myself and instead wallowing.

Mother sniffled. "Where is Lucy?"

He didn't answer for a moment, a tick in his jaw the only sign he was surprised at the question. "At home. Doctor's orders."

If anyone could make his visit any more bearable, it would have been his wife. But, seven months pregnant, she was constantly uncomfortable, as her sparse letters to me indicated, and was unable—or not allowed—to even get out of bed some days.

I did not envy her. I did not envy that she was tied so permanently to my brother.

"We will miss her." Mother patted Lucas' arm. "Helena, come greet your brother."

The stubborn ache in my throat, my chest, tightened. I had half a mind to turn around and retreat to my room. Let them have lunch, just the two of them. They wouldn't miss me.

Meeting them on the ground floor, I gave my dearest brother a clipped smile, if only to make my mother happy. "Lucas." My hands shook behind my back, clasped tight.

Those dark eyes, so similar to mine, looked down his nose at me. But he had no words for me, nothing to say. I could have sworn his lip almost curled, disgust flashing in his irises.

His disdain for me, so strong, even after months apart, was so unlike his fondness for me in childhood. A few years my senior, when we were children, I looked up to him, following him around like a puppy. We had played together all day; we were tutored separately, but in the same room, so he was always making me laugh with the funny faces he would throw at me.

Yet, as soon as his duty as the heir to the family name began to grow clearer to him, to become more tangible and real, he grew distant, until I felt I did not know him at all. It was solidified with Father's death, and further when he found out about Adam and me.

What would Mother think, huh? Father? He must be rolling in his grave.

Our butler grabbed Lucas' suitcase and hastily brought it out of the room, and it was as if Lucas had been here all along. The perfect boy at home with his doting mother, his ditzy sister.

"We will be late if we do not leave now." Mother sniffled, opening the front door. Our driver waited outside, the car idling against the curb.

The cloud inside my chest was circling, thunderous, seeping through my ribs, squeezing my muscles.

"I can just stay here." Instinct pulling at me to turn and go back up the stairs. The little girl inside me insisting my room was safer. Dark, comfortable, *lockable*. Mother turned to me with a sharp reply ready, but I interrupted her. "The reservation was only for two people."

"Nonsense." Lucas shot me a look. Shards in his eyes, daring me to refuse. "I'm sure we can convince the club to accommodate one more."

How dare *you*, he had said that night. I slammed my eyes shut.

He didn't want me there, for any other reason than to inspect me, to glare down his nose at me and figure out what I've been doing in his absence. *Whoring around.*

"This is not how you welcome your brother home." My mother glared at me. "You *will* be dining with us."

The club was busy at the lunch hour; the *maitre d'* was kind enough to add another chair to our reserved table, though upon our arrival, his face turned a flushed red at three people, not two. But it was Lucas, head of the Quintrell Company, and he could not refuse.

The food was untouchable. Though it looked delicious, my stomach rolled. Ignoring the salads, biscuits, and roasted beef brought out to us, I could hardly even sip on the chilled water served to me.

How I wanted a drink. A *real* drink.

The wealth in the room was immense, gold detailing all along the lights, gold-plated china, the clearest crystal glassware. The servers were all well-dressed and kept, even the buttons on their vests polished to shine, not a hair out of place. Gelled, made up. They never looked at us directly, averting their eyes downward, toward the floor, or at the dish in their hands.

Yet they didn't whirl like those at the church-turned-mansion on Long Island. Didn't appear out of nowhere with ambrosial gin. *Didn't work in a house where blood was being drained and served on ice.*

"How is the company?" my mother asked Lucas.

He gave some reply that his investments were paying off. And Mother wouldn't really know otherwise. She felt business was a man's responsibility, and as the woman of the family, it was none of her concern. A sentiment he mirrored.

"That child of yours will be lucky to take over," she laughed to herself. "One day."

Lucas nodded. "Yes. Sure. Absolutely." Like he was convincing himself of this, that the financial security was all for his children, and nothing more. "Unless, of course, Lucy bears a girl."

I abandoned my water glass, looking at him through my lashes. I had held my lips all day. The words came forth, quiet, "Can't a woman manage an estate?"

My mother shot me a look.

I swallowed the lump in my throat. "Is that not part of

what I'll be doing when I marry? Helping manage my husband's estate?"

The thought of marriage—of *me, married*—was unfathomable. The finality of it still hadn't sunken in, but I knew, deep within myself, I would not be marrying—I *couldn't*—because whoever Lucas chose would be just as insufferable.

"Your job as a wife is to manage the *house*. Keep appearances," Mother said, straightening her cloth napkin. "Remember? You must always be above reproach. You will do whatever your husband asks of you."

She had drilled this into my head countless times before, but her words still fueled a frustration within me.

"You wouldn't be able to handle managing an estate," Lucas muttered. His voice was low but its iciness scraped like knives in my skin.

Heat crawled up my neck. "And what would you know about what I can handle?"

At this, Lucas' look of disdain turned to a glare.

Those eyes locked on to me, and it was as if I could read the thoughts he pushed my way. That I should remain quiet, because he knew exactly what I'd done, what my mother feared, and he could tell everyone—but he wouldn't, at least not publicly, because he would never let what I'd done reflect poorly on him. What I did years ago, when I was still young and foolish. When my heart was easily captured.

He ran his tongue over his teeth, fist on the tablecloth.

"Anyway." He turned back to Mother. "I had the pleasure of visiting my future brother-in-law, and he seems to be managing quite well over in England."

"*England?*" The word shot out of me before I could stop it.

He had already chosen my husband?

I had thought I would still have time, that Lucas would be surveying the eligible men in the city, in our circles. That I'd be able to stall, to push the decision as long as possible. Or even that I'd be able to convince them to drop the whole thing, that his time was better spent with his wife, *away* from here.

But no, I was just a bargaining chip. A thing to be traded.

And the question was—what was he getting in return? Shares in some company? Status?

My mother gasped. She was just as surprised. "England? I suppose they do have quite the gentlemen over there. *Titled* men, no less."

Lucas gave her a calming smile, a hand on her arm. "I had a few empty days in my schedule and decided I would see a friend, who just so happens to be looking for a wife."

Sourness bloomed on my tongue.

"He's the heir of a barony."

"Oh, how wonderful!" Mother grinned, clasping her hands.

As if I wasn't there, as if I had no say in the matter.

As if it was decided.

It *was*.

"He's willing to make a visit over here, should we decide to secure an engagement."

I fisted my hands in my lap, grasping at my skirt. Nails digging into my thighs beneath the fabric.

How had this happened so quickly?

"Wait." I shook my head, forcing my voice to remain

strong, unwavering. "How can I marry someone I've never met?"

A shrug. "It happens all the time," he said. "You will not be the first, and certainly not the last."

Mother placed her hand on my arm, her face soft for the first time in months. There was a genuine spark of happiness in her eyes. "You will be fine, I assure you."

Yes, and you hated your husband, I wanted to shout. *Because* you *didn't get the choice.*

The fire within my lungs turned suffocating, smoke eating up all the breathable air. My heart thumped quickly against the cage of my chest, and though I willed myself to calm, it beat on, the rhythm like a runaway train.

Lucas kept talking, kept filling Mother in on my potential husband—the family's wealth, the grandness of their estate in the country, the past accomplishments of the heir—but I didn't hear it.

Mother was elated—all her fussing and primping finally coming to fruition.

Perhaps she was happy I'd be a whole ocean away. That I would quiet down and become someone else's problem, though she'd never say it.

What if I traveled all the way across the ocean just to find a bitter man that wanted nothing to do with me? I would be trapped, with a vast expanse of water in between me and the world I knew. Far away from New York and my family and Flora and... *Adam.*

"I don't believe I've been this happy since you married Lucille." My mother nearly swooned. Her hand found Lucas' arm, steadying herself in her seat.

He grimaced. "Yes, what a happy time in our lives."

"And is she happy?" I bit out, unable to stop myself. "Is Lucy happy?"

Lucas only laughed. "Lucy is content to do as she should—providing me with an heir."

"Is that all she is good for?"

Mother hissed my name.

Lucas waved a hand. "So what? This is tedious."

I scowled. "She is not your wife simply so you can *use* her." I believed the words wholeheartedly, but I knew it was foolish speaking them aloud.

"What do you think your husband would be using *you* for?" Lucas looked down his nose at me. "You will marry, and your union will be consummated, and he will bed you until you give him an heir. It is nothing new, Helena."

I wanted to vomit.

"Lucas," my mother said in soft reprimand, a glance around the room. "This is not proper talk for the table—"

"When he is your husband—when you are *his* wife—he is free to do with you as he pleases," Lucas went on. "*You* do not make that choice—you won't make *any* choices. Your husband will."

I stood from my seat. I was shaking my head, the room spinning.

"Sit down," Mother whispered. The patrons at tables near us began to glance our way at the commotion. She turned to Lucas with pleading in her eyes. "Son, please. We can talk further about this later—"

"No."

"Yes, do sit down, *sister*," Lucas sneered.

I narrowed my eyes at him and resisted the urge to throw

my glass of water in his face, knowing it would only ruin what reputation I did have.

But did I even really care anymore?

Instead, I whirled on my heels, nearly running into a server with a tray of food, about to place our luncheon on the table.

"Helena!"

Ignoring my mother's calling, I stormed out of the dining room, my heels clacking on the marble floor of the hotel's foyer, shocked and concerned eyes following me until I was outside, leaning against the stone exterior wall, bent at the waist and wheezing.

I sucked air into my lungs, a sour taste coating my tongue.

No. *No.*

I couldn't do it. I wouldn't.

I braced a hand on the wall, squeezing my eyes shut, trying to ground myself in the cold air around me. I had rushed out so quickly I had not grabbed my coat and goosebumps were sprouting on my arms, the light sweater doing nothing against the cool early-spring breeze. But I relished in it, in the lack of warmth. Like I was alone, like no one was touching me, no hands grasping at my throat, no hands pulling my wrists down, no glowers or glares digging into me.

My back hit the wall of the hotel, my head falling back. Pedestrians passed, trying their best not to stare at the hyperventilating woman without a coat in the cool weather, all on her own.

Heat bunched under my eyes, and I wiped my cheek, only to notice my face was wet. Angrily, I wiped my eyes, as delicately as I could, not to mess up what makeup lined my eyes.

How dare *he*. How dare Lucas even come here, under the guise of wanting to see me off.

He knew exactly what he was doing. Knew that it haunted me. Reminding me to behave, to stay in my place, lest he reveal the truth to Mother—

Adam's face flashed in my mind, my throat already tight with dread, with grief, with frustration.

Was it so wrong to wish the happiest time of my life had never happened, only so I would not feel the pain that I do now?

A sob caught in my throat, and when I opened my eyes, my breath was stolen.

Because there, across the bustling street, people and carriages and cars passing between us, was a familiar face.

Dark auburn hair framing pallid skin, strong cheekbones, concern tightening his jaw, those widening hazel eyes. Eyes that had stared into mine nights before.

A large carriage passed between us—and then he was gone, vanished, a fragment of my imagination.

FOURTEEN

I found my way home amidst the bustle of the city streets as night quickly descended upon the city, weaving my way through pedestrians and cars jam-packed into snaking lines down the avenues.

My tears had dried as soon as I saw his face—but surely I only saw him because I *wanted* to see him; like my spirit knew better, and summoned the image of him to calm the ache in my chest, the anger spitting through me.

Promise me.

I hugged myself as I wandered the streets, and when I returned to our house, the butler was surprised to see me walk up without Mother or Lucas behind me. They must have still been at the hotel, because the car was absent.

"Miss?" His eyes were wide when I slammed open the door.

Freezing tendrils wrapped around my limbs as I ran up the stairs. Something fragrant sat in the air, our cook already preparing dinner.

I just wanted to curl up in my room. Perhaps bore a hole into the floor and disappear.

Yet, as my bedroom door bounced off the wall, I stopped in my tracks. My handmaid stood at my vanity, a pair of earrings dangling in her fingers, held up to her ears.

She gasped, whirling around like a child caught stealing candy from the jar. "It's not—I—"

"Take them," I mumbled.

"You're home early!" She returned the jewelry to the box upon the vanity. "I swear, I—"

"*Take* them," I insisted. "I have no use for them."

Her jaw snapped shut, her curly black hair tucked neatly into a knot at her nape. "Can I ask what's wrong?"

"You would not understand." I fell onto my bed, exhaling all the air from my lungs.

"Perhaps I can help."

"No. Can you—just please get my robe."

She bowed her head and retreated to the wardrobe. I did not speak to her as she helped me out of my day dress, slipping the stockings down my legs, hiding my shoes away into the wardrobe. Undoing the jeweled clips in my hair, letting the waves fall around my ears. We were silent as she held the silk robe open for me and I slipped my arms through the watery fabric.

I had to bite my lip, so hard I thought the skin was about to break, to hold everything in. She left without a word when I dismissed her with a wave of my hand.

I *wouldn't* do it—this forced marriage to the baron-heir, who couldn't care less about me, who was probably in Lucas' pockets and advised to raise a hand against me should I even speak.

And then I despaired for Lucy, because I knew it was the life she must be living.

Their marriage was the example Mother wanted me to follow: Lucas, after taking Father's place as head of the company, decided he was ready to marry, because of course, it was the next logical step. Sometimes I wondered if he wanted a wife and child at all, but the match had been arranged years before, when Father was still alive. Lucille Barrow was all too willing; a shy, young girl from a budding family, who was enamored by the first young man to give her any attention.

I remember my brother remarking that she was quiet and pretty enough. And not long after the wedding, she announced she was with child.

The first time I met her, I pitied her. She averted her eyes when Lucas turned her way, did nearly the same with Mother and me, until I was able to corner her and insist that we were sisters—not strangers.

If Lucas expected me to comply like Lucy did, he was sorely mistaken.

But he knew that, no doubt.

Was this just a way for him to impose his fist on me, under Mother's guiding hand?

If I stayed in the house one more second, I'd suffocate.

Running my hands over my face, I left my room, half tiptoeing, half unworried if anyone saw me. My feet were bare as I stepped down the stairs, and down the hall, past the kitchen and the various other drawing rooms and parlors, and through the heavy door to the gardens.

The moment my foot touched the rough stone path, a weight lifted from my shoulders. Our garden wasn't terribly large, but it was a bit of sanctuary in the city, tall ferns and trees planted along the exterior and hiding the street. The cook had her own section near the door, growing herbs and garlic and some vegetables she used in our dishes, but the majority of the garden was flowers, things that couldn't be eaten, but only seen.

It became a place I could step away to after Father died. He used to let me into his study, to examine his books, to pester him while sitting on his knee as a child. But as I grew older, it became apparent that what went on in the study was none of my business, and after he died, everything important was transferred to Lucas' own study, the rest of the books and furniture left to the moths.

I walked down the curving path, rounding the stone fountain with the cherub raising its plump hand to the heavens. The water sat stagnant, a green film ringing the basin of the fountain, leaves and other detritus coating the bottom. A vine wrapped around the cherub, and my mind flashed to that first evening, to the nude woman and her writhing above the crowd.

If only I had known then who was staring at me from the balcony.

I trailed my fingers along the fountain and shivered when the frigid stone sent a zing up my arm. The air cooled, the late afternoon slowly turning to evening, and I had not realized how long I had stayed out, wandering the city. Stepping off the path, the dirt was damp beneath my feet, grass reaching up and tickling my ankles. There were benches placed around, moss growing up the sturdy legs. I made my way toward the sycamore in the far corner, letting my weight sink into the soft earth under its branches. If anyone came looking, I'd be hidden away, unless they came off the path to search for me. Just as I wanted it.

Traffic still buzzed from outside the garden walls.

And though I sat there for upwards of an hour, as the sun began to set and the sky turned to crimson, then violet, it wasn't until I brushed the grass next to me that I realized a single rose had been set curiously upon the ground—a deep maroon, stained black at the petal-edges, its long stem tucked into the roots of the sycamore. As though someone had left it behind.

When I reached for the stem, I pulled away quickly, pricking myself on its thorns, and bringing my finger to my lips, sucking away the blood it had drawn so easily.

That evening, I sat up in bed, facing the window, warm embers burning in the fireplace. I held the rose in my hand, twisting the stem in my fingers. I had snipped off the thorns, but couldn't part with them, and they were at the bottom of the small vase I kept the bloom in. Every time I pressed upon the stem with the pad of my finger, the spot where I was pricked, a sore reminder shot up my hand, the spot still tender, a reminder of the flower's sender.

It was a welcome pain. Like the ache from the passion of a lover.

Curled up in bed, cradling the rose to my chest, careful not to crush the delicate petals, I played through that first real outing that Adam and I had—how he'd been waiting for me, eager, staring up at the house like he knew exactly where I was inside—and every other encounter. The secret nights in the garden just below my window, when he'd scaled the brick and iron wall, throwing a rock at my window like he was Romeo, summoning me to him. The love we'd shared in the garden, the ways we dared to show each other, when damnation was just an opened door away.

And I wondered, as I drifted off to sleep, was our wrenching apart—his death—inevitable, too?

When I awoke to the soft gray morning light, the rose was cushioned on the pillow, right next to my head. The petals fragile and unblemished, a single drop of dew dripped from the bud, as though cut from the garden only moments before.

FIFTEEN

I couldn't stay away for long, and though I kicked myself the entire drive to the church-turned-mansion near the Sound, there was a thrill growing in my stomach that I could not ignore. I was walking directly into the monster's den.

Flora convinced me to bring her. Maybe it was a mistake to tell her that I was thinking of returning—and I didn't want to know if she made good on her promise from the other evening—but she arrived at my family's house with her usual chipper smile, and a promise to Mother, whose unbelieving and unapproving brow rose ever higher, to return me by midnight.

I was surprised Mother let me go at all. Though, surely, if Lucas had been in the room and not out on an errand, I'd no doubt be prohibited from leaving the house again after that "stunt" I pulled at lunch.

Flora's driver dropped us at the top of the drive, past all the parked roadsters gleaming in the moonlight.

She gripped my hand and grinned, pulling me from the car. "It's time!"

Apprehension still boiled inside of me. *You shouldn't be here.*

As we passed the gates, starting up the grand steps to the massive front door, a phantom finger traced its way down my spine. Everything told me to turn around—the memories of what I'd seen, all that blood dripping down pointed teeth, those bodies gyrating—

I couldn't expose Flora to it. But maybe I worried for nothing, because she had come on her own a few days prior, and who knew what she'd seen. She left Dixon behind again tonight. As she readied me in my room, setting my curls and applying my rouge, she avoided all my questions about him, her only tell the twitching of her right eye.

Though, as we ascended the steps, his absence left an exposed feeling at my back.

On either side of the path leading to the house were small gardens, providing seclusion amidst its tall ferns and vines. Electric lights hung above the path, and as we walked I saw the flash of a leg here and there, hands gripping beaded skirts, sharp gasps, heady giggles, deep moans. Once through the gates, the revelers couldn't help themselves.

"Are you sure we should be doing this?"

Flora stopped and took my hands. "Absolutely. What good would it do to avoid him?"

I sighed, because she was right.

It was eating at me, day and night, knowing he was here, *alive*. Even if I didn't understand.

Following her into that devilish foyer for the second time, Flora never let go of my hand, winding us through the crowd. She ignored the servers and their champagne, though I longed for a glass to prepare me for whatever happened this evening. She tugged on my fingers, whipping her head side to side, asking others, "Do you know of Thornton? Does anyone know where he is?"

A man in a gray suit, maybe twenty years our elder, burst forth a laugh at the question. "The question of the hour!" And he lifted his glass in cheers and turned back to his group.

Their yelling had garnered some attention, but the best answers Flora got were shrugs before people turned away from us.

The decorations this evening were silver, tinsel hanging from the chandelier, the electric lights flickering like stars. The massive ballroom held hundreds of people, all who gave us odd looks as Flora asked for Thornton's whereabouts.

"We'll never find him," I shouted above the din.

"Of course we will. He just needs to know you're here," she said, looking determined as ever and leading me toward the grand stairs.

"Are you sure we should go up there?"

She gave me a look. "I'll turn this house upside down looking for him."

Pushing through the throng, we paused at the second landing. The crowd of the ballroom was below us, but there were plenty of people on the second floor, leaning precariously against the banisters, wandering down side hallways. A woman leaned so far over the railing I thought she'd fall, but a man clutched at her dress, keeping her steady while she waved down at someone below, laughter streaming from both of them. Flora pulled me past the couple, toward the large hallway that branched off into smaller corridors.

The house was a maze. Surely partygoers had gotten lost before. I nearly did, when running away from what I'd seen the other night, taking a wrong turn a couple of times in my panic. One could probably extend their stay past the one night, find a spot and hide for weeks before they were ever found.

"*Where are you going?*" a deep voice demanded, and we both stopped in our tracks when a male figure blocked our way.

Dixon.

His sleeves were rolled to his elbows, his mahogany hair combed neatly, only one strand falling before his eyes, which darkened when they landed on us. He looked at Flora, then at me, his brows pulled so low I nearly expected a growl from him. He was often displeased with us, in his protective way, but the anger that radiated from him charged the air in a way I'd not felt before.

"Out of our way." Flora made to step past him, but his arm shot out, caging around her waist.

Her glare was sharp. "*Lloyd Dixon.*"

"I know better than to let you off on your own."

She pushed away from him and crossed her arms. "So you can go out when you want, but *I* need supervision?"

"No, it's—" He shook his head, stepping in her way again. "This house is not safe."

She scoffed. "Look around! It seems plenty safe to me!" The only threat, really, was the bad decisions one would make in such a lawless place. At least, to her knowledge.

He wouldn't budge. "All it takes is one moment. Slipping into the wrong room and you're done for."

"What are you talking about?"

So he knew.

His eyes glanced toward me, however briefly—so, he knew *I* knew.

Flora's hand settled on her hips. "We're trying to find Thornton."

"You won't find him."

"Yes, we will. Helena knows him."

I didn't want to get in between this lovers' spat, but Dixon's eyes narrowed on me.

"How do *you* know him?"

Dixon already hated him, it seemed, and I didn't know if telling him everything would do Adam any favors. Dixon probably thought I'd stumbled into whatever happened in this house and ran into Vince Thornton, somehow entangling myself in whatever dark world slept under the veil of reality.

I blinked. "It just happened."

Dixon turned back to Flora. "Come, let me take you back downstairs. We can dance."

"*Not now, Dixon.*"

He ran a hand down his face. "Flora—"

She looped her arm through mine. "I'll meet you later."

"Fine." He looked to the gilt ceiling, exasperation straining his jaw. "If you come with me, I'll tell Helena where he is."

We both paused, and I knew Flora was waiting for me to make the decision.

"I don't want you mingling with his crowd," Dixon continued.

"But Helena can?"

He muttered under his breath.

"It's fine." I decided, freeing myself from Flora's grasp. "I can manage on my own. I'll find you later?"

She nodded hesitantly, crossing her arms so Dixon couldn't grab her hand.

He leaned down to me, telling me some indecipherable message with his eyes, as his lips nearly brushed my ear. I felt his breath hot on my cheek, but it didn't make my toes curl like... like it had when Adam and I were young. In a whisper only I could hear, he said, *In the garden. Waiting for you.*

How he knew it, I wasn't sure.

And he moved away, pulling Flora to his side. *Don't drag her into this*, that message in his eyes seemed to say, before he guided her back down the stairs.

I was on my own, and maybe that was how it should've been. I had no idea what Flora would do if she actually faced Adam, how he'd react to me bringing someone along.

Was he really waiting for *me*? And how did Dixon know?

There were seedy dealings in the manor, maybe relating to Dixon's income—there was plenty of liquor in the building to make that a possibility—and clearly the revelers were either oblivious, or were just as ensnared in that web.

The glitz and glamor hid the murk well.

Steeling myself, I turned on my heel and made my way down, the only way I knew how to get outside. I still had yet to fully explore the grounds, but I assumed the gardens were behind the house.

The band in the ballroom continued to play, and the professional dancers beamed at the guests, whirling around and kicking their feet out, barely touching the ground. Feathers and silver beading swung around their bodies, men reaching for the strings of beads as though they could catch the girls dancing.

When I was a child, I'd read books under candlelight about fairies and their dances, how they could charm you to dance until your feet bled, and you wouldn't even want to stop. Your mind would be lost, thrown to the wind, with only the search for pleasure to move you. And the fairies would watch in glee, laughing at their human puppets.

Outside, I could still hear the music. The fountain bubbled, and a couple jumped in, still in their clothes. The girl wore a black number, lucky for her, and her stockings already had holes. The man fell, bursting forth with laughter as a wave of water went over the stone side of the fountain, and he pulled the girl on top of him.

Soon I came upon large iron gates, propped open, the borders of the garden lined with full hedges and cypress trees twirled toward the stars. Their height reached almost that of the spires of the mansion.

A chill wracked my body, a cool phantom embrace pulling me in. The breeze fell, and a stillness settled deep into the stones.

A few people mulled around, but at my entrance into the gated space, they looked up.

I felt like an intruder. Every face, I anticipated seeing him. I could hear them whisper as I passed.

I hugged myself as I wound deeper into the cypresses, a few sycamores scattered here and there. Once I traversed far enough, I realized that all the flowers around me, open and crisply white, were moonflowers. Fragrant gardenias and curiously bright lilies bobbed at me. The perfume of the blooms was so potent, when I shut my eyes I nearly felt my feet come off the ground, floating into the air. An enchanted fairy garden from my stories, luring me in to trap me in their underground revelry.

Every bloom perfect. Almost too perfect, maybe even artificial.

A stranger rounded the bend and my heart soared.

Until I saw his face.

It was not Adam.

But I did recognize him.

The stranger grinned, a sharp tooth glinting bright like the petals of the moonflowers. Hands in his pockets, he walked toward me, and though the nagging voice in my head told me to run again, I found myself rooted to the spot.

"Interesting seeing you here," he crooned.

He stopped only a few inches before me, too close for comfort.

But I refused to let him see the fear that made my pulse beat against my neck, my ribs. It must have worked, at least a little bit. He eyed the fluttering of my heart beneath my ear. His gaze felt like the sharp graze of a knife on my throat. Sharp like I knew those teeth could be. His eyes snapped back up to mine. "Not quite as scared, are you?"

"What is there to be scared of?" I challenged.

It was then I could smell the alcohol on his breath. Maybe he wasn't a threat, just an intoxicated man. Maybe I was overreacting and he wasn't one of *them*. A drunk man I could handle. I knew where to kick and make it count.

He inhaled deeply, like he was taking in the smell of the air. His nostrils flared. "Girls like you should always be scared."

"Is that a threat?"

He shrugged. "It's whatever you make of it."

Instinctively, I stepped back, but felt leafy thorns at my spine. A hedge. Cool stones beneath them—a wall. In the center of the gardens.

"I could Make you," he whispered, leaning in so I could see only his eyes. They were brown, but so close I could see the flecks of gold, the blackness of his pupils, so deep they nearly drew me in.

"Make me?"

He nodded once. He was staring at my throat again. "It will take only a moment."

"Not interested." I mustered as much strength and boredom into my voice as I could and moved to side-step the man.

His hand fell on my elbow. A sliminess snaked its way onto my skin.

"Just a moment, and you won't have to worry anymore," he whispered, and then his lips were nearly on my neck, and though I knew I had to run, willing my knee to jerk upward, screaming to *move*, I was still as stone, paralyzed. I lost all control of my movements as his nose trailed along my ear.

Move.

A large, pale hand landed on his shoulder and wrenched him back.

His eyes widened as he stumbled, but only for a moment.

I'd seen Adam glare, seen him angry before. The last time

I'd seen him, *before*, was the only time I'd seen a cool rage take him over. As though the life left his eyes, he darkened, and though he said nothing when Lucas berated him and threatened him, threatened *me*, I knew everything he wanted to say, because that fury in his eyes exposed him as the progeny of a devil.

I swore his pupils became black as the midnight sky above.

My would-be attacker paled even whiter than the flowers around us.

"Go." Adam's voice wasn't his own.

It only took the one word, and I was forgotten by the stranger. He didn't even look at me, eyes glazed over as soon as Adam appeared, and he turned to leave. I thought I saw claws at his fingertips, poised at his sides, stiff and ready.

I loosed a shuddering breath, watching my attacker retreat. "I had it handled."

Those predator eyes slid toward me. "You had that anything but handled."

"I don't need you to step in and save me."

I've made it this long.

Monsters hadn't existed before his return. Monsters that drew blood for their own pleasure just didn't *exist*. Until now.

The muscle in his jaw feathered. "I'm sorry."

"For what?"

The waning adrenaline made my fingers numb.

Maybe it was because we expected each other this evening, but the air between us felt different. I hadn't happened upon him by surprise—and he seemed to want to be found.

He was waiting. *For me.*

"For everything," he said.

I felt my resolve crack a little. I didn't want to forgive so easily.

"For leaving you. For waiting all these years. For letting you go through it alone."

"I wasn't alone."

His expression was pained, almost like he couldn't look at me, and it made me angry.

"I had Flora," I said. I wanted him to hurt, too. "I found ways to pass the time—people to pass the time with."

He knew what it meant, and he nodded. "It's my fault."

I was *years* past worrying whose fault it was. It was something I'd gone over in my head to exhaustion. In the end, it didn't matter, because I was still stuck with Mother wanting me to marry, still stuck with Lucas choosing the man I'd be tied to for the rest of my life.

A sob suddenly wracked through me, catching in my throat. "What happened?" Voice breaking, it came out a plea.

He'd been missing—I thought he *died*. On a battlefield, thousands of miles away from his home, on another continent, surrounded by other boys sent away to die. What were his last thoughts? Who shot him? Friendly fire, an accident, something completely preventable? Or was he taken? A hostage?

He looked like he wanted to come to me, to make the step forward and take me into his arms, but he didn't. Maybe he forgot how.

"I went to France," he began.

I suppressed the urge to tell him to stop. He didn't have to relive whatever it was—but I needed to know.

"It was my first time on the field, in battle, and before it even began, I was full of bullets. I don't remember a lot of it," he confessed, and looked at me through his lashes, as though he worried how I'd react. "There were bombs, and gasses, and I couldn't move, and I thought I lost all my limbs. Then I couldn't breathe."

He glanced upward at the sky, mirroring Dixon's exasperation from earlier. Something like worry lined his eyes.

I'd seen men come home from overseas. They never came back the same. Like they went to the war and came back a little less themselves, forgetting a piece of their soul across the ocean.

Lucas sneered at the men in the streets, and Mother never said anything, but her eyes said it all.

"I wanted to follow you," I admitted. Wanted to tell him everything, how I'd been dragged home by Lucas after Adam had left, locked in my room.

He shook his head. "I wouldn't have let you."

For a brief moment, the boy before me was the printer's apprentice I knew so well.

"I woke up dead," he said, returning to his past. His eyes glazed over like he was watching it all before him, like one of those moving pictures. "I *was* dead, but I could feel the ground beneath me again. Couldn't feel the beat of my heart, didn't need to breathe, but I could move. There wasn't any more blood. At least, none of *mine*."

He'd held a glass of red liquid a few nights ago. I hadn't wanted to accept it, to admit it to myself, that he wasn't just *living* amongst these monsters.

"You…" I didn't know how to say it. "You didn't come back the same."

"I'm not the same."

This was not my Adam. He used to be, but he was something, someone different. The dangerous glint to his eye told me so. It wasn't just the effects of the war.

"You have to tell me," I insisted. I couldn't go home without the truth. Couldn't return to Mother and Lucas and the prospect of this forced marriage without knowing wholly what had happened.

"Come here." He held his arm out to me. And at my hesitation, I saw something break in him. "I won't hurt you," he said, his voice so soft.

I put my hand in his and tried to ignore the shock I felt at his cool skin. His fingers fit in mine just like they used to, intertwining the exact same.

He led me out of the garden, and the guests watched as we passed, staring just like they did when I wandered in. Except now, their eyes widened at Adam, at our hands linked together, and they averted their gazes almost in a sort of reverence.

He was not the same.

The party on the lawn was slightly more subdued than before; a few people passed out against tables, the couple no longer in the fountain, a few articles of clothing discarded and soaked on the ground. Adam led me around the side of the house, down a walk I'd not seen before, and we ended up on a veranda. Huge marble pillars supported the roof. Electric lights strung there, too, to light our way.

"You live here," I said.

He nodded. "Yes."

"How long?"

How long have you been back?

He paused, and his grip on me tightened. "Two years."

But the parties had only been going on for the better part of a year.

"Why?"

He seemed to know what I meant and looked directly at me. I felt the same chill run down my flesh as I did that first night, when he was high above the crowd, and he found me, even when I must have been a speck amongst thousands. "To find you."

We rounded a corner, and the only noise I could hear from the party came muffled through the windows, the echoes bouncing off the trees on his lawn. Sounding so far away, like we had the house to ourselves.

He pulled me to a stop. "Look."

At first, through the window there was only darkness. But as my eyes adjusted, I could see that we looked in on a room—somewhere private, because there were only two people I could see. A couple—they held each other in a tight embrace. My cheeks burned as I realized I was a voyeur to their pleasure.

"I need you to understand," Adam was saying behind me. He caged me in to the window, his strong frame pressed against mine.

And as the woman bit the neck of her lover, I felt it. I felt the bite myself, the prick against my neck. I reached up as though to palm the wound.

Adam's hand fell to my hip. The touch so familiar I nearly wept.

The woman cradled the man's skull, and his arms

wrapped around her waist, pulling her even closer. He angled his throat to give her greater access. Rivulets of red ran down the column of his neck, staining his collar, running in streams down her arm. He fell to his knees, and she followed. I gasped, believing him unconscious, but he gripped her harder, and she was suddenly in his lap.

I did not know where the blood or her red dress began. And when she finally pulled away, the man gazed at her in hunger. He leaned up and licked his own blood off her lips. He had those knife-like teeth of his own, bared in a smile.

Adam's lips pressed to my throat, and he kissed the spot beneath my ear so gently, savoring the taste of my skin. I reached up and wound my fingers through his hair and shut my eyes.

If I willed it hard enough, I could pretend we were six years younger, and Lucas had never found out and sent him away. I could pretend we'd never parted. I could pretend he'd never died.

His caress sent heat straight through me. I knew he felt it too, his hand gripping my hips even harder, pulling me straight into him.

"I missed you," he said against my neck, ravishing me with more kisses. I never wanted to leave his grasp, never wanted to leave that moment where maybe everything could be okay. He'd returned, and he was okay, and I had yet some freedom.

I turned, wrapping my arms around his neck and bringing him down to me. His lips grazed mine softly. I pressed my forehead to his and just breathed in the scent of him. A smokiness, a familiar sweet smell of his cologne. The same from before—a scent he couldn't have afforded, but I'd gifted it to him and he wore it until he left.

A smile pulled at my lips.

He gazed down at me hungrily, but it was a different hunger from the couple on the other side of the window. They continued their bloodletting, but I could see now it was a feeding of passion, a frenzy of lust, and not the murder I thought it was.

And if this was Adam's world, then so be it.

"I want to kiss you," he said, echoing the first night we'd ever been alone.

My cheeks were wet, my vision blurred.

He didn't have to say anything more, because I stood on my toes and pressed my lips to his, and it was like coming home. I burned for him. Ached for the way he held me. Wanted him to make me forget everything I'd done these past few years, every night alone.

"I want you," I breathed, and before the words were fully spoken, he lifted me up, a predatory glint in his eye, and whisked me away.

SIXTEEN

He only put me down when he found a secluded spot on the grounds, away from it all. As he carried me, I couldn't look away from him. He supported me effortlessly, like I weighed nothing, and when he glanced down at me, there was a fire in his eyes that only burned hotter every passing second.

I hadn't realized how much I missed him.

His brow was strong, his hair only just now mussed, thanks to my wandering fingers. The auburn color hadn't changed, a red so dark it was nearly the color of wine. Without the gel, it was long enough to fall into his eyes. The time away had made his shoulders broader, his jaw stronger, his limbs muscled but lean.

He set me down on plush grass, gingerly, like he thought I might break, shrugging his jacket off and laying it on the ground. I'd had only a moment to catch my breath before he pulled me flush against him again.

"I should have found you sooner," he muttered against my lips, his fingers coming up to cradle my jaw.

I held his face in my own hands, his stubble, his plush lip. He was *real*.

"Yes, you should have," I said, making us meet again. He tasted like whiskey, something metallic. Our mouths moved against each other like we'd never forgotten how.

His arousal pressed against my stomach. The heat running through me pooled at my core, my muscles tightening in anticipation.

It had been too long.

Why had it taken so long for him to find me?

He slipped the dainty straps of my dress off my shoulders. The cool air on my exposed chest sent goosebumps across my flesh, his hands smoothing over my arms, leaving a trail of shivers in his wake.

I pulled his hair so hard I knew it must hurt, but I couldn't let go. Couldn't let him leave me, even for a second.

He nipped at my lip, sharp teeth threatening to puncture. His hands roamed down my sides, around my hip, and under my ass, before he suddenly hitched my knees up around his hips. I squealed, gripping onto him harder as we fell backward.

He loomed over me, the soft earth beneath me, a whisper of a breeze dancing between us.

I'd never felt so eager for anyone else, not even after I believed him dead. I burned for him the first time we did this, and the fire was relit, spreading through my veins, a want so intense I was shaking.

He just gazed at me with hooded eyes, like he was

soaking in the sight of me, beneath him, sprawled out on the grass. My skirt was around my hips, my stockings the only barrier between us as he settled between my thighs. My shoes had fallen off at some point in our haste, away in the grass.

"This is a sight I missed," he mused, untucking his shirt, the clicking of his belt sounding out. My toes curled.

When he was free, he fell back upon me, his mouth falling straight to my throat. He licked across my collarbone, sucking at my skin, biting at me just hard enough to steal my breath. I arched underneath him, my fingers clawing at his arms.

"Don't stop," I whispered, hands turning to fists in the fabric of his shirt.

His tongue trailed to my breasts. My eyes rolled back into my head at the sensation of his mouth on me, his hands roughly pulling my dress down so I was bared to him. He palmed one breast, squeezing roughly, almost to the point of pain.

Tears gathered at the corners of my eyes, the pleasure of having him too good, and we'd only just started. He was sucking, pulling my nipple into his mouth, until I was crying out, wrapping my ankles around his middle.

He groaned and ground his cock even harder against me.

"I won't stop," he said. "Once I have you again, it's only you. It was only ever you."

All these years, I'd been chasing this with other men that could never compete. Seeking *this*—this rush of desire, this visceral, mind-bending want.

And all these years, he'd been waiting for *me*.

The tears fell, trailing down my cheeks.

"I won't let you go again," he said, with so much urgency, a wild look in his eyes. "You've always been mine. You were made for me."

I nodded, because it felt so true, like it was written in the stars above us. We'd both been alive on this earth, and I didn't even know it, and now I felt so foolish for not believing that he'd find a way back to me.

My stockings were ripped apart, the flimsy fabric hanging on just barely to one of my knees, and he was pressing against me in a friction so delicious I wanted to scream. His soft flesh was hard, bigger than I remembered, and he was not even yet inside. My hips moved on their own, drawing him in closer.

"You have to say it," he demanded, bracing my arms onto the ground, holding me still. "Say that you are mine."

The head of his cock brushed against the apex of my thighs. "I'm yours," I sighed. "I'm yours, I'm yours." Repeating over and over like a prayer, willing it to be true.

And then he pressed into me, a burning stretch forcing my thighs even further apart. He took me all at once, sliding in slowly, forcing me to accommodate his size.

"I've been waiting for this," he said against my throat.

My thighs burned, my clit throbbing. I couldn't relax, my muscles squeezing him, even when I felt I was splitting apart. My breaths came shallow, and I knew if he were anyone else, I'd tell him to stop, that I couldn't do it. That it was too much.

But I wanted that burn, wanted to bleed for him. I wanted him to claim me again.

Tears kept falling, mingling with my ruined curls. I squeezed my eyes shut until his thumb ran against my cheek.

"Look at me," he whispered.

When I opened my eyes, he brought his thumb to his lips, licking my tear away, that sharp tooth glinting in the moonlight.

And then he started to move, slowly withdrawing, the friction bittersweet. My thighs shaking around him, I locked my ankles.

"Have you missed me?" he asked, dragging out. Pushing through my walls again, in and out, in and out. "I think of *nothing* but you." He forced his thumb through my lips, pressing down on my tongue, fingers bruising at my jaw. "These lips. This cunt. *You.*"

A sob broke from me, unsaid anguish spilling down my cheeks.

"You've been mine this whole time, Helena." Another harsh thrust. "Say it."

"*I'm yours.*"

His pace became urgent, claiming, stretching every bit of me around the hard length of him, forcing us together like two halves to one whole. The tears came freely as I struggled against his ferocity, writhing and pleading and needing everything he would give.

He withdrew suddenly, sitting back on his heels.

A jagged breath escaped me, shock at the emptiness and the cold air, before his hands were on my hips, flipping me over. His hand smoothed over my ass, my hip, before he lined himself up again. Sliding the head through the slick wetness between my thighs, spreading my arousal along his length, sending shocks through my spine.

And yet, he didn't fuck me.

Over my shoulder, through blurred tears, I met his eyes.

He was grinning, a cruel tilt to his lips as he held my hips still, denying me, over and over, reveling in my impatience, my need.

My hands turned to fists in the grass. "*Please.*"

A dark laugh. "That was all I wanted to hear."

And he sheathed himself inside me again, all in one vicious thrust. The new angle drew a groan from deep within me. He would never leave me, even if we were separated; he was mine, and I was his. His thrusts became a brutal, steady rhythm. My arms too weak to hold myself up, I buried my face in his coat, spasming against him, my cries muffled into the fabric. Powerless to do anything but *feel*. The heady glide of his cock, the cool evening air on my damp flesh, and then—a sharp prick at my hips, his nails digging into my skin.

My back arched as the pleasure built again, relentlessly maddening.

"Will you come again, darling?" he said through his teeth, reaching down to the nerves at the apex of my thighs. "I want you to come." Circling roughly, knowing just how I liked it—"Come on my cock."

My body would not deny him. A burst of pleasure shot through me, and I pushed my ass into him, urging him on, harder, *harder*. I must have said the word, because he just couldn't get *deep* enough, not even as pinned me in place, his hips slapping against mine.

I wanted this to last forever. I wanted him to fuck me, to make up for these lost years, until the sun came up.

And then we'd start all over again.

Nights lost to this all-consuming pleasure.

"*Fuck*, Helena," he groaned, his movements turning to

sharp jerks. A warmth filled me, his cock twitching with each pulse. I trembled beneath him, gasping for air, my eyes swollen, so wholly incomplete and put back together all at once.

He leaned forward, kissing his way across my shoulders, along my neck, finding that sensitive spot beneath my ear again. Lingering there, his lips warm, tongue fluttering against my skin. Still hard within me, his hips moving in a slow, subtle grinding.

I wanted him forever, now that I had him.

Wanted *this* forever.

Because how could I ever go back to my life before?

It terrified me, knowing what he was now capable of, knowing what world he dwelled in. As he sucked on my neck, he thrust once again, and again, his breath hot at my throat.

The unsaid threat that he could bite me.

And I *wanted* him to.

I wanted his teeth in me, wanted him to claim me in every way he could.

But after a moment, a deep breath, he pressed one more kiss to my pulse. "You have to come back to me," he mumbled.

"I haven't yet left," my voice breathy, soft.

"But you will."

"You said you want me to stay."

"Of course I do," he growled under his breath, grinding against me. Warmth seeped down my thigh. "But your friends are expecting you."

Was it too much to ask to stay in this dream world forever?

Adam placed another kiss on my jaw before he retreated. My stockings were ruined; my hands and knees ached. Limbs shaking from the aftermath, I paused when I noticed the blood at my hips, the little crescent cuts where his fingers had dug into my flesh.

If he noticed my blood, he did not call any attention to it. I quickly sat up, pulling the straps of my dress to rights, my heart thudding in my chest at the thought of how *unnatural* it was to thirst for—for *blood*.

Yet when I faced him again, a laugh flew from my lips. He was the most unkempt I think I'd ever seen him.

He glanced down at himself, his shirt ripped open, tie and belt discarded off somewhere in the grass. His cock hadn't yet calmed, still coated in our arousal.

He flashed me a smirk. Then he crawled forward till we were face to face. "You look positively ravished."

"I feel ravished," I breathed, and reached up to kiss him again.

He helped me up, brushing his fingers through my hair to help smooth my curls. I knew my lipstick was ruined, my eye shadow. He just used his thumb to wipe away the smudges.

And as he led me back toward the revelry, his hand in mine, I knew something had changed between us.

Yes, we'd changed. Years apart had done that.

But now...

I could not just continue to move on, not when I craved him so badly.

We rounded the corner of the house and my sight narrowed on Dixon and Flora, waiting, like they knew what we'd been up to. Dixon's eyes narrowed—at the man next to me—and Flora gave me a knowing grin, though she seemed a bit dazzled when Adam stood next to me.

He pulled me to a stop. "I'll let you go on," he said.

Dixon's glare was tangible even at this distance.

"Okay."

"Promise me," my lost lover said, pushing my hair from my eyes, cradling my face once more, fingers on my jaw, angling my face to him.

He didn't need to finish the sentence.

Promise me you'll come back. Promise me you're mine.

I leaned into his touch, breathing in his scent, the whiskey and iron now mixed with a sweet muskiness.

And I didn't want to leave.

"I promise."

SEVENTEEN

When Flora and Dixon pulled up to my house well past midnight, I half-expected Mother to be waiting on the stoop. But her bedroom window was dark—the whole house was dark, save for the window to the parlor, the electric lamps still lit.

"Good luck," Flora whispered with a grin as I climbed out of the car. She waved as they sped off.

Standing alone at the front door, my stockings long gone, my hair loose and undone, I steeled myself against what would be inside. Turning the unlocked handle—Mother never locked the door if I was out—I stepped over the threshold.

If it was not Mother who stayed up, then—

"Lucas."

My brother reclined in an armchair in the parlor, a cigar lit in one hand, puffing mindlessly as his eyes followed my entrance. He still wore his evening clothes, and his light brown hair was still slicked back, the only indication he'd been waiting awhile was the undone tie that hung around his neck, his collar open. His stare caught on my bare legs, slowly moving upward toward my neck. Creeping, checking every inch of skin. Like he knew. His cheeks hollowed as he dragged on the cigar.

I wanted nothing more than to fall into bed. But I knew him, knew he'd have something to say, and he'd force me to hear it, one way or another.

The house was quiet, all our servants having been dismissed, only a low crackling fire in the hearth to keep away the late spring chill.

Still Lucas said nothing. I wondered if he could hear my heartbeat. I wondered if he had men at the party, calling him at the first sight of me. I wondered if he knew of Vince—if he knew Vince and Adam were one and the same.

"You're late."

When I didn't answer, he scoffed, before pulling on the cigar once more. Smoke wafted toward the ceiling, the heavy smell crowding my senses. The air was so hazy he must've had a number before I arrived.

"Should I tell Mother?" He stood slowly, the cigar dangling between his fingers. Peeking at me through his lashes, waiting for my panic, waiting for my groveling.

I hated him. "I imagine you will."

"Hmm."

To him, it was inconsequential, if I was in trouble with Mother or not. She'd likely gone to bed hours before, whenever Lucas arrived home, pinching his cheeks and thanking him for watching out for me. And he'd have given her that smile that said he had everything under control.

He had *me* under control.

"I know where you went. I know where you and Flora get off to when you're out. But Mother? Does she know?" He sighed dramatically, shaking his head. "What will we do with you?"

"Hand me off to someone else," I said before I could stop myself.

His eyes flickered at my anger. "You're displeased." He stepped closer to me—the second time that evening a man had tried to corner me against a wall.

"You must know you're not getting out of it?" Lucas stopped before me. He waited, sucking in the tobacco once more, taking his time. Voice dangerously low, "You'll do as we say. Lord Wright Highsmith is already on his way." He checked his watch as if that mattered. "A few days' time. And this little act, this little *flapper* thing, will end."

Wright Highsmith?

My heart dropped.

"I'm not Lucy." My fury was bitter, hot in my veins.

"No," he said, smoky breath fanning my face. He glanced toward my lips, then looked me right in my eyes. "But you should be."

Eighteen

Lucas told Mother that I was not to be believed regarding a curfew, and she agreed without argument that it would be wise to keep me at home until *Wright* came.

Mr. Wright Highsmith, they said his name was. Heir of the Whitrow Barony.

I could only reach Flora by telephone. But as I rang her that next morning, I'd only been able to relay my betrothed's name to my friend, before Mother walked into the downstairs parlor.

"Who are you talking to? No more." She waved her hand at the telephone. "That girl will only drag you into more trouble."

"What trouble?" I demanded.

My mother's eyes narrowed. "She may not soon be a married woman, but *you* are. Hang up. You must ready. Lord Highsmith is arriving."

A ringing pierced through my ears. I thought I had a few more days.

Lucas lied. He hadn't told me.

He smirked from the doorway, leaning against the frame.

He hadn't told me the truth the night before. He hadn't told me Wright Highsmith was *on his way*.

His punishment dealt, my brother turned without a word, ushering my mother away, leaving me frozen in the parlor as the walls began closing in around me.

The maid raked her fingers through my hair. Gently, easing any tangles apart, the feeling grounding me amidst the tumult of my mind. She focused on her task, brushing out all the tangles, adding a barrette to hold the waves away from my face. She set out the gown Mother had ordered for me a few days prior, completed as quickly as the dressmaker could manage, just for me.

I hated it. The soft blue skirts went all the way past my knees, nearly to my ankles. There was a sash at the waist, to pull in and show off my figure to the lucky bachelor. A modest and humble gown, with lace accents and ribbons. In Mother's vision, I'd be the perfect docile lady: enticing to a man wanting a young, obedient wife.

The gentleman arrived earlier in the afternoon. I'd retreated to my room to think on what I was to do—I couldn't go through with this, couldn't bear to accept another man, not *now*—when downstairs came the sound of the front door opening and Lucas greeting our guest. A rich baritone voice traveled up the stairs. Deep, resonant, almost soft.

For only a moment I allowed myself the hope that he would not be as terrible as my brother.

A sharp tug on my scalp. I winced.

"Sorry," my maid said. "But you are all done. We should get you dressed."

As my dressing gown fell in a puddle on the floor, her eyes lingered on my hips, on the red marks slowly healing there, the only evidence of my night with Adam. She said nothing as the new dress came over my head, skirts falling and fluttering around my waist.

"You look beautiful."

At my silence, she gave me a smile that warmed her face. "Everything will be alright, Helena." She set about straightening the gown, pulling it into place, securing ribbons, tying the sash. "I truly mean it."

"Perhaps I am just being dramatic," I said.

"No, I don't think so."

I pressed my fingers against my eyes at the dull ache ringing in my skull, careful not to smudge her work. "What's your name?"

Her smile faltered for a moment. Like it never occurred to her that I'd ever ask. The dusting of dark freckles on her cheeks reddened at my attention. "Séraphine, Miss. Séra."

"Séra." I held out my hand. "Thank you. For everything."

She grasped my hand, her fingers tinier than mine, a chill to her skin. Her smile turned almost conspiratorial. If we were different people, if the roles were reversed, would we be friends?

A knock at the door and I ripped myself away, running my hands over my skirts.

"Helena?" Mother—her knocking paused.

Séra turned and tidied the vanity. It was covered in rouges and perfumes and jewelry and kohl, all instruments of my transformation into the perfect would-be-wife for *Wright Highsmith.*

His name still churned foreign on my tongue, in my thoughts.

"Yes?"

"It's time," my mother called. She opened the door, just enough to rake her eyes over me. Dressed in her own pastel evening gown, her light hair was braided at her nape. Disapproval did not yet wrinkle her features. But if I filled out the dress to her liking, if I fit her vision, she did not show it.

I could just walk out the door, I thought. *Wave down a taxi and save Highsmith the embarrassment of a runaway bride at the altar.*

Most anyone would stop a car for a desperate woman, would they not?

Someone surely would get me away from here.

"Come," Mother said, pulling me from my fantasies. "Let's go down to dinner. I'm sure Lord Highsmith would like to dine after all his travel."

"But—"

I wasn't ready.

I couldn't do this.

My shoes became glued to the floor, my tongue dry.

I'd met plenty of men before; how could this be any different?

But it was so, so different. All the other men I'd enter-

tained wanted a wife, sure, but they would lead double lives
—they wanted the freedom to continue their partying and
illicit drinking. Entertaining them was only that: *entertainment*. Someone to pass the time with. There was no threat of
permanence, no expectations, really, outside of the glamor of
the bars. Speaking to them, kissing them, letting them order
drinks for me, it all meant nothing, knowing I'd never see
them past daybreak.

Lord Highsmith—he was downstairs, waiting for his
would-be bride. Waiting for *me*.

"Oh, really, Helena, this is quite ridiculous," Mother's
patient facade fell, the lines between her brows deepening.

I opened my mouth to speak, but nothing came out.

Her hand enclosed mine in a vise-grip. "Let's go."

Séra kept her head down, cleaning up the bottles of
makeup, as Mother dragged me away.

And my plan to run out the door was thwarted, because
there, at the bottom of the stairs, standing next to a smug-
looking Lucas—there he was. Chestnut brown haloed by the
sunlight streaming through the window, he wore a gray suit,
a tie knotted at his throat. Cigar smoke drifted into the foyer
from the parlor where they must have been waiting. His
deep brown eyes met mine before his lips pulled in an empty
smile.

Every step downward was a strike against my heart.

And when he brushed his lips against my hand, it took
everything not to recoil, not to shove him away at the feeling
of his thin groomed mustache on my fingers, his warm
breath. "I am so glad to meet you," he said.

"Well!" Mother said, beaming at her visitor. "Mister—er,
Lord Highsmith, this is Helena. Helena, Lord Wright High-

smith." She gave me a look. "How *nice* of him to come all this way to meet you."

"I—" I choked on the words, but Lord Highsmith only chuckled. Then, I knew he mistook my silence for awe.

"Why don't we dine?"

"Wonderful idea." Mother gestured toward our dining room. "We hope everything is to your liking."

Lord Highsmith waved her concern away. "Your hospitality has been exemplary."

Lucas took up the rear of the group as Mother led my betrothed into our dining room, chattering away.

Under my brother's watchful eye, the hairs on the back of my neck stood on end, my heart crumbling in my chest. And he leaned in, sending chills down my spine, halting me in my steps. "Don't mess this up. Just behave, and good things will happen, *dear sister*."

NINETEEN

Dinner had come and gone, and I'd hardly touched my plate. Still there sat roast, potatoes, salad, all neglected.

I needed a drink. A cigarette. I sipped on the chilled cucumber water I had asked for, only able to stomach the subtle flavor.

"Sister," Lucas started. All eyes at the table turned in my direction.

I pulled the glass from my lips, heat rushing to my cheeks.

"You've barely eaten," Lucas continued. "Was dinner not to your liking?"

He hadn't even looked at me all evening. They'd all done a grand job of ignoring me, the three of them.

"Haven't had much of an appetite today." I avoided Lucas' stare.

"That's no good," Lord Highsmith intoned.

A white-hot anger reignited in my veins. I set my water

down. "Perhaps I'll go to bed. It is getting late." Glancing at the clock on the wall, the face read only eight-thirty. But Lord Highsmith didn't know any better, didn't know I had a habit of staying up until the sun rose.

Lucas' hand shot out to grip my wrist as I went to stand. "Stay. We were all just getting to know each other so well."

"Yes," Highsmith agreed. "A shame, to retire so soon. We've not yet truly spoken, you and I."

He turned to me with a proffered hand.

I stared, dumbly. "Truly, I—"

Lucas' chair screeched as he stood. "Perhaps we should give them some time." He gave Mother his arm. "Let us go to the parlor, and the two of you can spend some time together. Helena, why not show him the garden?"

A brow lifted, his instruction clear.

I looked between him and the baron-heir.

To the garden. Alone. With *him*.

Just take his hand. Then maybe I can feign sickness and escape to my room.

When his fingers met mine for the second time, there was no spark of attraction, just a solid, incongruous *wrongness* stemming from his skin against mine.

Fingers soft, unworked. *Not like Adam's.*

I tried to imagine the heir being sent off to war, and my mind went blank.

"The garden?" He motioned for me to lead the way.

We were close, his cologne strong and foreign, the fabric of his jacket impossibly soft—probably more costly than even Lucas would spend on a single dinner suit.

We must have seemed so small to him, our little budding American family.

"I'm sure it's nothing like the one you must have at home," I said, forcing politeness into my voice. Mother and Lucas left without a second glance, their voices trailing off down the hall. The servants filed in, taking away plates and glasses, much of the roast and vegetables leftover.

I showed Lord Highsmith down the hall to the garden's doors, the same ones I'd run through only a few nights before. A brisk breeze flowed between us, rustling my skirts.

We had no moonflowers, only roses and dahlias, heathers, daffodils. No nymph-like statues, no wandering nameless guests.

"The gardens at home are impractical."

"Oh?" I couldn't read him. He glanced around, not in distaste, but not in appreciation of the greenery, either. Perhaps he didn't know flowers at all.

"Acres of this." He gestured to the flowerbeds, the ruffling blooms. "When hardly anyone ever walks through. We keep gardens, I swear, only so we can employ the gardener."

"I see."

He glanced at me as we walked amongst the foliage. "Do you enjoy the outdoors?"

His direct attention was discomforting. At dinner, at least, there were others to keep conversation.

But now, we were *alone*.

I swallowed around the lump in my throat. "I suppose I do. I like this garden."

I liked the garden at Vince's manor. I thought of the rose yet alive in my bedroom, its withering thorns and few fallen petals the only evidence of the passing of time.

"If I lived in a city such as New York, I'd need a place to

escape to as well, I imagine," Lord Highsmith continued. We strolled along the path, and though it was somewhat quiet within the garden walls, we could still hear the sharp horns of cars, the sound of pedestrians only a few meters away.

"You live in the countryside?" I chanced a look at him. I had been avoiding his gaze, keeping my attention on the blooms around us, dull in the waning light.

"I do," he said. "I attended Cambridge, but when I finished my studies, I didn't return home right away. I explored the continent for a year and a half before I was called home due to the war. I haven't left our estate much since, though I've traveled to London for business."

"What sort of business?" I supposed I needed to know if I was to become his wife.

His brow raised, surprised I'd ask. "Well, we support a village. And with the war, the country needed soldiers. Railroads are still being built all over. We have our hands in most everything. My father has yet a seat in Parliament, which I am set to inherit."

"So, you will remain in London for much of the year? And your wife will stay at home? In the country?"

His eyes narrowed. "Somewhat."

I stopped, pulling my hand from his arm. My palms were damp with sweat. The light blue dress I wore turned ghostly white in the moonlight, the lamps weak in the darkness. It cast a ghoulish shadow across his face as he turned to face me. He still looked as put-together as he did before dinner.

"What do you expect of me?" I asked.

I needed to drop all pretenses. My skin was crawling underneath the dress my mother had picked. As we'd walked the garden, I'd only felt that the facade Lord Highsmith showed me was just that—a mask to hide whatever he truly felt underneath. Much like Lucas and his ability to show whatever side of himself he pleased.

Lord Highsmith's brows furrowed, and he adjusted his cuffs. "Well," he began, and he seemed unsure of what to say, like my forwardness was entirely outside of what he expected. What had Lucas told him about me? Had Lucas said how "unruly" I was? Had Lucas told him about Adam?

And did Lucas know Adam was back?

"When you are my wife," he began.

Not *if*, but *when*. It was decided. They'd already talked it through.

I forced my mouth to stay shut.

"We'll return to England, and we'll live on the estate." He straightened himself, and I saw a glimpse of the man whose every direction was used to being heeded. "My mother, the baroness, will guide you. She'll keep you busy with her work. She does much volunteer work in the village, manages the house—"

"Does she ever leave?"

"Leave?" His brows furrowed. "You mean to London?"

"Wherever." My hands shook. "Can she leave?"

He frowned. "She leaves if there's reason to."

"I see."

"Helena, she's a baroness. She has responsibilities."

It was the first time he'd said my name, and I wanted him to take it back, to *un*speak it. The syllables, the cadence wrong with his accent, his *voice*.

"She never had much chance to leave, anyway," he continued. "When she began to have children, I suppose, she became too busy with the nannies and the house that it became impossible to worry about much else."

"And must I have children?"

I knew the answer. I felt his incredulous stare on me. A scoff, almost a laugh.

"Why, yes—"

"Then this cannot be done," I said, and turned to take my leave.

A tight grip on my arm halted my steps, and I whirled around before he could say anything, willing as much strength into my words. "If you think you can lay your hands on me because my brother and my mother have given you leave to do so, you're sorely mistaken."

Ire flashed in his eyes, and the restrained, disinterested man he was not twenty minutes before disappeared. I saw the heir then, his real self, staring down at me, taken aback by my words. "*Helena.*"

I recoiled. "You may as well return to England."

"I will not." His grip only tightened, pain rocketing up my arm. If he'd handle me like this—could I expect him not to raise a hand to his wife? "This is atrocious behavior."

I tried to pull myself free, but his fingers dug in.

"You'd be wise to calm down," he said through his teeth, voice low. "It is already done."

It—the marriage contract.

I'd been signed away, and I hadn't even known.

"*I don't care,*" I hissed, ripping myself away. I marched back toward the door to the inside. The garden's walls only felt constricting, closer and closer, like they were moving in to trap me. "You can rip up whatever contract Lucas got you to sign."

"Really, Helena," Lord Highsmith called from behind. "This is ridiculous."

I bit my lip, holding back the torrent building inside of me.

He scoffed at my silence. "You only need to have one. Then you can take whatever man you'd like. So long as you're discreet."

And he could continue his gallivanting with any woman in the city, while I was stuck and locked away in the countryside. I didn't care to be so controlled, to have to hide what made me happy. I didn't want anyone's child if I did not want it, much less *his*. I didn't want his mother watching my every movement. I didn't want the responsibilities, whatever they were, of a baron's wife. I didn't care about the title, didn't care about the money. I didn't know a thing of England, or London, or Cambridge, or any of it. I didn't want to waste my life away as this man's wife.

The tempest burned, a scream begging to release. I needed to scream until I was finally heard. Until the sound of my anger seeped so deeply into their bones, a worm in their ear, that they couldn't escape my anguish, and they'd know, *they'd know*, just what they'd done to me.

Twenty

The garden doors slammed against the interior walls as I shoved them open. Mother came rushing around the corner as I stalked down the hall. My heart peaked at the sight of her, at the sight of Lucas following. In only a moment, they understood what had transpired.

"*Helena*." Mother tried to stop me, following me into the foyer and up the stairs.

"Quintrell," Lord Highsmith warned, calling my brother into action.

Mother grabbed her skirts, frantically trying to keep up. "Stop!"

But it was Lucas who caught up first, reaching the landing just as I did. He pushed me into the drawing room upstairs, gathering me in his arms and shoving me through. Mother protested before the door was slammed shut, the lock flipped with finality.

He was breathing heavily, and I realized I was, too, as I

backed away. His chest rising and falling, his jacket ruffled in his manhandling of me.

It was not the first time.

We could have stood like that, staring at one another without a word, for upwards of an hour. Me, anticipating his next move, and even so, too weary to run.

"I won't do it." The words, as I uttered them, sending chills through my flesh.

I had angered him before—he was only ever angry at me —but never before did I outright disobey him.

And yet, he did not move, did not say anything for the longest moment. He could not look upon me without a distasteful expression, as if the sight of me forced his brows lower, the corner of his mouth to slant, his eyes to narrow.

We'd been the best of playmates, always together as children. Until he realized he was heir to our name, and with that came power, and more money, and control.

With that, came everyone's scrutiny, and if he was held in society's good graces, his power could exponentiate tenfold.

And I, his meager sister, would be the property of another man. Out of his control.

His lip curled over his teeth. "You *disgust* me."

After so many years of hearing these words, I thought perhaps I would have hardened to his scorn, but that little girl that used to yearn for his company felt every slice, every stab of pain.

I forced my voice to remain strong. "I will not change my mind."

Lucas' hand raised in a claw, as if to grab me, but it

stalled mid-air, his fingers curled around an invisible neck. "I wish you were like Lucille. Submissive. *Pliant*."

"Lucy *hates* you," I hissed, longing for the words to wound him.

I *hate you*.

"Her *feelings* are irrelevant." He stalked closer. "She's an example to you, doing as she's told." Advancing on me until the backs of my calves pressed against the velvet upholstery of the settee.

Then his face came closer. His face, so like mine—our eyes the same hue, our cheekbones inherited from the same mother, the same complexion as our father—yet so twisted and distorted. And suddenly, his hands braced my shoulders, and he pushed me.

I suppressed a cry as I lost my balance and before I knew it, he was leaning over me, one knee on the couch next to my leg. My fist beat at his chest. "Luc—"

The shout died in my throat as he covered my lips with his hand, the other gripping one of my wrists so tightly I thought he may break it.

Our noses almost touched.

"You *will* marry, if not to save your own reputation, then to prevent the ruination of *mine*," he seethed. "I don't care what you do once you are his problem. You can continue to whore around and ruin yourself. But until then, you *will* stay in line."

I wrenched away with my free hand. "*Go to hell*, Lucas."

He laughed darkly, grabbing my face with both hands, his fingers digging into the soft flesh of my cheeks, my neck. Nails like talons—I had the sudden thought that he was worse than any monster my mind could conjure.

"What makes you think that you have the power to say no? What makes you think that you can defy *me*? I have tolerated you enough. I should've sent you away all those years ago. Girls get sent away all the time to learn subordination. Shall I ship you away now? Or maybe Wright will do it himself."

Spittle landing on my cheek, my ears ringing.

"Is this what you want?" He loomed closer.

I couldn't shake my head, couldn't move. "Let go—"

"Let me remind you, then: this did not end well for you last time."

Last time.

Nausea roiled in my gut.

"Wonder how *he's* doing now, huh?"

An angry sob stalled in my throat. Some of my fight diminishing. "Please—"

"Yes, you *should* beg for forgiveness." He shook my skull, his grip on my jaw firm. "Do you get it now? I've been gracious, letting you gallivant around these past few years. Am I not generous? And here I am, setting you up with a *baron*—and this is how you act?" His eyes shone with frenzy, his face so close to mine I could taste his breath.

My hands were free, but I was too stunned to realize I should push him off of me.

What if someone barged in? Would Mother do much else than wag her finger at her son?

No, she wouldn't. This I knew.

"And this is strength?" I whispered against his hand.

Hot tears lined my eyes, and it was only fuel for Lucas' fire. He sneered. "Ah, there it is."

His hatred was like a brand, and I couldn't stop the blurring of my vision, the anguish threatening to fall.

"This is what you'll do," he began again; "You'll make yourself presentable, dry your tears, then you will return downstairs and apologize to Highsmith. You are lucky he hasn't yet left. And from now on, you will *listen*."

A muscle flexed in his jaw as he leered down at me, utter contempt twisting his features.

Pulling my wrist free, I moved to slap him, an ill-advised, impulsive move; but he gripped me even harder. Red capillaries in his eyes, the irises almost seemed black.

Then—a light knock at the door.

A turning of the doorknob, but it wouldn't budge.

"Lucas, dear? Helena?"

He gave me a glare that said if I spoke a word, I would regret it.

Had she heard him through the door?

My chest heaved, trying to regain my breath, shuddering on an inhale.

He pushed away from me quickly, regaining his balance and straightening his shirt. He smoothed his hair back with a flat palm, the fire in his eyes slowly dying off. A deep breath, another. As if the menace in him was something he could summon and send away. The mask returned, the facade built up once again.

I was left crumbling on the settee, my heart pounding against my ribs. I dared not move as Lucas went to the door.

He turned to me one last time.

"*I dare you.*" His voice was barely above a whisper, but it rang loud and clear in my ears.

I dare you, I dare you, I dare you.
And then he was gone.

TWENTY-ONE
SIX YEARS AGO

"I hope your meal was satisfactory."

The voice was familiar, *too* familiar.

We were enjoying ourselves, Adam and I. We'd gotten into a new club, still mostly empty for the evening. No one to recognize us. No one to possibly tell Mother or Lucas. Except—

With those six words, my blood ran cold.

No.

No.

A man slid into the booth next to me. All I noticed at first was that he was wearing his evening jacket—he didn't intend on staying—as the side of his body bumped mine, his elbow nearly causing me to drop my fork against my plate.

And then—

Lucas cleared his throat. Leaned back in his seat.

Adam's eyes were steel as they met my brother's—but he said nothing. He had never met Lucas before, at least, not to my knowledge. Lips pressed into a silent line, hazel eyes narrowed.

Like he had expected this.

"More than, thank you," Adam said.

Run, I tried to tell him with my eyes.

Please.

I was ready to get on my knees, to beg my brother to leave. I knew what would be waiting for me at home. I had worn those bruises before. But—*please, not him.*

Lucas slung an arm around my shoulder. "Good," he said, so casually I flinched. "I told them to treat my guests like royalty."

We were alone in the room, the other tables set but empty. No other diners had been seated here.

It hadn't been luck. It had been Lucas' making.

I shut my eyes against the realization.

If I had known—

"So what's the con?" Lucas smiled, his hand on my shoulder tight, fingers digging into my flesh, as he stared right back at Adam. "You have me here now. What is it you want? Because surely it isn't my sister."

I wanted to separate myself from the limb, burn off the skin he touched.

Adam wouldn't look at me. He wouldn't *look* at me, I couldn't tell him—

"Come on, Vering." Thought outwardly he showed only a concerned brother, I knew what fury lurked underneath his facade. He clicked his tongue, a slight shake to his head. "Don't stay silent now. Talk."

He knew Adam's name?

My hands shook. "Lucas, I can explain—"

"What *are* you doing out with him? I thought you were with Flora?"

"It's not—I just—"

No excuse would be satisfactory, even if Lucas did believe them.

He *tsk*ed again. "So neither of you have anything to say then?"

I could only stare at Adam, memorizing the lines of his face, the angle of his cheeks, the little indentation where his dimple would appear. The slightly chapped texture to his lips, the way his auburn hair curled behind his ears with that cheap pomade. The shadow on his jaw at the end of the day. The way it felt against my lips, the slightly salty taste of his skin, the hardness of his muscles, the strength of his arms around me.

"I'm a bit disappointed, Vering." Lucas leaned back, turning his attention to my lover. "I thought surely you'd have known better. To get Helena tangled up with you— why not tell her the truth?"

Adam's hands, which rested on the table this whole time, had turned to fists.

"The truth?" But Adam wouldn't *look* at me.

"I love her." He finally spoke, voice calm and assured. "That's all there is to it."

Lucas laughed. "Love? What is this? You have *nothing*. You *are* nothing, Vering." His hand tightened on my shoulder, pulling me closer into his side. "Helena, truly, I am helping you out here. The faster this rake is gone, the better."

The spark I felt the first time he kissed me. The ease with which we fell into each other. The unruly way his hair fell in his eyes. The smell of ink on his skin after a day of work, the black stains on his fingers, the stains he'd leave on me.

Please look at me.

"You've swindled my sister. You think *love* is good enough?" Lucas crooned. "That's *rich*."

"It's enough," Adam said, the clench of his jaw the only show of his discomfort.

Lucas turned to me again. "If you think he loves you, you're more foolish than I thought."

Adam's throat slid. If he spoke, he'd only make Lucas' wrath worse. If he was silent, he let Lucas win.

"So, here's what we're going to do."

There was a click, and suddenly, Lucas was brandishing a gun, pointed straight at Adam's heart.

Father's old pistol.

"Lucas!" Before I could think, I was grabbing his wrists, attempting to wrench it skyward.

Then—

Those irises of fire flew to me, and the cool sharpness of metal pressed against my forehead.

"I should just kill you," he snarled, pushing the barrel against my skull. Right against my temple. "All you ever do is cause trouble."

A sob caught in my throat as I scrambled until my back hit the wall. "*Please.*"

The fact was, I had no idea if he could do it—if he could shoot me, kill me, point-blank.

"Is that what you want? Hmm?" The metal jabbed against the thin bone above my ear, sharp and steely cold. "A double murder? You and him together—then off to jail I'd go, and you'd be satisfied, wouldn't you? Finally getting rid of me."

A scream stalled in my throat.

It only ever felt like he wanted to be rid of *me*.

"Quintrell." Adam hadn't moved an inch. "What do you want?"

My heart was thumping, pounding against my ribcage, wanting out.

I couldn't breathe.

Lucas pulled the gun away from my head, and I sucked in air like I was surfacing from water. Slamming shut my eyes, I pretended I was anywhere else. Pretended the last five minutes never happened.

"What I *want*," Lucas spat, "is to solve this problem."

That gun was pointed once more, right for Adam's heart. Lucas was itching to do it.

"Alright." Adam stood. "I'll leave. You won't see me again."

Though he said the words to my brother, I knew they were for me.

I won't see you again.

My heart was shattering into a million pieces. But I couldn't let Lucas kill him.

Sobs shook my entire body. "*Please.*"

Lucas laughed again. "You're right, I won't. Because here's the thing." The upholstery of the bench shifted as he stood, the gun inching ever closer to Adam's chest. "You know what's going on overseas, right?"

My blood froze in my veins.

I wanted to vomit.

"You know what I did today?" Lucas' voice was low,

venomous. "I just so happened to be walking past the recruitment office. They said they're in dire need of men."

Adam glared. At his sides, his hands were in fists. But he didn't move, didn't speak.

"Want to finally make something of yourself?" Lucas grinned, pure malice in his eyes. "It's the honorable thing, isn't it?"

No. *No.*

"Lucas—" I had to get his attention on me, had to give Adam time to run. To get *out of here.* "You're mad at me, not him—"

"No, I've been *betrayed* by you." He narrowed his eyes at me. "I couldn't care less what happens to your little lover. But how dare *you.*"

I willed Adam to look at me, to understand—

But his eyes avoided mine, staring at the man who held a gun up to his heart.

"How dare you sneak around," Lucas sneered. "I've always given you the benefit of the doubt. But I was right— you were just waiting, *dying* to whore around, to ruin yourself with the first man that gives you attention."

I shook my head through the tears. "No, I—"

"What would Mother think, huh? *Father?* He must be rolling in his grave."

"I'll go," Adam said again.

"Then *go,*" Lucas hissed, "before I unload these bullets into you."

Through my tears, Adam's figure was merely a blur.

Just another thing to embarrass Lucas—my makeup running down my face, my skin red and blotchy with my hysteria.

"You leave in two days. I suggest saying goodbye to your family."

Two days. Until an ocean would separate us.

One moment, Adam was there, and the next, he was gone.

Lucas opened the chamber and let the bullet fall into his palm before pocketing the weapon. He sniffed, grabbing a glass from the table—a finger of whiskey—and downed the shot, throwing his head back, roughly setting it back down on the table spread.

His face twisted with disgust when he looked at me.

"Get up."

Adam—

He was gone.

Off to war.

Lucas gripped my arm, pulling me from the booth. I stumbled to my feet, but he didn't care.

"Sir—" The *maitre d'* stood in the doorway. He must have seen Adam leave.

"Shut those doors," Lucas demanded.

The man's eyes widened when he saw the state I was in, but he nodded once, and did as he was told.

Lucas pushed me further into the room. "You're lucky there's a rear exit."

There was a door against the back wall of this dining room, and suddenly he was pulling me down a dark hall, servers glancing at us nervously, and then I was outside, and a car was waiting, idling a few steps away. Lucas shoved me in, then barked something at the driver.

His glare like a dagger, like the gun against my head,

lethal and on the cusp of the point of no return. My heart had yet to calm, my fingers numb in my panic.

He said nothing else, but he showed me just how displeased he was when we returned home. He told Mother nothing, sequestered me upstairs, and struck me once—though it seemed enough to satisfy his anger.

I was locked in my room for three days.

I ate nothing. Sleep evaded me. And when the door was unlocked, Adam was already fighting against a foe he didn't know, all because I was foolish enough to think I could have something for myself.

I never saw him again.

Four months later, Adam Vering's name was listed in the paper's obituary, with only the date of his death, nothing else.

Nothing else for the poor printer's apprentice sent off to war.

Twenty-Two

I lay in bed, my quilt pulled up to my chin.

My tears had long run out, my throat aching with the passion of my hatred for Lucas. For my family. For my situation.

It was decided, then. My mother, my brother—they had made the decision. And I was to comply.

I could not sleep, could not rest, knowing what was in store for me. Knowing what I would soon have to do. Let a man that I knew nothing about claim ownership over me, force me to have his children, *stifle* me, if Lucas' treatment of Lucille was any indication.

I loathed him. I loathed *all* of them.

A sharp tap came from the glass panes of my window. I lay still, silent, should the sound come again.

And it did.

Another tap, though this time I may have seen something moving in the darkness beyond.

I threw the sheets off of me.

Down in the garden below, a familiar face grinned up at me, teeth sparkling in the moonlight.

I threw open the window. "Adam?"

He took no time at all climbing the wall up to the window, finding easy footholds and scaling the bricks.

"You cannot be here," I whispered.

But my heart fluttered at seeing him. At the memories of him and me in this very garden, six years ago.

"I cannot?"

"You will be skinned alive."

His fingers dug into the windowsill, a stray curl hanging in his eyes. "I would not allow it," he said matter-of-factly. "May I come in?"

I stepped backward, allowing him entry. Perching on the slim ledge, his large frame blocked out all moonlight.

He stepped down into my bedroom, his lithe figure moving with ease. And before I could think better of it, I threw my arms around him, burying my face in the cloth of his shirt.

Stunned, he didn't move for a few breaths. Then fingers twirled through my hair, twisting curls and cupping my head against his chest.

I knew that this was where I was supposed to be. I tightened my grip, shutting my eyes against the barrage of feelings that threatened to overwhelm me.

Then, he froze, still as stone. "What happened?"

How he sensed something was wrong, I didn't know. I shook my head against his chest. "Nothing."

He gently pulled me from him and searched my face in the moonlight, gaze sweeping over me from head to toe, his pupils dilating once they landed on the little red marks on my face. My neck.

"Helena—"

I wrenched myself from him, turning as if to hide what had happened to me.

"It's nothing."

Of course, it was something.

Perhaps that was the part that hurt the most: that I let Lucas have such control over me, *still*.

But what choice did I have?

I should not have let Adam in.

Would I even see him again after this evening? My fate was decided. Wright was waiting for me somewhere in this city, fully expecting my hand, as promised.

Suddenly I was gasping for breath. Lungs aching, my ribs constricting, sobs catching in my throat. Muffling the sound with a hand over my lips, squeezing my eyes shut, willing this all away—

His face fell to the crook of my neck, his lips tenderly meeting the sensitive skin there. He placed the most chaste, most gentle of kisses upon my flesh.

"Darling," he breathed into me.

Darling.

I could not do this.

"You expect too much from me," I said through my tears.

"I expect nothing from you," he countered, placing another kiss to the angle of my jaw. He turned me in his arms, gently pulling my hands away from my face. Through my blurry vision, I saw his eyes once more land on the bruises, his brow furrowing.

"Helena." His voice was soft, enchanting. "*What* happened?"

"It does not matter."

He looked furious; not at me, but at the words. "And yet it does."

"No—" I gasped. "I am to marry—"

"Marry who?" Something dark flashed in those eyes. "Deny them, whoever they are. Refuse."

"You do not understand."

"But I *do* understand." Pain twisted his features. He'd already gone six years without me. Falling to his knees before me, his hands wrapped around my waist, fingers digging into my hips, only to keep me anchored, pressing his face to the soft skin of my belly. "I understand that you are hurting. I only want to take it away from you."

How I wanted this. How I had dreamed of this for years. Knowing it would never come.

And yet.

My fingers instinctively wound through his dark hair. Would I ever get to touch him again after this night?

I hoped, when all of this was said and done, that he would find me again.

"You are driving my thoughts wild," Adam confessed, gripping the silk of my shift. He pulled me tightly to him, as if we could meld into one. And I let him.

"I am only glad that I know he had not killed you," I whispered.

An ocean would separate us again, soon. And maybe one day I'd be allowed a lover.

But I could not ask him to wait another six years, wait another eternity, for *me*.

His fingers tightened. "Stop this."

"Adam, we can't."

He looked up at me like I had just cursed him. "All these years, I did not let go. All these years, I could never forget you. Not even for a moment. I cannot forget you when I attempt sleep. I shut my eyes, and I see you. You are always there, Helena. *Always*."

Maybe in another life we could have been. In another life, we *had* been.

"Let us go away together," he said.

How I wanted to. My frustration burned at my eyes.

They'd find me. This city was not as big as it seemed.

Adam stood once more and cupped my face. Eyes searching me, looking for the answer. But I had none.

His soft lips met mine in the midnight glow trailing through the windowpanes. He tasted of that whiskey and iron and something sweet, and just like the first time we kissed, I became wholly wrapped up in him. My arms twined around his neck as his lips moved against mine.

I savored every moment. Committed it to memory.

The sharp point of one of his teeth scraped across my bottom lip, but I relished in the feeling. He tangled his hand at the back of my head and anchored me to him, angling my face even further backward. He pulled away for a brief moment to catch his breath.

"I could do this forever," he breathed.

Against my better judgment, I sighed with ecstasy. "I wish... I wish you could."

His mouth found mine once more, his free hand roaming across my back, pulling me closer to him, crushing our bodies together. I could feel the defined muscles of his chest through his shirt, through my thin shift. My breasts pressed against his chest, the fabric of my nightdress too thin to conceal how much I craved him.

He wandered with his mouth, pressing feverish kisses along my face, down my neck. He licked the sensitive part under my jaw, under my ear. Emitting a growl that sent bolts of pleasure through me, his tongue ravished the flesh of my throat.

I wanted him to mark me. I wanted that bite. I wanted him to leave behind evidence for everyone to see.

To let Wright know that no matter if he was successful in gaining me as a wife, he would not gain me as a lover.

That my mind would forever be elsewhere.

That someone else had already gotten to me first.

Adam pulled away, panting. His dark eyes begged for more, a hunger deep within them, his arousal evident in the press of his body against mine.

"What will it be?" His voice was hardly above a gravelly whisper, our breath mingling in the small space between us.

"What do you mean?"

I knew what he meant. But there were two sides within me warring, and I did not know which to choose.

"Will you come with me? Or will you let another man claim you when you could be free?"

"Free?" I could hardly mutter the word.

"I would never implore you to do my bidding, Helena." He pressed his forehead against mine. "The only thing I ask of you is that you let me cherish you. All I want is you, every day, every night."

I gazed into his eyes, those shining, icy hazel eyes, and saw my home there.

I pressed my lips to his.

The words did not even have to come out of my mouth. He had his answer. Triumph darkened his eyes, a near-sinister gleam in his irises as he gathered me into his arms. His mouth was suddenly upon me again, my body burning for his, as he swept me away into the night.

PART TWO

ARRIVISTE

TWENTY-THREE

I do not remember driving to the large house on the hill. I had the distinct understanding of being carried into a vehicle, but my thoughts were otherwise engaged on the man before me.

He whispered his promises to me, his breath tickling my ear deliciously, his tongue reaching out to stroke my neck. It was maddening, the way he consumed me. I wanted him to devour me. I wanted to devour him. We could feed off each other forever this way, in an endless cycle of lust, and I would never tire.

Straddling his hips, my slip bunched up at my waist.

"It is unfair that you are practically naked, and I am fully clothed," he muttered, before his lips met mine. He ran his tongue along my lip, sucking, sharp teeth teasing.

I pulled away. "That is fixable."

His head fell back against the seat with a groan. "We should wait—"

But the words were cut off when I captured his lips with

mine. I missed him. I needed him. I *wanted* him, more than I ever wanted anything. I *ached* for him.

I didn't want to think anymore about my family or the heir who thought he had a claim on me.

His arousal pressed against me, and all my thoughts fell to nothing. I did not care that we were not in the privacy of a bedroom; the feel of him sent jolts of anticipation up my spine and through my fingertips. I was absolutely electric and wondered if he felt it, too. Where we met, there was lightning. All my nerve endings were charged with an urgency to feel him, skin to skin, to get lost in his body. To give over to him. To let him get so deep within me that he was in my skin, forever in the cells of my body.

He rocked my hips against him, first slowly and then with such ferocity, sliding my core against the ridge of his arousal. My thighs quaked, tightening on either side of his hips.

"Adam." Gasping for air once more.

But he nipped at my breasts through my slip, his tongue massaging my nipples through the cloth. I melted.

"Vince," he breathed against me, teeth just barely sinking into my breast. "Call me Vince."

Crying out, I clutched him tightly to me, and suddenly, his hands were lifting me off of his lap, only long enough to swiftly undo the fly of his pants, and then I was sinking on to him. I took him slowly, his size stretching me to the point of pain.

"I can't—"

"Yes, you can," he growled, palming my ass, pushing me down until our hips met.

My muscles clenched in protest at the intrusion, a delicious burn settling in my core. My face fell to the crook of his neck, my breaths coming in short pants against his throat.

God, I had nearly forgotten what it was to have him.

He was made for me, filling me so wonderfully I didn't think I could move. I could finish just like that, with him stretching me and nudging that spot deep within that turned me into a mewling puddle.

If I moved, I would shatter.

He knew this, his hands guiding me, pushing me and pulling me along his cock. It quickly turned to a frenzy, the slick spot between my legs growing ever wetter, my heat hungrily taking him in, only to feel empty in the brief moments he retreated.

"I want to be dripping down your thighs when you finally come home." His dark auburn hair hung over his eyes, unkempt, his pupils blown wide. His sharp teeth poked at his lip, peeking out from inside his mouth.

He watched me move over him, his hands gripping so tightly on my hips, his nails digging into nearly the same spot as they had when we'd found each other again.

"Yes," I sighed.

His fist tangled in the hair at the base of my skull, wrenching my face away from him. His teeth skimmed my throat. Tears burned at my eyes, the pleasure so intense it bordered on agony.

He bit softly into my neck, and the strange sensation of his teeth pressing into my skin sent a bolt of fear through me. I was completely bared to him, completely at his mercy.

But he didn't puncture the skin, just held his teeth there, like he couldn't resist a taste. His tongue flicked out between the two knife-like teeth, my pulse beating erratically between his lips.

I almost said it aloud, that I wanted him to do it, to pass that threshold, to stop being gentle with me.

He pumped into me furiously, my hips slamming against his.

"Come, my darling," he hissed.

Hot tears escaped, streaming down my cheeks, and I screamed. The walls of my heat spasmed as he rutted into me, the head of his cock pounding against that deepest part of me. There was nowhere else for him to go, but he rocked into me, forcing himself to reach that most sensitive spot that sent me careening.

The electricity of our joining shot through my limbs, my inner muscles milking his cock as he slammed me down one final time. My orgasm came seconds before his. He groaned into my neck, his breathing turning jagged as he pulsed inside.

"Fuck," he breathed, thrusting once, twice, as if to make sure the imprint of him within me was permanent.

I wanted it to be.

I didn't want anyone else.

I fell limp in his arms as he released my hair, turning into a rag doll draped over him. My blood still hummed with energy, the heaviness in my chest dissipating as pleasure took over.

He clutched me to him, his own breathing slowing, one hand still glued to my waist, the other bracing my neck. I looked up at him, my vision still a little blurry, and for a brief moment, I felt I wanted to cry, overcome with the experience of joining with him again. Of finding him again.

His gray eyes shone in the darkness, reflective like a cat's. Studying me.

He twitched within me. A slow, languid thrust.

"You are exquisite," he whispered, his own energy spent, his head once more falling to the seat behind him. Brushing my undone hair out of my face.

My slip clung to my skin, damp with the sweat of our passion, the cloth over my breast still wet from his mouth. I wanted to tear it off of me, and tear his clothes off, and fall into a world where we had no obligations save to love each other.

Maybe we could. Maybe that's what life with him was.

I only smiled languidly in response.

His gaze was suddenly drawn to the window, and there was a flash of recognition in his eyes. "We're here."

But I didn't want to leave the warmth of his lap.

He braced my hips, helping me move off of him. The spot between my thighs was slick, and that wetness was already seeping out of me. I pressed my thighs together tightly.

There was no party this evening. The lawns were completely empty, save for the trees, the fountain. The car continued up the drive until we were before the massive front doors. Every light inside was on, the manor shining bright, maybe even visible from the atmosphere.

He tucked himself back into his pants before shooting me a smile.

He had insisted I call him Vince. It wasn't his legal name, at least, not the name of the boy I knew before. He was Adam Vering, and that was it. A printer's apprentice who had fallen in love with a girl, before being threatened with death by her brother, sent away to the war.

But Vince Thornton had been the man to come back.

"Are you ready, darling?" He grabbed my hand, his fingers warm and strong in mine, and I tamped down the thought of them touching me, spreading me wide.

I nodded, swallowing the small lump in my throat.

He knocked on the divider separating us and the driver —a foresight I am glad occurred to him—and in moments the driver was opening the carriage door to let us out. Even though the driver did not look at us, a blush bloomed on my cheeks. How much of that had he heard? I hadn't exactly been silent.

God, I should be mortified. A proper lady would.

The wife of a baron would.

Adam—Vince—turned to exit, but I pulled on his hand. "Wait."

"What is it?"

Glancing outside, the front door was being opened by another servant, and the interior light spilled out onto the driveway. Another set of footmen stood by the door, waiting.

I knew there were plenty of servants here—there never seemed to be a shortage of them.

All watching.

"I'm—" I glanced down to my exposed breast, my damp skin, my bare thighs. "I can't walk into the house like this."

"Ah." He looked around for his discarded jacket, crumpled on the floor, and pulled it over my shoulders. His figure was so broad that his jacket fell around me like a blanket, swallowing me up. "Better?"

I nodded, and he slipped his fingers through mine. When my feet met solid ground, I nearly felt my knees buckle underneath me. My muscles jelly, used and tired.

He quickly wrapped his arm around me, steadying me.

The servants continued to look forward, not acknowledging me. I knew they'd seen worse. They must know of the strange parties that went on upstairs, the bloodletting, the amount of *relations* that must have happened on the grounds every time there was a party.

Human and monster alike.

Vince ushered me inside, and the roof of the devilish foyer seemed so much higher when there were not hundreds in the room. The grand staircase was vacant, the large ballroom empty, our footsteps echoing against the marble floors. No ribbons decorated the space.

It was as if the parties never happened.

How could one *live* in such a big house alone? Especially with those demons and angels watching every move.

"This was all for you," he said, pulling me to a stop amidst the maze of halls, in front of a set of mahogany doors. The carvings in these doors were that of sentinels standing at guard.

His words made me dizzy.

"You're lying." I let a laugh slip out, but I knew he was not a liar, never had been before.

He held me in his arms, his hair still messy, sleeves pushed up to his forearms. He cradled me, his other hand caressing my cheek. I leaned into the feeling before his lips met mine.

It was a soft kiss, quick. But it was disorienting all the same.

"You wanted me to call you Vince," I said, looking up into his eyes.

"That's who I am." A pause. "Adam Vering died. Vince Thornton lived."

Perhaps he meant to disorient me. Perhaps he meant to dazzle me. Before I could say anything else, he pushed open his bedroom doors and shut them behind us, and though it was dark, I knew I was at the heart of this den of blood-sucking creatures, his eyes reflecting whatever light they picked up in a flash, before he lunged and was upon me.

TWENTY-FOUR

When my eyes opened the next morning, the canopy of a bed hung over me. Large, vaulted ceilings, bathed in sunlight which streamed through sheer white curtains. The windows were cracked, letting in a slight breeze, which cooled me, pebbling my skin.

It was the room of a king.

And not mine.

Not my room.

The realization of what I'd done came back to me in the span of a second.

My mother—Lucas—*Wright Highsmith*—

I bolted upright.

Vince lay next to me, his arm splayed above his head, and we were both naked, tangled in the silky maroon sheets of his bed. My slip lay forgotten in the middle of the floor.

I had let him take me.

No, I had run away. I *wanted* to come.

In only my underwear, no less.

My whole body flushed with embarrassment, remembering the pleasure he had brought me the night before, the absolutely sinful act we had committed in the *car*. The lovemaking we did afterward.

My whole body ached. Between my thighs, a lingering dampness remained, a soreness that spread from my thighs to my navel.

And he looked so peaceful now, his eyelashes lying across his sharp cheekbones, his dark, reddish-brown hair tousled against his pillow. In the daylight, his skin glowed. His muscles looked sculpted of marble, his whole figure that of Adonis, a dusting of dark hair across his abdomen and chest.

No small part of my heart cracked as I gazed down at him.

He was here. *He wasn't dead.*

I couldn't wrap my head around it, still, that the truth I'd accepted years ago wasn't the truth after all. That he was well, real—I could touch him, I could kiss him, again.

And I'd run away from my brother and my betrothed to do it.

I slid off the bed, careful to stay as quiet as I could. Waking him meant confronting last night, confronting what he was—and I wasn't entirely sure I knew how to feel about it.

Plush carpet dampened the sound of my feet hitting the ground. Two robes had been laid out on the armchairs near an unlit fireplace. Sliding my arms through one, I tied the belt closed, the fabric soft as spider's silk on my skin, a dark emerald in color. A breakfast had also been laid out, a steaming pot of tea and a plate of fruit. The citrus of Earl Grey permeated the air.

My favorite tea.

But my stomach felt hollow.

Swallowing down my unease, I glanced toward the bed once more. Vince hadn't moved, his chest rising and falling so imperceptibly, it was like he wasn't even breathing.

I slipped out of the room before I changed my mind and returned to the warmth of his side. The prospect of returning to that dream world, where there was only pleasure, where I could forget everything but his body and mine, nearly drew me back.

The hall outside was quiet, vacant, the polished floor icy beneath my bare feet. Looking one way, then the next, I had no idea which way to go, not remembering the path we'd taken last night. So I wandered, quiet as a creeping mouse, as I tried to trace our steps from the night before.

No servants greeted me, no sounds echoing down the halls; not the shutting of a door, the rasp of a broom, the squeak of shoes against the marble.

Yet I couldn't shake the feeling of eyes following me as I walked. A few portraits hung from gilded frames, every now and then, but none so direct and eerie as to feel like they watched my every movement.

Every door I passed was shut, dark mahogany interspersed amongst white and gold wallpaper. I turned the handle of a few and found most to be locked, some entire hallways hidden away. A few that opened held simply furnished bedrooms, their curtains drawn closed against the late morning sunlight. Though, from the thresholds, I could see the rooms were spotless—beds made, corners tucked tightly, not a speck of dust on the furniture. Like the rooms had been used recently.

I made sure to shut every door behind me. I wasn't certain if I was allowed to be prying, if I was even allowed down these halls. And I worried every time I opened a door I'd find something I wouldn't like.

They were all nondescript, empty, unremarkable, and I wondered when I'd find something else. This house couldn't possibly hold only bedrooms?

Turning one more door handle, expecting nothing, I nearly moved on after a quick glance within, until I realized I'd seen the space before. Seen those drawn curtains, that bed, that plush, deep red rug covering the entirety of the floor. My breath caught, and though the room itself wasn't much different from the others, I saw the memory of that feeding couple again, in the center of the room, arms wrapped around each other as she drank from two pin-prick wounds on his neck. Blood down her chin, the same color as her dress. His sharp grin as they switched roles, as he brought her onto her lap and laved at her throat.

The vampire couple Vince and I had watched that evening had been in *this* room.

The energy hung in the air, heavy and low like a storm cloud. No blood stained the floor, the furniture. All had been cleaned away.

I shouldn't be here.

Stepping out of the room, shaking off the memory, I shut the door behind me, perhaps too harshly. The sound of the door hitting the frame echoed down the hall.

I cringed at the noise before putting distance between myself and that room. The feeling of Vince pressing me against the window, kissing me while that couple fed from each other on just the other side of the glass—it awoke something within me, a fear, a fever, a thrill.

After—we'd fallen prey to that passion. And again, last night.

Coming around a corner too quickly, I ran into a hard wall, almost knocking all the air from my lungs.

But—no, not a wall.

A shriek stalled in my throat as I lost my footing. Quick hands grabbed me by the shoulders, steadying me on my feet with a light grip.

"You may not want to run in these halls."

Sinclair stood before me, those amber irises catching the sunlight in a dangerous glint.

The last time I saw him, he was covered in blood, showing off those knifelike teeth. I scrambled out of his grasp. "You!"

His brows quirked in amusement. "You," he echoed, amused, though there was no surprise in the expression.

"What are you doing here?" My feet carried me a few steps backward, my heart picking up speed at the shock of running into a vampire.

Alone.

Sinclair was a vampire, and I was alone.

A glance over my shoulder as if I could summon Vince, it appeared we were entirely, perhaps dangerously, *alone*.

"Too curious for your own good, I see." He was following me, one large stride at a time.

"I—"

"Couldn't stay away, could you?" That glint in his eye

danced, the corner of his lips turning upward. A tilt to his head, animalistic. "What were you looking for?"

"Nothing," I said, because it was mostly true—I didn't know *what* I was searching for, just that it was here, in this house.

"Oh, come now." He leaned his shoulder against the wall with all the casualness in the world. "You and I both know you've been rooting around in those rooms."

Outwardly, he was just a man, even if my instincts, my body, knew he was a predator. How easily they hid amongst humans—drinking with us, sleeping with us.

I didn't know whether to fear him or thank him for bringing me to Vince.

"I'm a guest here," I said, lifting my chin.

"Just a guest?" He crossed his arms. "I won't hurt you, Helena. But be mindful of who's around when you go running like that. You might inspire someone to... give chase." Another flash in those eyes.

"Who else is here?"

A noncommittal shrug as he pushed off the wall to standing again. "Right now, no one who will harm you."

Unable to stifle a shiver, I glanced away from his piercing stare. What had I gotten myself into? From one house so stifling, to another full of monstrous creatures.

I should've hidden away at Flora's. Vince had lured me from my home so easily, but I was not sure it was the best option. At Flora's, I'd be safe until my brother realized where I was, banging on the door with a team of cops behind him. A brief respite, until reality closed in again.

No one knew where I was. Not Flora, not Dixon, not my mother, not my brother or my betrothed.

And there was a vampire standing before me, every so often glancing at the pulse in my neck.

My eyes narrowed on him. "What is going on here?"

"Her curiosity wins out." He grinned.

My scowl deepened. "*You* were the one that brought me here."

"I did no such thing," he said, hands raised to feign innocence. "I merely made a suggestion. A push in the right direction. *You* would not have come here if you didn't already want to."

"You wanted me to see." He may as well have walked me right to the doors of that dark, red room himself. Pointing out the people in the robes, sparking that curiosity—he knew exactly what he was doing.

And he'd been put up to do it by Vince, one way or another.

Sinclair leaned a bit closer. I cemented my feet, unwilling to move. "And what *did* you see, Helena?"

Words stalled in my throat.

"It's drawing you in, is it not? I told you, we can give you *more*. Just around the corner, and you're there."

My tongue turned dry against my teeth at the thought. I had no idea, but perhaps something had been pushing me along, guiding me there without my knowing.

"You want to see it again." That amused brow still arched, eyes half-lidded. "You want to *watch*," the word charged, the accusation full of mirth, "so you can understand, yes?"

"Why—" The words died on my tongue.

"Because we need to feed, Helena," he said, voice lowering. "And why not share the pleasure of it amongst ourselves?"

"*There you are.*"

As though my thoughts summoned him, his voice echoed down the hall. Sinclair's gaze darted over my shoulder.

He was moving quite leisurely toward us, wearing a satin robe himself, parted around his bare chest as he walked. A faint bruising on one side of his neck, where I'd kissed him over and over again. Hair mussed, a shadow at his jaw.

Vince came to a stop right before us, his stare never leaving the other man, even when his arm came around my hips.

"The bed was cold," he said to me, voice softer.

"I didn't want to wake you." I turned in his arms, placing my palms against his chest, but he still didn't look at me.

"Thank you for watching over her."

"I am nothing if not dutiful," Sinclair drawled.

Vince's fingers tightened at my waist.

Much like my attacker had when Vince confronted him, Sinclair's eyes narrowed. And after a moment, he turned and walked off without a word, disappearing around that corner like he'd never been there to begin with.

"What was that about?" I asked after a few moments of heavy silence.

Vince's gray eyes lowered to me, pupils dilating. "Are you alright?"

"Why wouldn't I be?"

His mouth pressed into a firm line. "I thought you might've left and gone back."

He'd awoken to a cold, empty bed, without a note, without any real indication I would return—only the promise I'd chanted over and over in the midnight hour, and promises could be broken. I could not run from him now, not when I'd just gotten him back.

My alternative was marriage to a cruel man I did not love.

"Why is Sinclair here?" I asked.

"He lives here."

"Does anyone else live here?"

"Only the ones I can trust," he said. "Two others, besides him."

Two others. "You trust Sinclair?"

He nodded once.

"Why?"

A beat of quiet, hesitation, his gaze searching my face. "He's been one of my companions for some time."

How long had he surrounded himself with these *companions* while I believed him dead? Vince and three other vampires, living it up on the Island while I was wasting away in the city—

I stepped away from him, running my hands over my face. Mind whirling, thoughts spiraling, my overwhelm catching up to me.

If he trusted them, he *knew* them—he spent time with them.

While I'd filled my nights with liquor and empty kisses, just to keep going.

A muscle ticked in Vince's jaw. "Did you expect me to be alone?"

"I don't know."

"This will take time, Helena. To settle in, to get your footing. You'll find everything is well—"

"*No.*" I turned from him, pressing my fingertips into my eyes, holding back the onslaught of grief I'd ignored since last night.

Everything was *not* well.

The only reason I had my dead lover back was because *he was no longer human.*

His hands came to rest on my arms, gentle and soothing. "I know this is all so different. I will try my best to—"

"You don't get it," I snapped, spinning on my heels so we were once again face-to-face. "I thought you were *dead.* And my heart still aches, even when I can see you are here, right in front of me. Every moment I expect to wake up, for you to disappear, and then I'm stuck forever with *them.*"

Those gray eyes searched mine, his features the softest they'd been since last night. "I am real. I'm right here."

Then why doesn't it feel like it?

I still felt I'd wake up any moment and be in my room, at home, Lucas pounding on the door.

Adam is back. He's alive. He's here *with me.*

"I'm *mad* at you," I breathed, the words barely louder than a whisper. "I'm angry that I've spent so long so... *empty.* That Lucas threatened you all those years ago, and I did nothing, and then I thought you were dead. But you're not, even though my heart still thinks it."

He wrapped my hand in his, his skin cool to the touch. Bringing our clasped hands up to his chest, he pressed my palm to the skin there, feeling the soft, slow thud of his heart. Still beating, even if it gave away his secret in its slow rhythm.

He was no longer human.

"I will work every day to make sure your heart knows that mine beats for you."

And though the words melted a bit of my resolve, the anger still flared. "*Ugh.*"

Every time he was near me, he clouded my senses. Made me want to become that young girl again, hopelessly in love, thinking everything will be alright.

"I am betrothed," I said, hoping the words stung him just enough. "I am ruined. My brother will *kill* me." I tore myself away again, pacing the hall, the marble icy against my bare feet.

"He will do no such thing."

"I have a life!" I threw my hands into the air. "And now you've interrupted it—and I am learning that *nothing* is what it seems!"

His hands fisted at his sides, like he wanted to reach for me, to keep me from running. I realized his hair was not only mussed from sleeping, but from running his hands through it so many times this morning. Did he pace his room, worrying that I'd left?

Good. Maybe then he felt half the nerves I did.

"You don't get to just show up and act like everything is okay." My teeth nearly punctured skin as I chewed on my lip, the pain grounding. "You don't get to just decide when to pull me back in like this, not without an explanation."

Like earlier, he just watched me, the tilt to his brow, the line of his lips the only evidence of his concern.

"Say something!"

"What do you want me to say?"

"I don't know. Tell me everything? Like how? *Why?*" My anger bloomed into a wretched thing, the urge to hit something, my limbs restless. I kept my distance, worried if I came too close, I'd pummel him or let him say sweet nothings into my ear until I fell apart.

But the anger just simmered. Anger that I'd been living in anguish for six years, at the whims of my brother, and Adam had just left me there. *Alone.*

"You don't get to become something different when I'm stuck, the same I've been for the last six years." The last word cracking, stinging in my throat.

He exhaled a breath. "I will never forgive myself for what has happened. I feel responsible for how things happened. How you've been left alone, and for so long. I want to make it up to you."

"How?" My shoulders deflated. "What can you do about it?"

His eyes hardened, and he neared me, and I let him. Let him come close enough I could smell the cologne left over on his skin. An expensive, rich smell.

"I can't change anything," he said, "but I want you. I've wanted you since the day I set eyes on you. You must understand that all of this was for you."

All of this.

"Believe me, I *tried* to come home. I tried to figure out a way. And then," he glanced down at himself, "even though I didn't ask for this, it led me back to you."

I shook my head, hearing the words, wanting to melt

into him again, but wanting to stay angry, at the world, at *him*.

And then his fingers danced, feather-light, across my cheeks, wiping away the few tears that did escape.

"I just—I can't—" My lips trembled. "You don't know—"

"You are so pretty when you cry."

Lips brushed against my face, my eyelashes, his fingers twining into the hair at the nape of my neck. Pulling me to him like I knew he would.

"Let me make it up to you. Let me distract you."

Kisses to every inch of skin, my ears, in my hair. And though his skin was much cooler than any living man, his hands were the same strong hands I knew from before.

I leaned into him.

"Let me make this better."

When he pulled away, our breaths mingling in the space between us, he looked at me with near-black eyes. The monster within him gazed out at me, grinning, waiting.

TWENTY-FIVE

I spent the next day in bed, exhaustion taking over. When I awoke, it was already late afternoon, the setting sun turning the sky above us to a creeping indigo, fading into the dark.

And Vince stayed with me the whole time, peppering kisses on my bare shoulders, rubbing circles onto my back; comfortably silent when I didn't feel like talking, murmuring how much he loved me when I did. I'd doze, curled into him, and when I woke, he'd be trailing his fingers along the valleys of my side, around my hips, up into my hair.

His touch intoxicating, calming, a soft reminder that kindness did exist, and I'd just forgotten in the span of six years.

When I finally opened my eyes, facing the large window that looked over the grounds, a heaviness had eased from my limbs.

He noticed I was awake. "You need to eat, darling."

I hadn't eaten since the night before, like I'd undergone a transformation myself, coming to the manor; my needs were no longer the same in this dream world.

Grogginess clouded me as I pushed myself up to sitting, the world still hazy after my dreams of nothingness. Sleep had just been a lull from my tumultuous thoughts, a way to shut off the noise, the worries circling inside me like a shark does its prey.

"Let's get out of the house," Vince said as he sat up next to me, the muscles in his abdomen flexing.

We were both unclothed. The comfort I felt around him was unlike anything I'd felt around anyone else. I could strip myself to my barest form, and he wouldn't look at me with any scrutiny. Just appreciation. Just—seeing me for who I was.

"Okay."

His lips curved in a soft smile before he leaned forward and pressed them to mine. He slipped from the bed and held his hand out to me. "I want to take you somewhere," he said.

As I stood, my knees weak from disuse, I wondered what Sinclair was doing—what the other vampires that lived here were doing. When would I meet them? And would they truly not harm me? Sinclair hadn't ever tried, even if I was suspicious of him. The only one to attack me was the strange man in the garden—and given the way Vince had run him off, I doubted he was one of the more permanent residents.

"We'll have to go into the city." Vince led me to a doorway across the room that opened up to a closet. "But we'll be discreet."

He remembered.

He knew I feared Lucas and what he would do if he found me.

Before, I don't think he understood my fear, not until Lucas pointed a gun at him. He just didn't get it—not until we were found out.

I'm inclined to ruin you.

Now, I almost worried more for him than myself—how Lucas would react, knowing Adam was not actually dead. What destruction would come then?

"I don't have any clothes." I almost laughed, glancing at the simple silk slip that had remained discarded on the floor this whole time.

Vince grinned over his shoulder. "You do," he said, pulling open one of the many built-in wardrobes within the massive closet, to reveal dozens of dresses in every fabric and color imaginable.

I gasped, coming to stand next to him. "How?"

"Pick out whatever you like." A kiss pressed to my shoulder before he wandered to other shelves, shirts folded with crisp lines, whole racks of shoes at the floor. Suit jackets hanging neatly in a line. "I may have acquired some clothes for you. Just in case."

Just in case.

He had always expected to find me. He was waiting for me. Making a place for me in this house, in his room, were I ever to choose him.

I pulled a cream-colored number from the lineup. Lace sleeves, a satin skirt, a swooping neckline. And as I pulled it over my head, the expensive fabric falling like water along my flesh, it felt so right, it almost took my breath away. Exactly my size, snug where it needed to be, the skirt loose around my knees.

"This fits," I said, dumbfounded.

Vince turned to me from where he was buttoning his shirt. He grinned again, eyes sweeping over my figure. "I have my ways."

The driver pulled up to an unassuming building, all dark brick and yellow electric lights. A single doorman by a modest front door. No one else lingered outside, no cars parked along the sidewalk. I expected crowds, but wherever Vince was taking me seemed private.

When the car stopped—the same car in which I couldn't resist climbing onto Vince's lap the other night—he exited first and then offered me his hand. I was thankful for the satin gloves Vince had brought out, the wildly luxurious cashmere shawl that wrapped around my shoulders, as the brisk air nipped at my skin.

As we walked up the steps, the doorman made eye contact with Vince. He was dressed simply, a dark coat and hat, hands stuffed into his pockets, face mostly hidden by the dark. He nodded once, some understanding passing between the two of them, before he held the door open for us without a word.

Within, the warm yellow of the electric lights glowed in the nondescript lobby. An opening to the right, where stairs could be seen leading up, and a few shut doors to our left. Dark wallpaper peeling in the corners. The floor was tiled, alternating white and black, with a red runner leading toward the staircase.

Nothing like the dinner club I was expecting.

My fingers tightened around Vince's. "Where are we?"

He just turned to me and raised a finger to his lips. The building was quiet, like the walls sucked up any sound, my voice sounding out of place. Too loud.

We made our way up the stairs, steps muffled by the runner leading us to the next level. And at the top, another choice of two directions. He chose one, pulling me along, knowing where he was going.

It was then I began to feel out of my element. What was he dragging me into? And why did I feel, deep inside, that I didn't want to know what was behind all these doors? The further in we walked, the dimmer the lights seemed to get.

Vince stopped before a door that had no indication of what was inside. He ushered me in, and it took a moment for my eyes to adjust in the darkness.

"A table for two," he said to someone I couldn't see, his grip on my hand secure.

There was a muttered response before we were brought to a dining room—and I could only tell it was a dining room because of the candles that were lit on every table, the only source of light, barely strong enough to illuminate the silhouettes of those sitting.

Vince thanked whoever sat us, and pulled out a seat for me, guiding me down.

"I can't see anything," I whispered, holding onto the arms of the chair as I sat.

"That's the point," Vince chuckled, pushing the chair in and making his way to his own seat. I could only really see him once he was across from me, the flicker of the candle casting shadows across his features.

"You can see fine," I said, noticing the ease with which he moved around in the space.

"I can."

"Because you're..." The word sat on my tongue.

He looked up at me through hooded eyes, the candle-light glinting across those hazel irises. "A vampire?"

I swallowed, nodding.

"Yes," he said. "I can see in the dark."

We hadn't had this conversation yet. And I knew we needed to have it, but I feared what I would learn; I was scared that he might say something that made me fear *him*.

"Does that mean..." I glanced around, as though I could see through the heavy darkness around me. "There are others here?"

"Yes."

I couldn't hear anyone else's conversations, just the rumble of voices speaking low, whispers in the pitch black-ness. Suddenly self-conscious, I worried whatever creatures lurked around us could hear my every word—could even hear my *heart beating*.

Vince reached across the table, fingers soft on my cheek, pulling me back to the present. "It's alright," he murmured, thumb brushing against my skin. "I am right here. I won't let anything happen to you."

My hands had become claws on the chair arms.

"It's just you and me," he said, leaning back into his seat. "Just focus on me."

I linked my fingers with his, our clasped hands setting down onto the table. The tiny flame from the candle radiated a modicum of warmth, like a second caress on the inside of my wrist.

"This is a private club. No one here is looking for trouble."

"Oh." The words only eased my anxieties a little.

There were vampires living in the city this whole time. Enough of them to have their own establishments. Faces flipped through my mind—how many people had I met, out and about, that were *not* human?

"What else?" I asked, my free hand fisting in my lap.

His brow arched in the dark, the shadows dancing across his face.

"Is there anything else I need to know about you?"

"What do you want to know?" he asked, head tilting the slightest bit.

At that moment, a figure came to our table, setting a platter before me and two glasses, one for me and one for Vince. A roast, some greens, the scent of the dinner making me realize just how hungry I had become.

So they catered to humans as well, if they were able to prepare such a dinner. It was simple, but smelled expertly done, like something I could get at any other club.

Vince raised his glass to his lips and took a modest sip of the dark liquid that appeared black.

I didn't need to ask to figure out what it was.

It was jealousy that flowed through me—a feeling I couldn't fathom. How morbid, to be jealous he wasn't drinking *my* blood.

"Is this sufficient for you?" he asked.

I nodded, taking a bite, if only to bite my tongue. A thought came to me then as I ate. "Can you not eat food?"

His one hand steepled over the top of his glass, turning the drink absentmindedly as he watched me. Like it was a delicacy, a dark wine, not meant to be gulped down, but savored.

Whose blood was it?

"I can, but it doesn't taste the same. It's much like when you're sick, and it loses all flavor." He propped his chin on his other fist.

I could not imagine never tasting the sweetness of champagne, the strong bitterness of coffee, the sour burst of a ripe grape on your tongue. I couldn't imagine smelling the candied almonds on the street and feeling indifferent to their sweet cinnamon scent. A whole world closed off.

"Where do you get the blood?"

His eyes flickered. "We get our sustenance in many ways. Willing donations, either directly from the source, or in a glass, such as this. Often, we feed from each other."

"Or you attack someone."

His brows drew together. "Only the worst of us attack. It's uncivilized when there are other options."

I set my fork and knife down. "How long have you lived this way?"

His hand stilled on the glass. "Six years."

My eyes fluttered shut.

He'd gone away, and almost immediately, he'd changed. Lucas had sent him to his death and instead, he'd become *this*.

"What happened?" I whispered, my dinner forgotten. "What is it like?"

He thought about it for a moment, and the way his eyes searched me, I saw a glimpse into the past. For a brief moment, it was *Adam* in front of me, that intelligent mind churning.

He was so clever, always thinking about something, always mulling over something he'd read, wondering about bigger things than I'd ever even thought about. Big philosophical things that hurt my head. He had tried to talk to me about those things once, about his thoughts on the world, the universe, about the possibility of a divine god above us—or something else—and I had kissed him to make him stop, to draw his attention to me instead.

"It's an entirely different existence," he said, and I knew he spoke of more than just his change in appetite. His pause grew longer, and I knew he was hesitating.

"Can you tell me about it?" My heart fluttered just thinking about *what* he was now.

His eyes flickered as though he could hear it.

He was attuned to my heartbeat, to the flow of blood in my veins, the way a python is attracted to heat through the flick of their tongue. The way a shark can smell a single drop of blood through miles of water. Whatever transformation he had undergone had made him into a predator, one designed to hunt men.

And I had let him in.

"I will," he finally said. "But I cannot tell it all at once because then I think I'd go mad."

I nodded as though I understood. But I didn't, not really. "How many of you are there?"

"It entirely depends." His eyes darkened, like he feared my reaction. "There are considerably less of us than there are men."

I swallowed the lump growing in my throat, and his eyes found that spot beneath my ear. "All of you—transformed?"

"No. I am Made, as I was not born this way. Though, many *are*. They are... true vampires. Born."

My eyelids fluttered closed at the word. *Vampire.*

"We are all over the world," he continued, then cleared his throat. "Us and many other creatures. My Sire was Born long ago, and then six years ago, he Made me."

Vince adjusted in his seat, visibly uncomfortable.

Had he told anyone? Was I the first? Was it improper to ask a vampire of their origin?

And how many other *creatures* were there?

"I fear it's a terrible story," he said, glancing at me for my reaction. "I was away at war, and I was nearly dead."

That thought alone struck a fear in me, that I had almost truly lost him.

No matter that all this time I thought he was dead—knowing, now, that he wasn't, but he could have been—too many emotions circled within me, so many worries, such anger and frustration that any of this had happened *at all*.

"That was when my Sire found me and... *Made* me. Drained me of what little life I had left and buried me—the ground was unholy and desecrated with the violence of the war, stained with the blood of every other soldier that had fallen, and some that had lived, and it was in that ground that I changed. Every bit of soil soaked with that wretchedness. Imagine that—earth so profane, so synonymous with suffering, with anguish, and then *rotting* there. I was cursed as soon as I arrived, as soon as I touched that ground, and perhaps that's why he chose me amongst all the others."

He looked off into the room, smoothing his hand

through his hair. Perhaps it was too intense a story to tell here, of all places. His hearing was more attuned than mine. Any other vampire could listen in on us.

I opened my mouth to tell him that if he couldn't bring himself to speak it now, I would understand. But he kept going, his hand a fist on the table, his voice low:

"I had no knowledge of any of this happening. My consciousness was long gone, my blood near spent after that battle. I was as good as dead. And though my spirit was still tied to my body, it was nearly free to move on to the next life, if it exists. But *he* took the last drops for himself. Drank what little blood I had left, stole me from my fate. His bite is poison if he wants it to be, and I suppose there was something singular about me amidst all those other dying men on the field. He buried me. I died in that soil—"

His voice caught, and he said nothing for a moment, his jaw flexing, until he looked at me directly with those icy eyes. "That is why I am no longer Adam Vering. That is why you must understand I am no longer that boy.

"I *died*. My mortal flesh is dead, but I live on, reanimated by the poison that was in my Sire's bite. It pushes every human cell out over the span of an evening, and when I awoke, I was no longer a man. I was new, reborn, but dead all the same.

"I renamed myself. When I awoke, I was half-delirious. But I knew, if nothing else, I could not let *him* know who I had been. I couldn't tell him who Adam Vering was. I did not know my Sire, didn't trust him not to find my family or —or *you*, and that was not something I'd risk. I had to mourn myself—you mourned me here at home, safe across the ocean, but it hasn't crossed your mind that *I* had to mourn my own death, my own humanity."

My food sat untouched before us, my hunger from before gone. In all my misery the past few days, disbelief that he'd hid himself from me, I hadn't considered what it made *him* feel. It had not crossed my mind that what he'd become was something he hated.

That maybe he had wished for death.

I had cried too much the past few days; I did not want to spill any more tears. "Stop. Tell it to me later."

"I want you to understand," he said, fingers gripping mine once more, "why it took me six years to come back to you."

I *hated* Lucas. Hated what had happened to us.

That was what I mourned the most: what could have been if Adam and I were never found out. He had died, and I'd not known it. I would have *never* known it, not for sure.

"I would've died, over and over again, for centuries, if it meant I would get this moment." He looked at me directly. "If it meant we'd be together once again. I'd become a specter if just to follow you and know you were alive and well. I wouldn't let death get in the way of my loving you."

TWENTY-SIX

An hour later, our meals abandoned, he stood and came to my side to lead me through the pitch-dark room. A hand at my elbow, another on the small of my back. I didn't feel strange eyes on me anymore, like the room had cleared out, and we were truly alone in that midnight dining room.

Candles had begun to flicker out, one by one, as the evening went on, until only a few dim smudges of light remained.

Out in the hallway, silence greeted us once more.

"What is behind all of these doors?" I asked.

"Some are guest rooms."

Just like in his house?

"The other floors lead to other clubs. This building is a hotspot, of sorts."

"Other clubs?"

A small smirk at his lips, nearly indistinguishable in the dark. "For those with... alternate appetites."

I said nothing more as we traced our steps. His fingers held mine tightly, squeezing every so often as though to remind me—or himself—that he was there.

Out on the street, the night had turned even chillier. The doorman inclined his head as we passed. Vince reached a hand out, holding a few bills in between two outstretched fingers, which the doorman promptly plucked and stuffed into his pocket. Another nod in thanks.

Adam Vering would never have been able to just hand out a sum that large like it was nothing.

An evening chill swept through me, a cold breeze raking its fingers through my hair.

Before I could say anything, before I could even shiver, Vince shucked off his jacket. "Here," he said, draping it about my shoulders, dark like a cape.

"Thank you."

He wrapped his arm around me, pulling me to his side as we walked down the street.

"I needed to take you out properly," he said. "It was my turn to pay for our dinner this time."

Though his tone was teasing, I knew he was remembering our past. The meetings at cafes, far on the other side of the city. Stolen kisses in the garden outside my family's house. His strange appearances on my street, when I'd have to run outside and shoo him away, for fear he'd be seen— and he'd say that all he wanted was a kiss.

The number of people on the sidewalks was minimal in the late hour, but still substantial, the nightlife in the city still rearing. Almost out of habit, I peeked at them between my lashes. Angling my face downward. Watching for any flashes of recognition, I eyed each passerby warily.

Vince said nothing else. We walked in a companionable silence.

An older couple caught my eye—it was not so much the expensive furs they wore, the gold around their fingers and necks, but the sneer at their lips, as they passed us by, peering down their noses. Not at me, I realized. At Vince.

He said nothing, only the tick of his jaw betraying his vexation

Did they know him?

Were they… vampires?

I gleaned over my shoulder to spot them again, but they were long gone, swallowed by the crowd.

"Who were they?"

"I don't know."

"But—they seem to know *you*."

He was silent for a moment as he led me down the street. "A great deal of people have learned my name in the past months. Some may *think* they know me."

A question burned in my mind: did *I* know him?

He must have sensed the direction of my thoughts. He glanced at me out of the corner of his eye, softening ever so slightly. "You are the only one who has ever truly known me."

I wasn't sure if I agreed.

"None of your partygoers ever seem to personally know Vince Thornton." I remembered asking around, what seemed like weeks ago, trying to find him amidst a sea of people, and I was met with laughter. "Why even throw the parties?"

The words stalled on his lips. "Because I hoped you'd come one day."

A pain seared through my chest. I'd been drinking my way around the city, when all I had to do was *find him*.

"Will you keep hosting them?"

"Only if you wish it."

We'd found the driver, parked some blocks away from where we'd dined. When he saw us, he started the vehicle, the engine roaring to life.

Vince opened the door, holding it wide for me.

"What about... the other parties?" I didn't know how to word it, what exactly to call whatever happened in that room between all those vampires. But Sinclair said they were for feeding, for pleasure, for sharing. Some sort of bloody bacchanal.

For a moment, Vince froze.

"I saw it."

He couldn't be too surprised, too worried. He'd shown me that vampire couple, after all. He'd revealed more about his world, about how he'd been Made, and somehow, I knew the two were related.

"What are they?"

His lips pressed into a line. "You will know soon enough."

TWENTY-SEVEN

My eyes snapped open to the mid-morning sun streaming through the windows. It was quiet, entirely too quiet.

Blinking the sleep away from my eyes, I rolled over to find the bed otherwise empty. The sheets lay tangled and unkempt. Cold to the touch.

A chill settled over me, even though the embers warmed the fireplace across the room. Tea was again set out for me, along with fruit and a few pastries and butter. Perhaps a servant was coming in while we slept, setting out the breakfast for me and tending to the fire.

The night before was hazy; I couldn't much remember even getting into bed, much less falling asleep. But my body was sore, an ache low in my belly. The ghost of peppered kisses on my chest, my neck. My elegant dress from the evening in a heap on the floor.

I took my time stretching, waking my limbs. Nibbled on a pastry while I considered what to wear in the massive closet. Pulling on a comfortable day dress of warm pink, I slipped my feet into comfortable woven stockings that went over my knee, then into house slippers.

Where did Vince go? I knew he slept—despite his change, he still needed to, even if perhaps the need was no longer as great as it was for me. But I wondered just how long I had lain alone in the bed, arm subconsciously stretched out as though waiting for his return.

And—how did he spend his days? What did he do in between parties before I'd arrived? I almost couldn't fathom him doing anything else, like I still expected to find him with ink staining his hands, the India soaked so deep, becoming part of his flesh.

Sometimes, I missed the way those painted fingers looked against my skin. Like he had a darkness within, seeping out.

I left the empty room behind and made my way into the hallway. It looked exactly as it did when I'd been snooping the other day—except for the whisper of voices tumbling down the hall. Too far for me to make out, but just loud enough I thought I heard a woman's laugh amidst the muddled noise.

Who else was here? Vince had said there were two others, besides Sinclair, who he trusted enough to let live here.

Two other vampires I had yet to meet.

I followed the sound, my curiosity pulling me like there was a thread in my chest, reeling me in. Past those watching portraits, gloomy landscapes, statues of Venus and Adonis, blazing electric sconces, even in the middle of the day. A confusing twist of corridors, as though meant to disorient, distract.

But the echo of the voices guided me, and I was before a doorway.

A sitting room, the windows thrown open, bright with white sunlight. Smoke wafted through the doorway, the smell rich and dark, and a phonogram played a small tune, background noise to the chatter.

I found Vince immediately—standing before the windows, looking out at the grounds. His back was turned to me, his arms crossed over his chest, and even from the distance, I saw the furrow to his brow, lost in thought. Dressed casually, the sleeves rolled to his elbows.

The conversation died. Vince turned at the silence.

Three figures sat around the table. The first, no surprise —Sinclair, smoking with a newspaper pulled open across his lap, lounging back in his chair. The second, a striking woman with chopped dark hair and severe cheekbones. The third—

"Séra?"

She stood immediately as I entered, gasping with delight. "Helena!" Smiling brighter than she ever had at my family's house, she wore a soft rosy-hued dress, the fabric rippling around her as she came to me. "I am so happy to finally see you!"

Dumbfounded, I was unsure what to say.

She seemed not to notice. "And more than anything, I am happy to be out of that house." She laughed. "I hope you forgive my saying it, but nothing is as comfortable as your own home."

I blinked. "No offense taken."

"Let the girl breathe," Sinclair mused, never looking up from his paper.

"And this is Veronica." Séra held out an open hand to the strange woman.

Her arms were bronze under the electric lights, her dress an elegant black, but the beading was extensive—expensive. "Nice to meet you." She had watched the whole thing coolly, her own cigarette at her lips.

"You too," I said, my mind still whirring.

Séra was here, with them—

Séra was a vampire. A fact that had somehow slipped between the cracks. And she'd been with me, at the house, alone, in my bedroom.

She didn't seem any more surprised to see me than Sinclair.

She knew. They were all unsurprised—like they'd known I'd be coming.

A hand settled on my back, strong and grounding— Vince.

These were the three that had been with him this whole time.

"Sinclair, Séra, and Veronica reside here. I trust them, so you can trust them, too, should you need anything."

How did this come about? Where had he met these three, and *why* had they earned his trust? And why did they live here? Did they not have their own places?

Séra clasped her hands together, a grin still plastered across her features. "I can't wait to prepare you for the party! Just like old times."

"Party?" It seemed I could only manage single-syllable words.

"Give it eight hours and this place will be packed full of people. I haven't attended in *months*. I'm positively *dying* to dance again."

Vince's fingers curled against my back. We had just talked about this, but I hadn't expected—

"Séra just returned this morning," he said to me, as though he could read my thoughts. "She insists."

"Well, why not?" she asked. "It's been how long since we've thrown one?"

"A week," Veronica intoned, finger tapping against the table.

"It's alright," I nodded, convincing myself. Parties meant crowds, hundreds—thousands—of people. Anyone could see me, recognize me, run to Lucas—ruin this whole thing. It had been two days and *nothing*, no sound from him, no police showing up at the door. I was waiting for him to show up with Father's gun, and maybe, this time, he would pull the trigger.

"It could be fun." I forced a smile.

"We'll make it fun." Séra grinned at me again, a flicker of mischief in her eyes. Maybe she was the same girl that readied me for my nights out before, but I had a feeling I had yet to truly know her. Our alliance perhaps had never ended, after all. She would know what was going on at home, at least for the last day or so.

Vince moved to stand in front of me. "Are you sure?"

There was no real reason for them now. Not really, not when I was here. In his arms.

But—if I wanted to know what was going on, to understand just what happened at those bloodletting parties deep in this house—

I looked up at Vince, meeting those steely eyes. A lock of his hair fell across his forehead, not yet held back by pomade. He hadn't shaved, either.

"I understand if you need some time—"

"No, I want to," I said.

"We should go pick out our dresses," Séra said, giddy with excitement. She nearly hopped on the balls of her feet, coming to hug me, almost as if she couldn't help herself. "I have so many that would look great on you."

"Do let the girl breathe," Sinclair huffed, straightening the newspaper.

"I was not expecting—*this*." I laughed again as Séra linked her arm with mine.

She'd never touched me so casually. Not without permission. But it was as though barriers had fallen overnight.

"Don't worry." Séra grinned, a sharp fang poking at her lip. "I don't bite."

TWENTY-EIGHT

Séra's closet was larger than the one I'd had at home.

Home. No, that place wasn't my home any longer. Hadn't ever been one, really, not since I was a child, since Father was still around.

An anxiety had settled itself into my chest, wrapping its spindly fingers around my heart. It squeezed when it wanted to, reminding me of what I'd done, at seemingly random moments, pulling my attention away from Séra's soft hands and kind words.

"Were you ever going to tell me?"

Séra smiled as she opened the wardrobe doors. "Eventually. Probably."

"How...?"

"Because he asked me to."

Vince asked her to become my maid.

He had a set of eyes on me for months now. Someone who observed, who often never spoke, who had access to every part of the house. She had made me feel comfortable, like I had someone to talk to. She knew how I butt heads with Mother, how I snuck out, *where* I went.

And then Sinclair—our meeting as though it were an accident, a stranger's suggestion to return to the party. To *find* the vampires.

"He told me your story, about your brother, and I wanted to help."

I said nothing, feeling the weight of it, wondering what else there was for me to uncover. She continued on, reaching for dresses, rifling through, pulling a few and laying them out. Dresses of every color, fabric, and length stuffed the closet full. What splendor she'd really had this whole time, while she was playing at being a maid.

"When he came back, really, I wanted to kill him," she said so casually, and I wasn't sure if she was exaggerating. "He's quite terrible. And *Lord Highsmith*—ugh."

"Is he still there?" I couldn't help but ask.

"Highsmith?" She popped her head out for a moment.

I nodded.

She rolled her eyes. "Yes. He and Lucas are figuring out some sort of plan. Your mother is quite emotional, but Lucas is refusing to let her call anyone."

No wonder the cops hadn't shown up.

"Does he know—"

"He doesn't know where you are," she said, a bit softer, giving me a placating smile. It warmed her entire face, and I suddenly wanted to hug her, to feel someone other than Vince against me. A friend.

She darted back into the closet, continuing her search. "I'm thinking something daring tonight. A statement piece."

Daring.

Ten minutes later, she had me dressed in a blood-red gown, shorter than anything I'd worn before. It barely covered me, its beaded trim falling just below my behind, brushing against the sensitive skin of my thighs. It was silky and smooth and cool to the touch, and exposed the near entirety of my back, crisscrossed with more beads. Mother would have fallen over if she ever saw me dressed like this. I was truly the harlot she feared—one wrong move, and I'd expose my breasts through the fabric at my sides.

But I didn't feel exposed. Inspecting myself in the mirror, I peeked over my shoulder at the way the dress fell across my back, how it fluttered out when I turned, how it glinted in the dim electric lights of Séra's room.

Flora would love it. And in that moment, I missed her. I hadn't called her—so caught up in everything, I hadn't told her I was alright.

She was the one part of my old life—if I could call it that—that I didn't want to leave behind. My dearest friend, my *sister*. She would want to be here.

I ran my hand over the beading on my stomach.

"You should wear that every day," Séra said, watching from the vanity, a hand on her hip. "I've never worn it. You can have it."

Our eyes met in the mirror. "I love it."

She patted the vanity. "You need some rouge," she said, while I sat. Running her fingers through my hair, she brushed the waves out and applied gels and a golden headband that sat just across my forehead, like a crown.

As she worked, her brow wrinkled in concentration, I noticed red markings on my neck—faint, barely there, almost like little bruises. The light purple from Lucas' hand, but the red love bites from Vince, like he'd tried to cover up the brutality with his tongue, his sharp teeth. To claim my pain as his own pleasure.

The dress displayed the markings for all to see, and I had the thought that it was as Vince intended.

"I hope you won't be mad," Séra said, reaching into a little jewelry box. She then pulled out a set of earrings, glimmering in the light, and I laughed, feeling my anxieties lift a little.

"You kept them." The set I'd seen her try on in my room, a night that felt like eons ago.

"I thought maybe you'd want them." She smiled.

"I meant what I said—you can have them. I think they'll suit you better, anyway."

She tucked them away, rooting through the box. "I have plenty to choose from. More in the wardrobe."

"I'm done up enough as it is," I said, turning my head to see her handiwork in the mirror. She'd applied rouge to my cheeks, a ruby red to my lips. Pitch-black lined my eyes, with little wings sharp like knives. She'd taken a pencil to my brows. I looked part seductress, part pouty actress, like the ones in the moving pictures. "Why could you not have done my makeup like this at the house?"

She gave me a look. "Because then I would've been fired."

The faint sound of a trumpet, beginning a jazzy solo, rang through the house, heralding the guests who must've been spilling into the house, parking their expensive cars along the drive, ready for a night they would forget by morning. We were so far into the house, it was difficult to hear, but she grinned at me through the mirror, her teeth more elongated than I remembered.

"It begins."

It was not long before Séra was supplying me with glass upon glass of gin, throwing them back herself, but holding her own like they were water. We'd descended the stairs as the foyer was filling with people, the scents of their perfumes and smoke, the sounds of their shouting voices and laughter permeating the massive ballroom. The servers were stationed around the room, flutes of champagne at the ready.

Sinclair joined us for a moment, offering us both a cigarette, before placing a kiss on Séra's forehead and retreating back upstairs.

I knew where he was likely going.

That damned room, where I'd found him; that cavern of indulgence and blood and consummation. Writhing bodies, mimicking the ones dancing down in the ballroom, the men and women with carefree masks adorned, drinking their worries away, while inhuman beings drank from each other, perhaps even from unwilling victims, right above. Shameless feasting.

"We should go with him," I said, sipping on my fourth drink of the evening.

I wanted to see it again, and maybe it was perverse, but I wanted to watch. Women and men biting each other, puncturing a spot on the neck where blood flowed freely, thick and red and spurting, and tongues lapping it up, the promise of preternatural strength and vigor.

Séra looped her arm with mine, bumping our hips together. "It's more entertaining down here," she said, her fingers lifting the glass again to my lips, watching until I swallowed more of the heady liquid before she was satisfied. "People make fools of themselves in the most entertaining way, if you stay long enough to watch."

I couldn't feel the burn of the drink any longer. My belly was warm, my muscles languid, though my mind was yet sharp.

"Where is he?" I wondered aloud, almost shouting over the din, the crowd becoming increasingly more packed, all of us bumping into each other's shoulders. Séra moved with grace, avoiding every other body in the room. I was clumsy in my half-drunk human state. Vince—I hadn't seen him since the afternoon.

Men ogled at us as we passed, not even hiding their staring, their gazes traveling up our thighs—no stockings—to the short hems of our skirts, hoping that they'd get a glimpse of what was underneath. To the way the fabric hugged our chests. Women staring, perhaps in jealousy, in envy. One woman caught my eye and winked her long lashes, pulling a blush to my cheeks.

"He must be busy." Séra pulled me toward the dance floor. "People call in the evenings," she revealed. "He'll show up, don't worry."

We became part of the throng, our feet hardly touching the floor as we joined the dance floor. The room spun, the gin clouding my head.

A few stray hands found my hips, my arms, and I only laughed, every sensation electrified as the alcohol settled in.

I'd lost my glass and Séra was holding my hand while we

threw ourselves into the music. We found the band amidst the crowd, a large string bass, a piano, a trumpet, a sax. The bass player grinned when we made eye contact, and I knew then he lived for these parties, as much as everyone else in the crowd. He fed off the energy, creating a beat for revelers to move to, and took in their dancing like it was worship.

Séra moved like a trained dancer, like the professionals hired to entertain at these things. I probably looked ridiculous, but I didn't care, letting the bass player and his band move my limbs through their music.

Hands gripping my waist, I nearly spun to shake them off, but the fingers dug in and a face nuzzled into my neck.

"I am sorry to keep you waiting," he said, his voice low, only for me to hear.

I reached up to wind my hand into the hair at his neck, my back pressed to his front. His hands doing nothing to stop the spread of heat to my core, my thighs.

"Then you must dance with me now," I said, turning and looping my arms around his neck.

His eyes darkened as they took in the front of my dress, the way the fabric fell between my legs, parting at my hips, the beading that caressed my curves. "I'm inclined to do something else," he said, his timbre sending shivers down my thighs.

Laughing, I moved my hips, letting the music take me once more. He watched hungrily, and though he didn't dance, the odd one out in the crowd, no one seemed to notice, parting around us like we were a fixture in the room and not just another couple to bump into.

"Séra picked it out!" I shouted, swaying and letting my skirts whirl around me.

He pulled me closer, halting my movements. His lips found mine, his kiss harsh, his hands winding around my waist so that I couldn't back away. His tongue found mine, forcing entry into my mouth, and though we were amidst a crowd, I couldn't stop. Indecent and indulgent.

I gasped as he nipped at my lip. My fingers played with the curls around his ears, with the collar of his shirt.

I wanted to undress him here, now, so everyone else could see how beautiful he was. So that they could see he was mine.

When he pulled away, his eyes fell to my neck. He smirked. "I have something to attend to, but I'll find you again."

And with one last kiss on my lips, he left me, his eyes lingering for longer than was probably wise.

Promise me.

"I told you!" Séra said, next to me once more. "I told you he'd love it!"

I was lightheaded, but I felt freer than I'd ever had. I had no thoughts, no worries, other than the fun that was to be had in this room.

Neither Lucas, nor Lord Highsmith, could keep me from drinking and dancing and kissing who I wanted and taking men into my bed, taking *Vince* into my bed—I was unstoppable. The weaver of my own fate.

I shrugged off years of control as I danced. My breaths came easier, my limbs moving freely, and if I were truly trapped in a fairy world, forced to dance forever, I did not think I'd care.

Séra was the first to stop. Sweat gleamed along her hairline, but it only made her shimmer. She grabbed my arm, pulling me out of the dancing crowd in search of a drink. It was not long before we found flutes of champagne and threw them back.

My thoughts moved in a barely coherent line, one after the other: thirst, hunger, *Vince*, vampires. Blood, champagne, *sex*, Lucas—*no.* My head was spinning. I might've toppled over, if not for Séra's steadying hand.

She laughed at my stumble, leading me to a spot to lean against the wall. "Perhaps a rest?"

Séra was right—listening in on others' troubles, I found myself thoroughly entertained by drama that was not my own. A respite from the whirling thoughts overtaking my mind.

The licking of lips, imaginations running wild. The sharing of pipes and cigarettes, of glasses of gin; the sharing of dreams and desires and secrets. A woman whispering into a man's ear, her hand covering her mouth as though to hide the words in the noisy room. The red blooming on his cheeks, the darkening of his eyes, his hands finding her hips. Her delighted cackle as his lips found her neck. Groups of girls sticking together, until they were weeded off, one by one, by drunken suitors. Young boys, barely out of their teens, gazing with wide eyes, star-struck almost, at the scenes before them.

Above it all, the chandelier glimmered. Every bit of the room shone, waxed to a sparkle, like diamonds and crystals were set into the gilded walls. Gleaming drapes hung from the ceiling, pulled back from the large floor-to-ceiling wrought iron windows, the fixtures a remnant of the building's original purpose. The devils still writhed on the ceiling, seemingly having moved from the last time I gazed at them.

I pressed a hand to my eyes. "I'm going to go find some water," I told Séra.

"One can stay hydrated well enough on champagne," she grinned, but waved me on.

I teetered on my heels, stepping through the crowd, blinking to clear my eyes. Though I was unsteady, I knew I wouldn't fall, an arrogant confidence keeping me upright. Why wear heels to these things, anyway?

I found a server some ways away, standing at attention near the stairs. He only glanced at me briefly while I reached for his tray, short crystalline glasses with a clear liquid. I grabbed one and took a sip, before my nose scrunched at the bitter taste. Most definitely not water.

A hand came from nowhere and took the glass from me. "Here," a male voice said, offering me a different glass.

Dixon, my savior, my sentinel, frowned at me as I drank the water he offered, giggling at my mistake. His hair was still combed, his gray eyes searching my face. "What are you doing here?"

"What are *you* doing here?" I slurred, before gulping down the water.

"Apparently keeping you from losing your wits," he said through gritted teeth. "Is this where you've been this whole time?"

He took the glass from me and set it on the tray of a passing server who promptly disappeared.

"What's it to ya?" I grinned.

"I should have known." He shook his head again. "Your family is furious."

"What's new?"

"Are you okay?" he asked, his firm hands landing on my

shoulder and keeping me steady. He looked me in the eye, trying to find some evidence of hurt, of mistreatment.

"I'm fine! I just had to get away, that's all."

Dixon's serious face never wavered. "Flora told me— about your brother and the betrothal. Helena, I'm sure we can talk some reason into your family—"

"I don't want to talk about it." I tried to push past him to find Séra again.

His grip on my shoulders tightened, just enough to keep me in place. "She's been worried about you. *We've* been worried about you."

"I'm *fine*."

"When you didn't reach out to her, she called me right away. Said I had to find you."

"Well, I'm here. Tell her I'm okay."

"*Are* you okay?" he asked again. "Do you know where you are?"

"For Christ's sakes, Dixon, I left on my own." This conversation was sobering me up more than I wanted.

A reluctant pause. "I know you have a history with Vince."

"Flora told you?"

"But he's not the man you knew," he continued.

I tried to push past him again.

It was nonsense. He worried too much. And what would *he* know?

"He's dangerous, Helena."

I rolled my eyes. "Yes, you've said this before, and yet here I am. Completely fine, alive and well."

"You don't know what he does, who he is."

"And are you going to tell me?" I asked, hands on my

hips. Staring Dixon down, though he was taller than me by a good few inches. His eyes flickered, but his mouth was pressed into a straight line, and he didn't say anything.

"That's what I thought." I scowled.

"Even if you know the truth, you're not safe."

"What, are you in on it or something? I know what *you* do, and Flora is perfectly safe, is she not? You're saying he's worse?"

Dixon laughed darkly under his breath. "We are not even *remotely* the same."

"Unless you aim to tell me what's so bad, I'm leaving. Enjoy your evening—"

He grabbed my arm again.

A sigh stalled in my lips.

Dixon was not a bad man. He watched over Flora and I, with a cooler head than most, keeping us from trouble.

And normally, he was right.

He was mistaken this time.

"Helena." He said my name with such gravity. "I don't know how much you've been told, what you've seen, but you're not safe here. The people here... they're not like you—"

"What, like vampires?" The words slipped from my lips before I could stop them. Damn whoever was overhearing our conversation.

Dixon's eyes widened, then hardened, all in a second.

"Wait—" I nearly laughed again at the ridiculousness of it all. "Are *you* a vampire?"

His silence was damning.

"You *are*." The effects of the liquor left me. Suddenly, I was totally sober, the room righting itself, my mind clear.

I should have known.

"Lower your voice," he hissed. "This is not something you can just say aloud—"

"Does Flora know?"

"No." His eyes flashed. "And if you breathe a word of it to her—"

"Don't you dare, Lloyd Dixon, threaten to keep me from Flora." I scoffed, wrenching away. "You don't seem so concerned about your own criminal enterprise and how it affects her. Why don't you mind your own business?"

"Because this *is* my business."

A shrill scream from two feet away, and suddenly a pair of arms were circling me, the sweet scent of rosy perfume pervading the air around us.

Her hug was like coming home.

Flora.

She wept, crooning my name. A happy sob wrenched itself free from my own throat. I threw my arms around her slim waist.

"My god, Helena, where have you been?" She cried tipsy tears, drops landing on my skin, right where Dixon's hand had been, holding me to her so tightly I almost couldn't breathe. "I thought we'd hear that you were being held for ransom!"

"I'm okay," I repeated for the third time that evening.

"I'm so glad you're safe," she breathed, pulling away to get a look at me. She wiped under her red eyes, careful not to smear her makeup. "I'm such a baby," she said.

"No, it's my fault—I should have said something. It all just happened so quickly, the last few days have been a blur."

Flora sniffled. "I understand. And I understand why you

ran away. We came here tonight because I thought—I thought if anyone knew what had happened, it must be Vince. But I see we didn't even need to hunt him down."

I nodded, squeezing her fingers. "Thank you."

She huffed out a laugh and pulled me into her chest again, her blonde hair tickling my cheek as she hugged me. "You must call me if you need me."

I promised I would, holding her tight.

Dixon caught my eye over her shoulder, sober and solemn, his arms crossed. He didn't have to say it, didn't have to remind me never to let Flora know of this world of night we'd found ourselves in.

These creatures would drain her before their lips even touched a vein.

I hugged her tighter before pulling away and smiling. "I have someone to introduce you to."

The haze of gin finally abated around midday the next morning. Vince lay beside me, naked under the sheets. The house was silent, the sun streaming through the windows at a noontime peak.

I slept the morning away again.

I stretched my arms above my head, the sheets falling to my waist, trying to relieve the soreness of my muscles.

Vince hardly stirred, only turning his head on the plush pillow. He was beautiful, an angelic quality to the way his hair fell on the pillow, his sharp teeth hidden behind those pink lips. I touched him, feeling the cool skin of his cheek, the stubble there, the fullness of his lip. Paler than he'd been as Adam, maybe just barely. But the muscles of his shoulders and chest were leaner, stronger, more defined. He had an energy, a vigor, he hadn't had before.

Before.

My life was now divided into two: *Before* and *After.*

I had to watch for many moments before I saw his chest rise and sink with his shallow breath. If I felt his neck, I knew his pulse would be faint, slow as though he were still on the brink of death.

I slid out of bed, grabbing his discarded robe to cover me from the chill of the morning. As I slipped my arms through the sleeves, I saw on the tea table a range of morning papers, a steaming teapot, and a small dish of toast, butter, and jam.

My stomach growled. I hadn't eaten at all last night— only drank, and then danced it all away.

I sat upon the couch, pulling my feet up, and relaxed into a pillow as I sipped on the tea. And I hardly read the papers, the politics all too confusing for me, but this morning, I picked up the neighborhood daily, like some greater force was pushing me to read it, controlling my moments.

The teacup nearly slipped from my fingers when I read: "*Quintrell daughter's disappearance.*" My eyes skimmed the page, jumping over words. I knew this was Lucas, knew he was trying to control the story and his image before there was speculation. Because of course my absence was noticed, or if it wasn't yet, he wanted to get a handle on the news before people began to realize I was *missing.*

Lucas Quintrell, head of the Quintrell Company, happily writes that his sister, Helena Quintrell, is away from town, caring for an aunt, before she spends some time taking a tour of the Continent. He and their mother thank all neighbors for their well-wishes.

I crumpled the paper in my fist, my teeth grinding. I should've expected it.

He was looking for me. Had no idea where I was, but rather than let my absence go noticed, rather than tell everyone I was missing, he lied.

A small part of me *wished* he'd told the papers I was missing. Then I'd know that he, my mother, maybe even Wright Highsmith, cared for me a little.

There was no concern for me—they would've sent the police looking by now, would've told everyone to keep an eye out for me.

I stood and threw the papers into the fire.

TWENTY-NINE

"You can go out in the sun. You still have a reflection. What about iron? Wooden stakes?"

I had been peppering the afternoon with questions—how could I not when I had such a creature resting between my legs? In between kisses, when he was able to take his mouth off of me, when I was able to catch my breath, reality would creep in and I'd remember that he was no longer human, and it would settle into me, deep and heavy, an impossibility that had somehow become the truth.

This particular question earned me a laugh. His eyes gleamed.

"My atoms don't suddenly defy physics." He pressed a kiss to my shoulder. "Besides, anyone getting stabbed in the chest with a sharp piece of wood would probably die."

I curled a lock of his hair around my finger. "I've read the fairytales."

"So it seems." He wrapped his arms around my waist and pulled me closer. His body was still warm with the aftermath of our morning and afternoon. But he just held me, keeping me close, his head cradled against my chest, like he was listening in on my heart.

His auburn hair shone in the soft sunlight. I never thought I'd be able to run my fingers through his hair again.

His shoulders were broad, wider than they had been when he left. We had been *kids* when he'd been threatened, separated. A young man, little more than a teenager, punished for falling in with a rich girl, and sent off to die.

My hands flitted across his shoulders. There was strength in his muscles, a rigidness that couldn't be hidden by clothes.

He lifted a finger to my chin, bringing me back to him. "I am as real as ever," he said, like he knew what I was thinking. He always had a habit of that. Our minds must have been intrinsically linked. "I haven't changed *that* much."

"But you drink blood."

A hum rumbled in his throat.

"Will you drink my blood?" I said it before I could think better of it. To ask such a question felt lewd. And his eyes darkened for a brief moment, like the thought either excited him or hurt him. I couldn't tell.

"I will."

The promise shivered through my limbs, my body reacting before I could even fathom the words, the silky caress of lust, an awareness suddenly of his sex against my leg. Another new first for us—consuming me, consuming my lifeblood. I often found him staring at me, at my neck, my thighs, almost lost in thought, pupils dilating.

"Until you say the word, I will be thinking about it every moment. I *have* thought about it every moment since I was

Made." He propped himself up on his elbows, strong hands bracing on either side of my face, his palms sending a chill through my cheeks. "I've thought about you every second since I went overseas. You must know that I hunger for you, darling."

His stare was intense, his words causing heat to flush my face. Blood. Rushing to my cheeks, warm.

Once more, his eyes flicked toward my neck. His throat slid. "The first coherent thought I had after I was changed was, how do I get to you? *How can I drink you?*"

He leaned forward, nose tracing along my throat. A breathy laugh escaped me, nervously, secretly thrilled. I pushed on his shoulder. The daring part of me wanted to see what he would do, *how* it would happen, but my fear overwhelmed me.

What was I doing?

He was not Adam. He'd told me as much. How could I expect anything to be the same? He wanted me. Wanted to take my blood, for his pleasure.

He said he hadn't changed that much, but the only part of him I truly recognized was his face.

He eased down onto the bed next to me, untangling our limbs. "But you must say it, or I won't do it."

"If you bite me, will I change too?" I whispered.

The horror of it flashed in my mind. I'd have to drink blood, too. I couldn't imagine—

"No. It takes more than a bite—otherwise, the world would be overrun with us, and we'd be stuck with no real sustenance."

"How strange," I said, my voice barely above a whisper. I traced the soft curve of his lip with my finger, the sharp edge to his cheekbone, the cut of his jaw. He shut his eyes like he was a prize dog being pet by its master.

"Mmm," he hummed again.

I thought for a moment.

"Do you have a coffin?"

He groaned, face falling into the crook of my neck. Nipping, pressing soft kisses to my throat "So many questions. Shall I bite you now, to sate your curiosity, my darling?"

Already clutching him close, trembling in his arms with an acute need, I couldn't imagine it—the prospect sunk deep into me like a stone, turning my stomach. Though this man before me looked so familiar, *felt* so familiar, I couldn't dismiss the little voice in my head that told me it was all a ruse, too good to be true.

THIRTY

"May I join you?"

Startled from my reading, I looked up to see Sinclair in the doorway of the small parlor room I'd curled up in this afternoon.

"Oh." I blinked. "Yes."

He strolled into the room, procuring from his pocket his case of cigarettes and a lighter. By the time he sat at the low couch across from me, the cigarette was burning cherry-red between his lips. He took a long drag and reclined back in his seat. Then he gestured to the book in my hands. "Anything interesting?"

In truth, I hadn't gotten more than ten pages, rereading the same passages over when my mind wandered. "No," I said. I set it down on the tea table between us. "Just one of those whodunits." It had been one of the only novels with its pages cut from the bookshelf across the room.

"Ah. Keeping your mind sharp?" He nodded, inhaling

the smoke again. "That's good. You will need your sharpest wits about you here."

I frowned. "Yes, you keep saying this."

"Because it is true." A shrug. "I only care for your safety."

"Or has Vince told you to keep an eye on me?"

A noncommittal gesture, a sparkle in his iris.

"What, is this house so dangerous I should expect to be attacked while taking tea?"

"While he's occupied, he asked me to keep watch. A precaution."

"Hmm." It seemed over-cautionary to me. "I was safe enough the other night."

"It is not *us* he wants to protect you from."

The passage from the newspaper played over and over in my head. I could read it again in my mind as though I held the paper in my hands—

He and their mother thank all neighbors for their well-wishes.

How conceited could Lucas be?

I knew he would tell his people to keep their eyes open. He'd been able to find Adam and I once before.

I sighed, busying my hands by refilling my teacup. A citrus scent bloomed in the air. "My brother is hardly a threat to *you*."

He flashed his teeth in a grin. "Glad you think so. I like to think we're quite scary." A pause. "But Vince seems to hold some concerns. So, here I am."

"And what is *he* doing?" I saw Vince only briefly before lunch, as he dressed for the day and I roused from sleep. A quick kiss to my cheek and he was gone.

"Taking some calls."

I stirred some sugar into my tea. "And who's calling?"

Sinclair gave me a look. Said nothing.

I huffed, sipping my tea. "Am I to know nothing of what goes on around here?"

"He's become an important man in our circles. And with that..." He seemed to think for a second, a word on the tip of his tongue. "With that *notoriety* comes responsibility. Duties. There are things he must attend to, things to be kept in order. Perhaps too many duties to list for you over an afternoon of tea."

He met my gaze, tapping his smoke against the ashtray. His strong nose, his striking cheekbones, his hair curled upon his brow, giving him a boyish charm—all of it a ruse to draw me and any other unsuspecting mortal in.

"You were Made, weren't you?"

He laughed in surprise. "Yes."

"Who Made you?"

"That's a bit personal, isn't it?" But his eyes twinkled in amusement. "Séra. It was an accident."

"An accident? Is such a thing possible?" I asked, sitting forward in my seat.

He gestured to himself, a sweeping hand toward his body, presenting himself as evidence. "It's possible when you are bedding a young vampire who cannot control themselves. Séra Dupont Made me, perhaps five years ago now, if I am remembering correctly." He had kissed her forehead the night before, and I knew there was some affection there, a relationship of sorts. But—I had seen him with an entirely different couple the night I'd first witnessed a bloodletting. Séra most certainly was not there. There must have been an agreement between the two, though she didn't seem the slightest bit interested in anyone else at the party.

"Do you regret it?"

"I regret that I had not asked for it yet," he said. "But I would have, eventually. And I regret that Séra had to come to terms with what she'd done."

"You love her."

He nodded.

"Is she Made, too?"

He gave me a look. "Did Vince not tell you anything?"

My blank look must have been answer enough.

"She's Born. She had family in the south—Louisiana. And some in France, I believe."

"What about you?" It felt dangerous to ask these questions, prying into the life of a vampire who I did not yet know very well. But if Vince trusted him, then I decided I could, too.

That muscle in his jaw ticked again. "They don't live far."

"Do they know?"

He shook his head, breathing in against the cigarette again. Putting it out against the ashtray. Lighting another.

He turned to me. "What else? I know that's not all that's bouncing around in your head."

I bit my lip. I had so many questions, and I wasn't sure if Vince was *able* to answer them all. "What are your origins?" I asked. "There must have been... a *first* vampire, right?"

"We came about as any other species, probably. Though I suppose the only thing remarkable about us, besides our strengths and our extended lifetimes, is that we can infect others, like humans, and bring them to 'our side,' as it were."

"Extended lifetime?" Those were the words that I had caught on.

"Yes. We live much longer than our human counterparts. All of us in this house are young. We're still considered fledglings by some, and will be for a few decades. We can live to many hundreds of years, if the histories are to be believed. Vince's Sire—"

His words stopped short.

"*What?* What about his Sire?" I had the distinct feeling Sinclair meant to keep something from me—had almost exposed too much.

If he were alive, his face would have reddened. "Vince's Sire is an old vampire. I'm not sure even Vince knows his age."

"What's his name?"

A pause, heavy hesitation, the air brimming with the unspoken word. And then: "Andreas."

And he left it like that, no surname, no title. The weight of it, heavy between us, the cadence of the word echoing in my ears.

"Many of us believe that we come from the damned," he said. "That when Lucifer fell, so did his companions, and from those fallen, we were Born, millennia ago." Sinclair trailed off, staring towards the window, a crease forming in his brows, some sullenness falling over his thoughts. "From what I know of Vince's Sire, I believe that must be our genesis."

The more that was uncovered to me, the more questions appeared.

I felt wholly in the dark. I did not know how Vince spent his days, I didn't know what these *duties* were;

Andreas, Vince's life these past six years, his intentions now —the truth of it tucked away. But how could I know Vince if I did not know his past?

Why would he bring me here, only to keep it all from me?

"Why did you tell me to come back?" I crossed my arms. Flashes of red and writhing figures in my mind's eye. "What was I seeing?"

His stare met mine. "I was only tasked with getting you here." A deflection, a half-answer.

"By Vince?"

He nodded once, his neck stretched to the side, two fingers lifting toward his face, bringing the burning menthol to his lips. But he didn't inhale. "By Vince. To be where you were, and to convince you to find your way here again. To make myself available to you." He laughed under his breath. "I went to so many parties." Shaking his head, he crossed his legs, ankle resting on his knee.

That bitter, slimy taste rose in my mouth again. "Our meeting was planned."

Another beat of silence, another glimmer in his eye.

"And Séra?"

He blinked slowly, languid, like he had all the time in the world. There was no emotion there, only a watcher's eyes, a *predator's* eyes. I didn't know when this change in demeanor happened, only that it had, and I suddenly felt like a rabbit in a cage, up for the taking.

His tan cheek dimpled. "Hired months ago, when a spot in your household conveniently opened up."

The facts were there all along, but I just ignored them,

too caught up being with Vince again, too preoccupied with gin and love and the thrill of it all.

I tamped it down.

It's nothing.

It didn't mean anything.

I was beginning to make a big deal of nothing.

He loved me, had *always* loved me.

I took a breath and plastered a quick smile on my face. "And Dixon?"

"Who?" Sinclair nearly dropped his cigarette.

"Lloyd Dixon."

He had been so vehement against my being here; he had seemed ready to drag me out of this house himself. But he knew Vince, had come to the parties every time Flora and I did—and must have come on his own. There was a familiarity between the two, even if Dixon insisted Vince was dangerous. He had been the one to tell me Vince was waiting for me in the garden.

But Sinclair rolled his eyes. "He's not one of us."

"One of...?"

"He's a high and mighty Born vampire. His coven and ours do not... see eye to eye."

I stood, my limbs becoming jittery from just sitting. A chill ran down my arms, and I wished I had grabbed one of those sweaters from my wardrobe. While I walked away, I felt Sinclair's stare follow me, smelled the tobacco from his cigarette.

The view from the window was the gardens. It was early evening, the sun making its way toward the horizon, not yet having hit the equinox. The cypress trees swayed, their blue-hued leaves stretching toward the clouds. From above, all the colors of the gardens were in view—pink and red and bright green bushes, the glowing white of flowers that would soon bloom in the evening darkness. The dark green hedges lining the stone wall boundary. The wrought-iron gate. The brilliant fountains at the center, one with a peculiar marble nymph at the center, who seemed to shine in the dimming sunlight, like she was about to come to life.

I ignored the point at which I felt Sinclair's view—on the back of my neck—and leaned against the windowpanes, their glass already appearing melted with age.

"I do not mean to offend," Sinclair said, misunderstanding my frustration, the lowness of his voice edged with humor. But he remained on the couch. "I understand he is a friend of yours—"

"What is going on here?" I turned to him fully, the window at my back.

"Here?" He looked around the room like he was missing something. "We're speaking."

"No." I narrowed my eyes at him. "What is going on that I don't know about?"

A raised black brow. "Clarify."

"Don't insult me," I scoffed. I made to leave the room, feeling heat in my ears. "If no one wants to speak plainly, then I'll figure it out on my own."

Sinclair sighed. "Ask Vince. Lest he behead me for revealing too much."

THIRTY-ONE

That evening I stood in a silk robe and nothing else while I waited for Vince to return.

Dusk lingered in a deep rosy hue above the tree line while I ate my dinner alone, only the soft breeze from the open window to accompany me.

Unease still seized my ribs in a vise-grip.

Vince had been orchestrating our reunion for the better part of a year. He knew where I was, knew exactly how to get to me, yet he'd waited to make a move until—

Until my brother came home to marry me off.

Involving others, playing this game of secrets.

Maybe Dixon's warning held some truth.

By the time the bedroom door opened and his arms wound around my waist from behind, the sky had turned to indigo.

"You're waiting for me?" His lips brushed my ear.

"What else is there to do?"

He hummed. "Perhaps I'll take you out on the Sound tomorrow."

I pulled away. "I need to speak to you."

"Of course." Leading me away from the window, toward the foot of the bed. "Anything."

I sat upon the duvet, the robe falling open at my hips. He pretended not to notice, slipping off his jacket and loosening his tie.

I had worked myself up, waiting for him. "Where do you get your money?"

For a moment, he only stared at me, pausing his movements as he undressed. Then he laughed. "My money?" Throwing the tie toward the couch, it landed on the floor in a heap, along with his jacket and shoes. "I earned it. Does it matter?"

I sat back on my elbows. "How?"

Perhaps it hadn't crossed his mind that I'd ask these questions, but I was growing tired of being left in the dark.

He stood straight, his hands going to his belt. "Being Sired by a wealthy vampire has its benefits." He discarded his belt and trousers. Then he was placing his knee on the bed, leaning forward, eyes flashing when they landed on the loose tie of my robe.

"An... inheritance?"

His throat slid. "In a manner of speaking."

The bed dipped with his looming form. He was caging me against the mattress, his legs spreading my thighs, his strong arms on either side of my head.

"I want to know." I whispered. "You are so different—I just need to understand."

After a second, he leaned down and pressed his lips to mine. He kissed me gently, his fingers brushing through my hair, just as he used to when we were teenagers. *When he was Adam.* And I was once more falling under the spell of his fingers.

"I will tell you everything," he murmured, his mouth trailing to my neck. I craned back, giving him full access to my throat.

My conversation with Sinclair was forgotten as soon as Vince's fingers slid under my bottom and pulled our bodies tightly together. He was growing hard, and the spot between my thighs slickened with need. Always ready for him, always eager. Trailing down, down, down. His tongue found my nipple, stoking pleasure. A hum of approval rumbling in his chest before he moved lower, his teeth brushing against my navel, holding me in place.

"Don't think I've forgotten," I managed to say between breaths. My back arched off the bed as his tongue swirled devilish things against my skin.

"Of course not." Pushing my robe open, baring me to him completely, he darkened with his desire. "You look absolutely delicious."

"Then eat me," I challenged, my voice barely above a whisper, not thinking of what dangerous words those were to say to a monster.

He revealed his teeth in a dark smile before he dove, pulling me roughly to the edge of the bed. I slid against the duvet, squealing at the sudden movement, before he was hoisting my thighs to his shoulders and staring down at me like it was the first time.

"Be careful what you wish for, my darling," he purred. Then his tongue was upon me, licking a stripe up my center, a graze of those sharp teeth against my flesh. The promise of pain, of pleasure.

I wanted to tell him to do it, to bite me, damn the consequences, but I couldn't speak, my voice lost. Tangling my fingers in his hair, tugging him closer, whimpering beneath him, spreading myself wider, his tongue greedily drawing pleasure out of me, then slowing down as I came nearer to my orgasm.

I groaned when he dipped into my center, pushing against the resistance there.

"Please," I gasped.

His laugh was teasing, tongue gleaming with my arousal. "Please *what*, darling?" Eyes dark, pupils completely dilated, the bit of the grayish hazel iris gone as his hunger took over.

What would it take for him to snap?

"Please, I—*please*." Murmuring his name, knowing I was *so close*.

His eyes were near-black as he crawled over me, settling his hips between mine. Pressing the head of his cock to my entrance, a sheen of sweat sparkling at his chest, his hair ruffled from my fingers. He watched me writhe, high off the desire he'd stoked in my blood.

My brain was short-circuiting, like a live electric wire with no ground, energy with nowhere to go. I couldn't catch my breath, held at the precipice, unable to fall.

He gazed down at me, the harsh angles of his face stern and unmoving, eyes trailing over my breasts, over the spot where his strong hands held me down, held me open.

I fisted my hands in the sheets, trying to buck my hips to get some relief. "*Please*."

"You're beautiful when you beg," he murmured, just

barely moving forward. His cock pushed at the band of resisting muscles, but stopped again. I knew I was wet enough, my heat slick with my arousal, that it would take nothing for him to spear himself into me. And yet, he watched me writhe, enjoying my discomfort.

I wanted to curse him, but the pleasure I felt when his flesh parted mine was enough to make me forget everything.

Make me forget.

"Do you like it when I do this to you?" he asked, cocking his head to the side. He gripped himself, running the head of his cock between my folds. "Do you like it when I deny you?"

I didn't know how to answer. Frustrated tears gathered at the corners of my eyes.

"You'll never be able to have anyone else's cock," he said. "You'll never be able to fuck anyone else," entering me one inch, "without thinking about me."

My head swam, but it was like I had become nothing but a mewling puddle. *I'm yours, I'm yours.*

"I am going to ruin you for anyone else," he promised, slowly pushing in halfway.

It still wasn't enough.

"*Please,*" I begged.

His hand snaked towards my throat, thumb finding the thudding pulse in my neck. His eyes were unrecognizable, swallowed in shadow, so dark, so lost. Could he sense the fear coursing through my veins? The oddness of it, coalescing with the heady lust clouding my mind, the need for more, for *all* of him, whatever that meant.

He watched my pulse flutter against my skin before he roughly wrenched my chin to the side. His nose trailed over my pulse. "I want to eat you." I felt him shake, like he was holding himself back. "I want to consume every bit of you, so you can't leave."

Black stars appeared at the edges of my vision.

Do it.

He slid further in, inch by agonizing inch, until he was fully seated within me, his hips pressed flush against mine. My breath came in pants between us, stars clouding my vision. The delicious stretch alone pushing me toward that edge.

His teeth scraped my throat. "I want to drink you, so no one else can have you."

I'm yours.

How could he not see that? How could he not see how utterly lost I was for him?

Lewd noises echoed in the room as he began to move, nudging his hips forward and back while his fangs threatened to pierce my skin.

And when I shattered beneath him, a low growl rumbled in his chest. "That's it." Whispers of filthy things into my ears, promises to ruin me forever, to hide me away, to keep me forever for himself; praising the softness of my flesh, how well I fit around him. How well I gave in.

I was still numb when his hips slammed to mine and he came. Teeth pressed—*there*—against my pulse.

Please.

I may have begged again, may have uttered the word, may have tangled my fingers in his hair once more and held his mouth to my throat. His tongue circled, idly, teasing himself with just a taste, but never pricking through my skin, even as his hips continued to thrust, slickening my thighs with both our arousal. Only a thin barrier between my veins and the knives of his teeth.

"Do not forget who I am," he said, his grip bruisingly tight. "Who I am *to you*."

"How could I forget?"

"Remember those words when you ask me your questions again."

THIRTY-TWO

My whole body was flushed a rosy pink, spent and sated, as I regained my wits, naked upon the bed. He'd withdrawn, stalking off to the washroom. And his words settled like poison ready to stop my heart.

Do not forget who I am.

The sound of running water, his feet padding across the floor as he returned with a warm cloth. My limbs hummed with pleasure, and I would have stayed in that bed all evening if he hadn't stopped kissing me.

His eyes found me first, his pupils back to normal. "Let me." And he was reaching down, gently swiping between my thighs, cleaning up the mess he'd made of me. He pressed a kiss to the corner of my mouth.

"I want to show you something." He couldn't hide how his eyes lingered on my thighs. "The roof."

"The roof?" I blinked.

"Yes. We must dress."

"I thought you said I could remain naked in this house if I wished it."

"*I* wish it," he said, pulling me from the bed, his hands strong and sure, leading me toward the wardrobe. "But I've grown selfish. I'm not sure I'm ready to share you yet."

I gazed at him through my lashes. "Yet?"

His eyes darkened. "*Ever.*"

We changed into our nightclothes, hoping to stave off the chill evening wind in layers.

"Wait," he commanded, pushing me to sit on a cushion. He rifled through a drawer before producing a thick pair of knit stockings. Then he knelt before me.

Without words, he lifted my ankle, setting it upon his thigh, and gingerly pulled the stocking over my foot, up my calf. With every brush of his fingers, every gentle touch, heat pooled low in my belly. Perhaps *I* was the insatiable one.

"We can't have you freezing." His gaze trailed along the creamy skin of my legs.

"No," I agreed, holding my breath.

He handled me with such care, those strong and brutal fingers barely touching, yet deftly warming me up all the same. They were luxurious stockings—everything in the closet was new, never worn, from the most famous tailors and dressmakers in Manhattan and abroad.

I didn't think Wright would care to ever spoil me the way Vince did.

When he finished, he leaned forward, his lips pressing a kiss to my knee. "Shall we?" He stood and offered his hand.

"I'm not going to have to climb the side of the house, am I?" I asked once we were in the hall.

"We're not animals," he laughed. "We'll take the elevator."

"You have an *elevator*?"

"Of course."

Down the main hall, away from his quarters, and toward the massive library.

He held my hand, our fingers interlocked. "I had it built into the house," he explained. "The architects recommended installing another in the foyer, if I was going to have so many guests, but I was quite partial to the elegance of the grand staircase. I thought the machinery would only subtract from the view."

But when we stepped inside, I couldn't hear a whir or any clanking from the engine running the elevator, the doors *ding*ing open a moment later.

In moments, we were on the concrete roof, the deep blue of the evening sky spread over us like a blanket, and I still felt as though I were floating, mind thoroughly scrambled, stuck in the reverie of our bedroom.

The stars shone through the haze from the city lights in the distance. The tip-tops of skyscrapers sparkling monoliths against the clouds. The wind grabbed at my hair, twirling it around my head, yanking on my skirt, the insistent breeze this high biting through my clothes, as I approached the small barrier wall.

The grounds sprawled out below us, seemingly on for miles, up to the Sound, the driveway a thin gray snake, the gardens a child's sandbox.

I sensed him stop a foot away from me. When I looked at him, he was gazing out on his lands, eyes squinting against the breeze which tousled his dark red waves. He was looking toward the city, unblinking.

The city that harbored dreamers and criminals, silly little girls hoping for their Prince Charming and young men waiting to be struck by the realities of war. It stood like a fixture of the earth, unmovable, a mass of iron and glass, twinkling with electric lights. From within, it was never-ending.

And there it was, so small, reduced to a few tall buildings in the distance.

I realized his face had transformed into a scowl.

I did not blame him. I knew the life we came from, the struggle he'd endure growing up, a struggle I hadn't had to experience myself. No plans to leave, just to work, to print his papers and pamphlets, to just barely make it. To survive.

And here he was now, so entirely, completely *different*.

Did he even think of his family? Did he ever wish to return to them? To his life before?

When I touched his arm, he softened, pulled from his thoughts. "I thought you might like it up here," he said, gaze still trained on the distance.

"It's quiet," I said, voice barely above a whisper. If I spoke too loudly, it would feel like a shout.

"Too quiet."

I leaned on the half-wall, hugging myself against the cold. That nagging feeling was back, a sourness in my stomach. I swallowed it down.

"I never really liked the silence this far out," he murmured. "I could not make myself return to the incessant noise of the city. I couldn't do it, not after I'd spent so long away."

Six years away.

Six years of believing him dead.

He took a breath as though to prepare himself, then braced his palms against the wall, his smallest finger brushing against my hip. "I'm going to tell you more about me, about my Sire, but I don't want—" A tick in the muscle of his cheek.

I cupped his cheek, his cold flesh, with my palm. "It's alright."

His eyes shut. "I will not make a promise I cannot keep. I will not tell you that what I've come from is not terrible, that I am not equally terrible."

I found myself deathly still, scared even to breathe.

His eyes opened, but he did not look at me. "He was the only one I knew for the longest time." His throat slid. "When I awoke, I saw only *him*, or the poor unfortunates he brought to—to feed me. Villagers close enough to the battle-fields, people that hadn't fled. There wasn't anywhere for them to go, so they were stuck like we were, hearing the guns all night. The screams. And if they disappeared..."

I tried to imagine myself there, to put myself on the battlefield. In the trenches. But I couldn't.

"My Sire wouldn't kill them himself. He'd come down into the cellar—yes, he kept me in a cellar—and throw them at my feet. I didn't have a choice. And they didn't under-stand, of course. Didn't understand. I looked like another victim in my bloody soldier's clothes, but they didn't know, underneath the filth, I was healed, I was living—undead.

"And no matter how much I resisted that first year, no matter how much I tried to ignore the smell of their blood, to drown out the sound of their hearts with my own screams, I would still do it. My body would move on its own, drawn to their pumping blood, the smell of their fear. My teeth changed, and my hands grabbed them like I was some puppet, and I was forced to eat them. To watch myself drain them. And only after months of his feedings, of him pulling me away from empty corpses, before I was able to stop on my own. To tamp down the hunger just enough, so that I could hear a faint heartbeat after I stopped. Impossibly slow, like mine."

When he looked at me, his face was hard, some mask having replaced the softness of his skin. "I tell you this so that you know what I am."

"I know what you are."

He shook his head. "You only think you know."

Hesitantly, I put myself before him, blocking his sight of the grounds, of the city behind me. "Then *tell* me."

I reached to brush a strand of hair behind his ear, but he suddenly gripped my wrist with brute strength. All it would take was a flinch and he'd crush the delicate bones in my hand. Those hands, which had murdered so many. That mouth, those teeth, that had eaten, drank, *consumed* so many souls.

Turning so his nose brushed the inside of my wrist, smelling, breathing in deeply.

Scenting my blood.

"I couldn't come home," he squeezed his eyes shut, "because if I returned before I could control myself, control my bloodlust, then I'd find you. I wouldn't stop until I did, and *everyone* would be dead."

His tongue darted out, deep red between his lips, licking the spot where my pulse fluttered against my skin.

"Do you understand I am a monster?" he asked, jerking me to him. "Do you get it? That I would *kill* anyone for you?"

I couldn't speak. He held me fast, tight, his grip caging me to him.

"I *want* to kill for you. I would turn myself into a demon for you. And I wouldn't be sorry. I'd be glad to do it, to rid the world of every last person, just so I could have you."

The words of a madman. Terrible. Vile. And yet it felt so good to hear him say those words. To hear he wanted me so deeply.

"You are..."

"*Yours*," he murmured, once more running his nose over my jaw, my neck, drawing a shiver through me. "I've made myself yours. I've *always* been yours."

"I wish I had known," I whispered, because if I tried to speak aloud, my voice would break.

"I would've stolen you away years ago, if I could have. I would've come to you in your bed, and shown you just how much I longed for you, before stealing you away from *him*."

"He doesn't matter," I said. "Just show me who you are now. Show me your new world. Everything. I want to know *everything*."

He kissed my neck. "You must know how difficult this is for me. How much I've wanted to show you, but how much I feared you'd run."

I held his face in my hands. "I'd never run from you."

He shook his head again. "I am not who I once was."

"And I'm still here," I insisted, resting my forehead on his.

"You want the truth. You want to see it all. Tomorrow,"

he said with conviction, his fingers tightening around me. "I will show you this dark world we've found ourselves in. I'll show you how cursed we've become, if it pleases you."

"Yes," I whispered.

He kissed me once, smashing his lips to mine, forcing his tongue between my teeth. Pulling away just as quickly, stealing my breath.

"Are you sure?"

How could I say no?

"Then—I have something for you," he said, reaching into his pocket, producing a small velvet box. "I want you to wear these."

Two red rubies shone in the moonlight. In the shape of teardrops—drops of blood, glinting like his teeth. Encased in gold and polished to a shine. Maybe even one-of-a-kind.

I gasped. "Vince."

"Wear these, and they will all know," he was saying, voice hardly above a whisper. A promise. "My protection. My *heart*. But know that if you wear these, if you step into that room, you cannot retrace your steps. You are mine, forever."

The moment my finger danced across the ruby, a jolt scattered up my arm—and I knew, with a single touch, I tied myself to him, for eternity.

THIRTY-THREE

My eyes snapped open to the mid-morning sunlight illuminating the room with a soft yellow glow. I was bundled deep into the sheets of the bed, feeling as though I awoke amidst a pile of clouds.

And I was alone.

I realized what had pulled me from sleep was the ringing of a bell on the wall, incessant enough to be annoying, sharp enough to startle me awake. In my sleep-addled brain, it took me a moment to realize it was the telephone, and another to realize I should answer.

"Yes?" I yawned, putting the receiver to my ear.

"Miss," came a male voice, one I didn't recognize, but immediately knew it was a servant, a butler perhaps, if Vince even had one. Monotone, unenthused. "You have a visitor. Shall I offer them tea?"

"A visitor?"

"Yes, ma'am. She says she's a friend."

Flora.

I rubbed my eyes and glanced at the clock on the wall, ticking toward eleven in the morning. "Sure. Yes. I'll be right down."

After I hung up, I changed into a minty day dress with fluttering sleeves of gossamer. I hadn't been able to decide between the hundreds of dresses in the closet, so I just reached and grabbed one, finding a pair of white low heels. I brushed through my hair and deemed it good enough.

I could not tell what clothing Vince had pulled from the closet for the day. Every shirt was folded immaculately, jackets hung in a neat line, shoes shined and presented on low shelves. It was like a department store, except it was all his, all *ours*. Endless options to choose from every day, and I didn't think I'd be able to get through my half before it all went out of style.

As I left the bedroom, my steps echoed in the halls, and I made my way toward the front of the house, the bottom level, where I'd met Sinclair and Séra and Veronica. I did not have to wander too far before a well-dressed older man, standing at a corner, gestured for me to follow him. "This way, Miss."

"Is Vince occupied?"

A small part of me wanted him to join, because I knew Flora had questions—and I didn't know how to answer them.

He paused, as though surprised I'd spoken to him. "Yes."

He led me to a small tearoom, down the hall from the dining room. Gesturing for me to enter, he stepped aside to reveal a door ajar.

As soon as I pushed it open, Flora stood from her seat, setting down her tea. "There you are!"

I couldn't help but smile at seeing her. "You woke me up, so this better be important," I joked, wrapping my arms around her.

"Is sleeping more important than seeing your best friend?" She pressed her cheek to mine. The warmth of her skin was a small shock, and she smelled of lavender and citrus and everything good. "You've been hiding from us, holed up in here."

"Not from *you*," I said, squeezing her tight.

"I know," she conceded, holding me at arm's length. "I just miss you *terribly*."

We took opposite seats, a full tray of tea and cakes and sandwiches between us. I could see she'd already begun to nibble at the food.

"Dixon doesn't know I'm here," she said, reaching for her teacup.

"Then should I expect him to come crashing through the window?"

She giggled. "Maybe," bringing the teacup to her lips. She wore her usual soft red lipstick, her light hair curled for the day in even waves.

I poured myself a cup and dropped in a cube of sugar. "How are you two?" I had not really gotten a chance to ask when I'd seen them last, being a bit too drunk, and Dixon too preoccupied with glaring at me.

"We're fabulous," she said. "But what about *you?*"

"Better than ever, I suppose.

I feel I can finally breathe."

I hadn't heard anything else from Lucas or Mother or Wright since that lousy letter in the papers. No other announcements in the news, no ransom letters in the mail.

As though I had disappeared from the face of the planet and they'd gone on with their lives.

Flora just beamed at me, her hands clasped in her lap, and I saw it clear on her face that she was bursting at the seams.

I rolled my eyes. "Alright, out with it. What do you want to know?"

"Everything!" She leaned forward, eyes sparkling. "One moment you were there, the next, you're gone, and Lucas is brooding even more than usual. What happened?"

I sighed. "Lord Highsmith arrived—"

She gasped. "Is *that* who that was? I stopped by the house to see you a few days ago, and Lucas just grumbled that you were away for a week or so. There was some guy with him—that was Lord Highsmith?"

I nodded.

"Who Lucas wants to marry you off to?"

I nodded again.

Her face scrunched. "He's not even *that* attractive."

I breathed out a laugh. "I don't think Lucas picked him for his looks."

"So, you two met?"

"We *more* than met. It didn't take long for him to start sounding like Lucas. And when I made it known I was not interested, Lucas... made it known that was not an option." I remembered the feeling of his fingers around my neck, looming over me, shaking me. Wright's insistence that Lucas get me under control.

How was Mother so blind to it?

I realized a sadness had settled deep within me, a soft,

almost imperceptible sensation; a kernel buried underneath all the other emotions, but still there nonetheless. Sadness that this was how it had to be. Sadness that I couldn't confide in my mother, sadness that I couldn't *love* my brother.

"And—Vince?"

I shut my eyes for a moment, letting the memory of that night wash over me. "He *saved* me, more or less, and brought me here. And I've been here ever since."

Flora's hand fell to my knee. "I'm glad you have him. If I were able, I would've hidden you away long ago. But perhaps you'd be too easy to find."

"Perhaps," I laughed.

She sighed, glancing around the room. "Surely there must be a lot to explore here. Have you found the secret dungeon?"

"Dungeon?" My face heated. There was no way she knew—

"There *must* be secret catacombs under such a gloomy house. Chambers hidden behind bookcases, tunnels with skeletons."

"No dungeons," I laughed, though I suppose I didn't know for sure.

She hummed. "I wonder what Dixon's house in England is like?"

"Probably much of the same."

"No, he's told me his house is a little old-fashioned. He's said..." She trailed off.

"What?"

A blush turned her cheeks pink. "He's said that Vince's house is... *excessive*."

"Perhaps there's some truth to it." But it was also grand, wonderful, and enthralling. Just like Vince.

"He told me he's never coming back." A pause, then a sly quirk to the corner of her mouth. "And I'm not supposed to come back, either."

I exaggerated a gasp, hand to my chest. "And here you are! What a bad girl!"

"Perhaps I *like* being bad."

"You like Dixon worrying for you."

"And what of it?" she said innocently.

"Just don't get me in trouble with him."

"He's the least of your worries."

I faltered, my hand reaching for my cup but stalling mid-air. "What do you mean?"

Flora blinked at me. "Oh. Did you not know?"

"Know *what*?"

She sighed. "I wish I had a newspaper. Lucas has come out with it. He's put a reward on your head. *One million dollars.*"

THIRTY-FOUR

A high pitch ringing swallowed all sound.
One million dollars.

To get me back.

While I struggled not to choke on my breath, not to let out the keening wail building in my chest, all I could think was that my brother would not offer such a sum because he cared for me. That warning from Wright Highsmith, the way he had called for my brother the moment I refused the baron-heir—no, their hearts were not broken at my disappearance. Whatever their agreement had been, it was worth a million dollars to drag me back, force me into marriage.

I shook my head, mostly to myself, turning the information over and over. "That can't be right."

"What, the money?"

"He wouldn't—"

"Maybe he's had a change of heart? Maybe your mother finally smacked some sense into him?"

I'd been at the party a few days prior. How many people

had seen me? How many people had caught me *with Vince*? They'd know *exactly* where to find me. And if Lucas found out about Vince, about *Adam*... I did not want to imagine how my brother would enact his wrath.

"Dixon wouldn't—"

"No!" Flora nearly rose from her seat. "Why would he send you back to your brother for a measly million?"

One measly million.

"You know how much he doesn't like Vince." I sighed, standing and wiping my palms down the front of my dress. "I have to go tell him."

The only place I knew to look was his private study, the one Sinclair had led me to that night weeks ago. My memory of the layout of the house was still fuzzy, but when we turned down the hall, I recognized the statues against the wall, the portraits hanging, watching us as we walked past. The hall was silent, except for Flora's gasps at the decor and our footsteps.

As we approached, the door swung open. Like he heard us coming.

When he saw Flora, I swore his eyes flashed. But he plastered on a smile and held his arm out for me, pulling me to him.

"Hello again," Flora beamed at him. Bright as always.

The room was the same—a fire burning to chase away the chill, the curtains drawn closed still, no breakfast, only glasses of a deep red liquid set on the table. And Veronica, sitting on one of the couches, silent as we entered. We must have been interrupting something, because papers were scattered across the table, which she cooly reached for and pushed together in one pile when she saw us.

"I hope you've been—oh." Flora's words to Vince were stilted once she realized there was one more in the room.

"Flora, this is Veronica," I said, suddenly feeling out of my element. "And this is... Vince."

To my surprise, Flora didn't react to the change in name, only crossed her arms and quirked a brow at the man she used to know as Adam. She sized him up. And he let her look her fill, her eyes landing on the glinting watch at his wrist, the golden cufflinks, the pinstripes on his pants, the dark, expensive suit jacket laying on the couch.

"You look different," she said simply.

He blinked.

Flora turned to me. "Doesn't he?"

"And you look marvelous, as always," he said, letting the charm seep into his voice. Sending me back in time, to the first moment he'd met her at one of our lunches, before dragging me into an alley and ravishing my neck with his lips. "It's like you haven't aged a day."

She rolled her eyes, but couldn't hide the flattered smile that pulled at her lips. "Don't try *too* hard."

"Can we help you with something?" Veronica spoke up, pressing her lips into a thin smile. If Vince and Sinclair and Séra tamped down their preternaturalness in an attempt to play human, Veronica felt no need. "We were in the middle of something."

I turned to Vince. "Did you see what Lucas said? In the paper—"

"This?" Veronica grabbed one of the many newsprints on the table and handed it to me. "We discussed it earlier."

I grabbed it from her, the delicate print crinkling in my fingers, the ink greasy against my fingertips.

REWARD FOR FOUND SOCIALITE.

Lucas Quintrell, owner of the Quintrell Company, is announcing a One-Million-Dollar Reward for the return of his sister, Helena Quintrell, who has gone missing after leaving the city to visit family. Quintrell says that his sister is likely somewhere in the state, and any information as to her whereabouts will also be rewarded.

It was a warning, more than anything. That I had to watch my back, that he *would* get his hands on me again.

He knew I would see it.

"And?" I felt panic rise in me, but glancing at Vince, he seemed unbothered.

He shrugged. "What of it?"

"Were you not going to say something?"

"You saw the paper, did you not?"

I narrowed my eyes at him. "And what did you two *discuss*?"

Vince reached for me, a placating smile pulling at his lips. "So angry," he said, amused.

"I'm being serious."

Veronica sighed. "Perhaps we should leave you two to talk?"

"Perhaps that would be best—" I began, but Vince waved her off. "What's there to talk about?"

"*What's there to talk about*?" I shook the paper at him. "There's a reward for my head."

He again didn't seem to understand. But some realization dawned on him and he laughed. "Are you afraid you'll be found?"

As though the notion were ridiculous.

He shook his head. "You won't be found. Not if I don't want you to be."

"Do you not remember...?" My voice cracked.

I saw the mirth leave Vince's eyes. He directed his false smile at Veronica. "Maybe a moment would be a good idea."

With a roll of her eyes, she led Flora out into the hall, a delicate hand to my friend's back. I couldn't turn away from Vince, couldn't do anything but stand there with my hands in fists at my sides. When the door *snick*ed shut behind them, Vince's smile faded. He studied me, adjusting his sleeves, turned partially away from me.

It was the first moment I felt I didn't know what he was thinking.

"Do you have no confidence in me?" he said, utterly unreadable.

"Excuse me?"

He lifted a shoulder, making a slow circle around the couches, toward a cart with a decanter and glasses. "It's just that—and correct me if I'm wrong—*you* wanted to run away. Yes?"

I nodded, biting my lip.

"And *you* came to me. Yes?"

Suddenly feeling like I was in an interrogation. Like I was being questioned for my actions, like maybe I'd done the wrong thing. My teeth bit into the flesh of my lip harder, drawing pain and the taste of iron.

He was in front of me in a second, grabbing my fists in each hand, soothing my fingers open, thumbs brushing against the half-moon indentations from my nails. "And yet you're still so scared." He cocked his head to the side, a lock of his auburn hair falling over.

I was so scared.

"You don't have to be frightened anymore, Helena." His palm came to rest on my cheek, and I'm not sure if it was a supernatural compulsion or just the familiar comfort of his touch, but the weight of everything finally surfaced, and then tears were brimming my lashes.

"I'm tired of this," I said, unable to speak above a whisper. "I'm tired of feeling like there's a demon looming over my shoulder."

"Not a demon anymore," he said, one corner of his mouth quirking up in a smile. "Just a vampire." And he leaned forward to press his lips to my forehead.

My fists bunched in his shirt, and he didn't seem to care that I was wrinkling the expensive fabric.

"You can let go here," he whispered to me. "You don't have to worry about him or anyone else from the outside. Just worry about *me*. Worry about *us*. I will take care of the rest."

I looked up at him through my blurry vision, wondering just how he would take care of it if someone reported they'd seen me. If Flora accidentally let it slip somewhere. If the cops showed up with guns blazing—*Could a vampire even survive a gunshot?*

I shut my eyes against the light of the room.

"Remember what I said, my darling." I felt his lips on me once more. "I'd kill them all, just for you."

Thirty-Five

Within the hour, Flora and I had made our way down to the docks at the Sound.

The salty breeze opened up my lungs, the warmth of the sun like a hug at my shoulders. I closed my eyes and leaned back on the plush blanket we'd brought with us. The hard planks of the dock poked my spine as I lay down.

We hadn't changed into bathing suits, but the water was too cold, anyway. My feet hung off the dock, my bare toes skimming the icy water. Flora joined me, laying down so our shoulders brushed. The dock swayed beneath us, just barely, the wooden beams creaking.

Vince still had yet to come out here with me, preoccupied with his work. It occurred to me then that I never really saw him leave the house, not besides the few times we'd gone out at night. He stayed sequestered within the manor walls, working, feeding. Not even during his parties did he seem to venture out, not since we'd found each other.

He was the beating heart of the house, stuck in the

center, making all the other parts work. A well-oiled machine.

I sucked in a deep breath of the seaside air, holding it inside me until my chest burned.

"Are you alright?"

I squinted against the midday sun, rolling over so we faced each other.

"I know I already asked," Flora prefaced, "but truly—are you okay?"

I gave her a smile. I couldn't tell her anything, not like when we were young girls, whispering and giggling in windowsill moonlight while the city slept below us. "Yes."

"I worry about you. You aren't usually this shut in."

"Well after the news today, I doubt I'll be going out and about much as it is."

"I just mean—" She paused, thinking. "I just mean that we always went out. We were always busy. And now..."

"Flora." I sat up a little. "Lucas is looking for me. I can't —I *won't* go back."

My brother would have to drag me back, kicking and screaming.

"Sure, but who's going to rat you out? Who's gonna recognize you? All it would take is a little makeup, maybe some hair dye." She lifted a shoulder. "I'm just saying, Vince has money. He could pay anyone off who *did* recognize you."

I paused. "You think I stay at the house because of him?"

"I don't know, doll. I know things have changed." She sat her hand on my arm again, her slim fingers cooler than the touch of the spring sun shining down on us. Her eyes glittered. "Just don't go changing yourself."

I shook my head. "I won't. You *know* I won't."

"But for Adam?" Her expression turned sheepish. "For Vince?"

I opened my mouth to speak, but she cut me off. "Why the name change, anyway?"

Out on the Sound, the waves were undulating, a dark grayish-blue, shining bright like serpents' tails under the sun. "Because his parents don't know, I suppose." Maybe it was partially true.

"His parents don't know?" Flora was quiet for a moment, as though it was a truth she hadn't considered. I wouldn't have understood, either, if I didn't know who he really was now.

"So, what, they think he's still dead?" She whistled, turning to look out at the water too. She leaned back on her elbows, her blouse sleeves ruffling down her arms. "I can't imagine."

I almost agreed, but—I had run away, hiding right under my family's nose. "He's gone through a lot."

Flora sat up fully, raising her hands. "I know. That war did something to a lot of people." She blew out through her teeth. "But Helena, how does someone just come back filthy rich?"

"He invests," I said pointedly.

She shot me an incredulous look.

"You cannot judge when your own man sells *liquor*," I pointed at her chest. "Which is *illegal*, if you didn't know."

She laughed at my stern expression, pushing my finger away. "As though legality is the same as *morality*." She leaned in close, smiling her warm smile at me, bronze skin glowing under the sun. "As long as he treats you right."

"Of course he does." I flopped back over, throwing an arm over my eyes to shield out the sun.

"*But?*"

I peeked out at her again. "But what?"

"But—I don't know. *But I wish I could go out with you every night.*"

I laughed, watching the clouds move above us. "I do."

"*I wish I'd run away to your house.* Wouldn't that be great? And Dixon could take us away, sell everyone off. Take us on a tour of Europe." She nudged me with her arm again. "We still could. You could come with me when I leave—I'll convince Dixon to buy tickets for the next boat."

"Wouldn't you like that?"

"It would be an adventure! My best friend, my man—"

"You're serious about him."

She hummed, sitting silent for a moment. "I haven't been talking to anyone else. Not for some time."

"Flora! You're in love," I crooned.

It felt good. Like we were girls again.

Her hand came to cover my mouth. "Hush, or he'll hear you."

"Would that be so bad?"

"He figures everything out," she grumbled. "Before I can tell him, he'll just know. Like he has someone listening *everywhere*. Feeding him everyone's secrets."

"Hmm."

"I want to tell him." She looked out at the water.

"I think he knows," I said.

She turned to me again.

"He's very protective of you. He's serious about you, too."

She thought to herself for a moment, watching waves lap against the dock, the clouds rolling above us, hiding the sun, then revealing its light. We hadn't had a moment where it was just us, no one else, in so long. Where we could speak plainly.

And the truth just sat there on my tongue, almost bursting from me.

But Dixon would kill me. I might lose her, if she knew.

"What about the two of you?" Flora rolled over on her side, facing me. Propped herself up on her elbow. A small smile pulled at her lips. "Will you two marry?" She had asked me the same thing about Adam, all those years ago.

"I don't know." I tried to imagine it. Me, wearing the most beautiful white dress, the most luxurious that money could buy, and him, dressed in a priceless suit, standing at an altar, making vows for forever. The only ones in attendance, the vampires that lived here—Flora, if I could invite her, and maybe Dixon, if she dragged him along. A small wedding on this very shore, the house miniscule in the background, just as dusk was beginning to blanket the Sound.

And they would all drink from their crystal glasses a deep, rich blood, and Flora wouldn't notice the peculiarity. And—would he have to change me then? Could a vampire even wed a human? And if his life was *extended*, as Sinclair had revealed, what did that mean for me, if I never changed?

Vince had yet to put his teeth into me. Had yet to drink my blood. I still didn't quite understand who he was, why he kept so much from me. So many secrets that were still locked deep within him. And though tonight he promised to reveal it all to me, to show me *everything*, I still worried—that he would never open himself up to me, that there would always be little truths hidden away, truths I'd need to uncover.

And if I were a vampire, did I want an existence such as that for the rest of my years?

I wanted a simple life. A simple love. Just me and him.

But nothing about us was simple. It never had been.

"Whatever you decide," Flora said, smoothing hair away from my face, "I'll be your maid of honor."

I smiled at her. "I would have no one else."

THIRTY-SIX

That red robe changed everything the moment the silky fabric draped over my collarbones. Brushing gently against my ankles as I swayed before the mirror, the same dress Sinclair had worn, dark maroon crushed velvet, with only a thin sash at the waist to keep my modesty. I did not realize it then, but this was the moment of no return: a human, donning the bloodred robe of the vampires. A human, on her way to dance with the dead. A human, in the thrall of her vampire.

Were not prey drawn to their predators in nature?

Hair unbound, rubies dangling from my ears, I ignored the fluttering of my stomach as I left the safety of our bedroom. Veronica waited for me in the hall, dressed in a knee-length, elegant black number—not a robe.

"Someone has to oversee things," was her explanation.

There were already people milling about the main halls, wandering down corridors and into rooms. Curious gazes staring at the surrounding opulence. That had been me, once.

"Should I not... hide?" My clothing was not very conspicuous.

"For what?" she asked with a glance in my direction. "The party will be nothing but fading memories in the morning."

I said nothing else, and neither did she, her expression unenthusiastic as we went on. She looked straight ahead, either oblivious to my inspection or ignoring it, her nose straight, eyes high on her face, the black of her dress accentuating the soft tan of her skin. I had yet to see her smile.

Without thought, I knew the way, even if Veronica was not my guide. And then we were before the devilish doors.

I held my chin high, squared my shoulders, walking with a confidence I did not feel.

"Keep your head on straight," she warned.

No sounds whispered from the other side, no voices, only a silence that seemed to listen back. The chill of the marble floor beneath my bare feet tethered me to every breath that filled my lungs. Another breath, and another, until I pushed open the heavy wooden doors and stepped over the threshold, into a den of vampires.

In a moment, I was surrounded by a hundred sets of predatory eyes, all flicking in my direction at the interruption of the doors opening. The room was dim, the lights soft like candles, and every surface was plush and deep red.

Bodies writhing over each other like snakes, hissing, groaning in ecstasy.

The vampires soon returned to their drinking, their

fucking, only a choice few remaining staring at me. The strange human who'd interrupted.

Last time, I hadn't passed the threshold.

Tonight, I joined them.

The doors fell shut behind me with finality.

Heat from the numerous bodies like a caress, an invitation to shed my robe. But glancing around, I grew conscious of my frame—the swell of my hips compared to the narrow waists of the women, their swollen breasts, the curves of their bodies worshiped by roaming hands.

Not far into the room, a trio blocked my way. Two men and a woman—one man in the middle, receiving and giving, while the woman speared herself on his cock, and the other male behind him shoved himself inside. She had raw bites on her throat, blood dripping down her collarbone, in between her breasts. The man in the back looked at me, a devilish glint in his eye as he pumped himself in and out.

Heat rose to my cheeks.

Was it my body they wanted? Or my blood?

As I walked, a soft hand slid up my calf before disappearing. I whirled around to see a woman on her hands and knees grinning up at me, her sharp teeth piercing her lip, a dark red stain at the corners of her mouth. An invitation to play in her smirking lips.

But Vince had told me to find him, and that's what I intended to do.

I spotted Sinclair at a couch near the wall, where he sat —this time, not with another couple, but with Séra. Her robe was falling off her shoulder, her light brown skin exposed to the dim lamplight. He fisted his hand in her hair as she licked a stripe up his neck, then bit down. I saw the flash of pain in his eyes, then the influx of lust. His pupils growing until his eyes were black. She moved to straddle him, the robe parting for her as she feasted on his blood.

Seeing them, watching the others, brought a maddening dampness between my legs. I squeezed my thighs together, my muscles clenching involuntarily.

A fierce yearning burned inside of me. I wanted this. I wanted to be feasted upon.

And then I saw him.

Across the room, almost too dark to find in the shadows, he stood, pushing off from a large black chair—a throne, of sorts—where he'd been watching, observing his court of the damned, in his own bloodred robe. It was like that first night, when he found me amongst the crowd of humans downstairs, when I'd wandered into his web, and he had zeroed in on me amidst all the other souls. Like our souls called to each other.

And as he stood, the whole room seemed to realize it.

Their fervor lessened, and though they didn't stop their feeding and fucking, they became attentive to his movements. Glazed eyes watching as he stepped toward me, one foot after the other, the crowd parting around him.

When he reached me, his eyes were pitch-dark.

The frenzy of those around us had left him wanting.

And here I was.

He towered over me, and I reached up for his chest, his broad shoulders. He remained still, waiting for my every move. We had a silent conversation, his feelings clear in his eyes, that he wanted *me* to make the choice, to make the move. He wanted me to choose him, to choose this world.

I swallowed a lump in my throat as my hands met the planes of his bare chest under the velvet. His neck was bare, the white skin unblemished, unbroken, unscarred—as though no one had drunk from him there. When everyone else in the room was scarred with bites, the evidence of feeding visible in the flash of an electric light.

My hands moved up to his shoulders, and in doing so, his robe fell, cascading down his back, exposing him to the whole room. His arousal pressed against my stomach, and I had half a mind to kneel, to take him into my mouth and show him just how much I wanted to be part of him forever.

But he grabbed my elbows before I could touch him further, before I could move.

I nearly melted when he grabbed me, almost weeping with want.

"Take me," I whispered, only loud enough for him to hear.

In a second his hands were beneath my thighs, hoisting me up in the air, my legs around his waist. I gasped as his arousal found me beneath my robe, brushing against that sensitive part of me that made me shiver. I almost cried. But he didn't enter me. He teased me, building my neediness, the tip of his cock nestling in between my legs, but never inside.

I threw my head back as he carried me, his strong hands supporting all my weight, his robe forgotten on the ground. He brought me back to that dark chair in the shadows. And he sat, pulling me onto his lap, my knees on either side of his hips.

"Are you sure of this, my darling?" He gripped my thighs roughly, pulling me down onto him, his cock stuck between our bodies, rubbing against the apex of my thighs, drawing that dampness out of me. Readying me.

"Yes," I breathed.

"They answer to me," he said, watching me writhe, watching me succumb to my lust. He only had eyes for me, his pupils zeroing in on the pulse at my neck. His nostrils flared. "And now, to you."

I didn't quite understand the nonsense spilling from his mouth, especially as he lifted me just enough, notching himself at my entrance.

"They were Made by blood of my blood. They bow to me. To *us*." And then he was pushing on my hips until his cock speared inside, one inch at a time, before I was fully seated on his lap, my muscles crying in protest at the intrusion.

It was all too much—the eyes of so many on me, watching me with him, while they all fed on each other.

I understood it, then. The biting, the sucking, the drawing pleasure from each other, all at once—it was a cycle of life, of energy, of giving and taking.

My hips ached with the need to move, to show Vince *he* was my life force.

I was a fool to think I could've lived without him. Without *this*.

Hunger bloomed around me, the creatures wanting my blood, but not able to have it.

"Don't you like it?" he hissed at me, barely able to restrain himself. I'd never seen him so taken by his blood lust. "Show them—you own me. Show them who's in control."

My breaths came shallow as I lifted myself, my muscles barely able to move, and came back down on him. "But—"

"Let them know it's *you*." He thrust upward into me harshly, his breath hot on my neck.

Our joining was hidden behind fabric, but anyone who looked would know.

They would all know what we were to each other.

"Show them just *why* they're all damned." He licked that spot beneath my ear, laving at the flesh, right where my pulse pressed against my skin.

"Who are you?" I whispered, rising to my knees. The friction as his cock left me drove me mad.

He roughly shoved me back down, and his mouth was on mine in a second, drawing my shout into him.

I burned.

I burned for him.

"I am their god," he growled, pulling away long enough to nip at my neck. His teeth were sharp, a moment's press away from ripping my flesh, but he held back. "And you are mine," he mumbled against my skin.

The word *Sire* broke through the jumbled haze of my mind. *Andreas.*

I squirmed on his cock, the sensation too much for me. He leaned back in his seat, hungry eyes watching as I moved to ride him, as I lifted myself, spearing myself down on him, over and over again. "They worship you?" I asked, breathless, my hands falling to the muscles of his stomach, moving my hips back and forth.

"They live, breathe, and they die because of me," he said, steel in his voice. His features turned harsh. He exuded the power of a Sire, a vampire who created and ruled above others—how had I not seen it before?—and I was suddenly shattering, my muscles clenching around him, the electricity shooting through me from nowhere.

He groaned, his hands falling to me again, forcing my hips to still. My heat gripped him, wanting more of him, wanting him *deeper*.

I couldn't breathe, my body so flushed with pleasure, that when he stood, holding me up, I knew if he let go my legs would buckle. He held me steady, and he looked about the room, catching the eyes of many of the vampires, who quickly looked away. Watching *us* as they continued their own fucking.

"Follow me," he whispered, his arm around me. I could do nothing but obey as he led me to a recessed door, and suddenly the blood party was shut away, and we were alone.

I dropped the robe as soon as the door closed, and Vince's eyes darkened. "I will never tire of looking at you, my darling."

He was not finished, his cock still hard, jerking in my palm when I reached for it. My own arousal coated him, slick and warm.

"Why does it seem like Veronica is in charge?" I asked, continuing my movements. Feeling the ridges of him against my fingers, wondering at how something so big could fit inside me.

His predator eyes landed on me, and were he anyone else, I would know to be afraid.

"Because," he said through gritted teeth, "no one becomes immortal without our approval."

"Both of you?" I asked, moving my hand slower, enjoying the hardness of him in my palm.

"Blood of my blood," he said again, and I understood.

He admitted it so easily, as though nothing could be a secret if his cock were in my hand. I could ask him anything, and he'd answer.

I leaned over and kissed his jaw, tasting the sweet salt of his sweat. A pang of jealousy went through me—he had bitten someone else, had changed someone else, and it had not been me.

But before I could dwell on it, he lifted me again, and suddenly, my back was flat on cool stone, immediately sending shivers through my body. He pushed my legs apart, and I realized I was on a table—an altar of sorts. Reminiscent of the original use of this building.

Heat simmered beneath my skin as he slowly climbed over me. I wrapped my arms around the back of his neck, his face inches from mine. My legs splayed open, waiting.

"Do you want to change me?" I asked, lifting my hips just enough to feel him, urging him on.

He hesitated, keeping himself just out of reach.

"More than anything," he said, and entered me in one rough thrust.

My back arched off the stone, a cry dying in my throat. Hips pressed flush, grinding into the rough coolness beneath me, an ache building between my thighs. Again, again, and again, plunging deep, powerful, until he withdrew—and with his unnatural strength, he flipped me over onto my belly. Pinned between his forceful thrusts and the stone, suppressing the screams bubbling up from my lungs.

He covered my mouth with his hand, his breaths hot

against my ear, muffling the foul sounds that came out of me. Hips snapping to mine—moving with a frenzy, nearing his own peak.

I pressed the back of my skull against him, opening up my neck, eyes rolling back into my head.

He growled, a truly animalistic sound, and I felt him near the tender flesh of my throat.

"Temptress." The words a low, guttural hiss.

The beast took over. Suddenly, his teeth pierced the flesh of my throat, tearing right under my ear. I cried out, the pain like a knife, a slash. Hot and sharp, piercing deep into my skin.

Vince was a vampire, a creature meant to *kill* humans. And he had his teeth in me.

I shattered immediately, my core spasming on his cock at the bite of pain and pleasure all at once. My orgasm came from nowhere, without any effort, like the puncture of his teeth was an aphrodisiac.

Quivering, my hands came to the stone in an attempt to push myself up, but I was wholly at his mercy as he came into me from behind, holding me in place with his mouth.

I had the brief thought that he would kill me. Vince would kill me—and then what? What was all this for?

His teeth still in me, his cock still rutting into me, he drank, and drank, his fingers like claws against my mouth, holding me still. I couldn't move, only succumb to his want and lust.

And the fear disappeared, as though I were drunk, and the warmth made me pliant. I ached, spent, and there was a comfort in letting go, in giving up control. My vision became fuzzy, the dark of the room growing.

He pulled away from my neck. "I can't even begin to describe to you how you taste," he growled in my ear, both hands finding my hips.

I was lightheaded, submissive to the sensations of him pistoning in and out.

When he came, he shuddered against me, and I felt his heart beating rapidly, faster than I'd ever felt from him. Like he was alive again. Wetness seeped down my thighs, mingling with the sweat between us.

In the haze of lust, disappointment sobered me, just enough. I turned, my cheek smushed, my heart slow, still breathless. "You didn't change me."

"I didn't." He straightened, still hard within me, his hands against my spine to keep me down. The darkness of his eyes seemed satiated, the wildness dissipating.

"You said—"

"I cannot Make you when I have only just tasted you." He licked his lips, his elongated sharp teeth stained a deep red. He struggled to catch his breath, his chest still heaving, his body playing at being alive, as he'd been six years ago.

He pulled away from me then, his release dripping down my legs. His large but gentle hands came to my shoulders.

"It will wear off," he said, his voice softer than before.

"I don't want it to wear off," I sighed dreamily again. "I want you to bite me."

He swallowed. A trail of red ran down his chin. *My blood.*

He drank my blood.

"I will not kill you. If I drink too much from you, you will die."

I turned, using all my strength to brush my lips against his. "Then you can Make me."

He pressed his lips against mine firmly, and the tang of my blood spread on my tongue. I half-expected it to taste as ambrosial as he said, but I tasted only iron, like I'd bitten my lip too hard. He was careful not to graze his teeth against my lips, his kiss gentle, his animal fed and sated. Pressing his forehead to mine, he loosed a breath, his big hand caressing my cheek with a tenderness I hadn't realized I missed.

"In time," he whispered.

There was a hearth in the room—which I realized now must have been an imitation of the old sacristy—and Vince summoned a servant to build a fire and bring some blankets. Chills wracked my body, and he cursed under his breath as he wrapped me in the furs and cashmere.

It was charming, almost, how he eyed me warily, waiting for the moment I would lose consciousness.

I nibbled on some pastries he ordered—too many for me alone, slowly regaining some semblance of normalcy after the warmth from the fire and the sugar from the sweets.

Death had been closer than I thought. He had taken so much from me, that when I stood, stars danced in my vision, the shadows of the room clouding over.

His amber eyes traced the column of my neck. "You will scar."

Pride bloomed in my chest, but I only shrugged.

"I will never regret marking you," he said, his eyes flicking up to mine. He sat naked upon the blanket on the ground, one leg bent, his arm resting on his knee. "Even if it will eventually fade. You are already healing."

I reached up, and felt that the punctures were already closed, not like a fresh wound, my skin smooth. "How?"

"My teeth. They heal as I tear the skin, so that when I'm done, there's only a vague red mark. A byproduct of being a killer that lives and hides amongst its prey."

"But the others out there..." I trailed off.

"We can choose whether to heal or not. And while I wanted to see that pretty crimson blood spill all over you, I... didn't want to overwhelm you."

I took another bite of the pastry, the sugary, buttery breading crumbling on my tongue.

"We typically wait until the end of the evening to heal up wounds," he explained, cocking his head to the side so boyishly I saw Adam for a moment.

"And when shall we do this again?"

He paused, lips quirking, suppressing a smile. "We convene at least once a month, more often in the summer. During the parties."

A chill traveled up my arms. "And no one notices?"

"Sure, some notice. Friends gone missing past midnight, only to return home the next day not quite right. But no one suspects a thing—it *is* a party. For us, it's a blood bank."

I starkly remembered the man in the garden, pinning me, threatening to feed from me, before I truly understood what was happening. He had disappeared after that, after Vince had scared him away. I hadn't seen him since.

"And," he continued, "it draws others to us. People who want to be Made."

The pieces began to fall into place, the full picture

before me, begging to be put together. Dixon's insistent warnings, the blank stares of the servants. Vince watched me, a dark smile growing as he saw I was beginning to understand.

"You Make them, and then they serve you." He had said it himself, had said it before, that he was their Sire. "You deal in immortality."

"I give them true life," he said, his teeth glinting in the firelight, and I saw then his vicious cunning, how he had returned home but made an entirely new place for himself. "If someone wants it, who am I to refuse? Making the choice to become immortal—is that not better than it being forced upon you? As it was for me?"

There was truth in what he said, but I knew there was more.

He bent the truth. *Made* the truth.

"What do you do?" I asked, fists tight under the blankets.

He watched me, every muscle at ease, the portrait of nonchalance.

At his hesitation, I shed the blankets, letting them fall around me, and rose to my knees before him, so we were face to face. His mussed auburn hair fell away from his eyes as he looked up at me with the eyes of a king. There was no concern there, not for the topic at hand.

The version of him from Before was small, was meek in a way that was only learned from being stuck at the bottom rung. Adam was quiet. He'd been ready to take the blame for running into me on the street.

But now, Vince moved through the world unapologetically. He made his choice, he found me, and his transformation years ago hadn't only been physical. In these six years, he'd built his own empire, right under our noses.

I held his face. "Your darkness calls to me," I said, seeing him, *truly* seeing him. "You want to burn everything."

He nodded once, eyes flicking toward my lips, almost close enough to touch.

"You want to destroy *them*."

He said nothing, but it was answer enough.

I hadn't fully comprehended that this was no longer Adam; hadn't understood that Vince was an entirely separate being. One had been killed, destroyed. His fragility had died with Adam. His caring, his empathy, his curiosity for the world. None of those books had been cut open. Every moment had pointed to this, to reclaiming what was his, to taking it all from those who didn't deserve it.

"You own them."

His hands came up to rest on my waist. "The price for immortality is everything. The price is ruination." He fell forward into me, his head against my chest.

I saw him now. And the weight of it all was no longer solely his to bear.

Outside this room, they fed off each other, drinking blood and giving each other their bodies. They were creatures undead, invincible to the world. They could not be killed, did not have to eat food to survive. They didn't need sleep, didn't need humanity any longer, save for the blood.

It was a sort of trick. They thought they were indestructible—and in doing so, they had forsaken everything that made them weak before. They had forsaken their humanity. Becoming a vampire, an immortal, was isolating.

And in this isolation, is where Vince was feeding.

Until they were as blank-faced and dead inside as the servants fueling the parties, waiting on humans indefinitely.

A laugh threatened to spill from me at the irony of it all.

His eyes flashed, and he wrapped his arms around my waist, pulling me to him, our bodies flush.

"When will you stop?" I asked as he laid me down, looming over me. I became dizzy with need, again.

His lips descended to my neck, sucking on the spot he'd bitten. "When I'm dead."

THIRTY-SEVEN

Upon awakening, I could feel it in my bones that the house was empty. The bed was cold again. I knew Vince was gone before I truly came to my senses. I had the distinct memory of him pushing the hair from my eyes, kissing my face, and whispering that he would return.

But when I opened my eyes, a dark red rose, almost black at the tip of the petals, sat against my pillow.

The sweet smell of the flower seeped into me, wrapping itself around me like a hug. I set it gently on the table beside the bed, careful not to crush the petals.

It was just like the one in my bedroom—the one I'd found in the garden, then on my pillow, back then.

He had been watching over me. Visiting me in the night.

I dressed hastily and pulled my shawl tight around me.

No voices echoed down the marble halls, only a few of the dead servants scrubbing at the floor, dusting light fixtures. The servants fluttered about, cleaning the floors in the wake of last night's party. None of them looked up at me as I passed.

How strange to walk amongst monsters that had no power to hurt me.

I made my way to the colonnaded veranda outside, greeted by a soft rumble of thunder out in the distance. The sky was a deep gray, a large collection of near-black mountainous forms along the horizon. Every few seconds, lighting would flash from within, bringing with it the delayed grumble of Mother Nature.

I leaned against a column, the marble a stark white against the hazy green of the lawn. The large fountain before the stairs to the porch still bubbled, the drive swept of all evidence of the previous evening's carousing, no cars left behind, no stray scarves or shoes.

A breeze picked up the ends of my hair, warning me to return inside. The rumbling continued, those dark clouds creeping ever closer. The water of the Sound, gray and bleak, roiled at the growing storm. The humidity was tangible, a suffocating force, stealing the air from right before me. My short skirt billowed around me, tossed around by the wind.

I shut my eyes and felt the tempest growing, welcomed the unsettling show of power. A moment later, water sprinkled from the sky, falling from that darkness looming over the manor.

I stepped down from the veranda, fully exposed to the elements. Tossing my hair, my skirt, tugging at the fabric, growing violent, gripping at me, pushing against me with invisible force, leading me along.

Yes, yes, more, more.

The wrought iron gates of the garden creaked as the wind rattled against the bars. Unlocked.

The cypress trees swayed, the moonflowers shut against the dim light of the afternoon, protecting their waxy soft petals from the gusts of air. The gravel crunched under my shoes.

In the daylight, it became clear this was not simply a garden. Of course it wasn't, nothing in this house was as it seemed. And if it'd been a church, then this must've been the graveyard—a detail I'd missed my first time within the gates, the midnight hour obscuring the true nature of these stone paths.

The flowers were overgrown, and amongst them, large flat stones jutted upward. Marble, concrete, granite... all peeking over the closed blooms, wanting to be seen, remembered.

The one closest to me was stained emerald with moss. The moonflowers grew uncontrolled around it, their vines wrapping around the stone, creating a wall of greenery so thick I had to pull the branches away. It was plainly decorated, with a simple border, the name of the buried carved so shallowly I had to run my fingers over the relief to read the name. The years underneath were lost to time.

Scanning the gardens, I saw many more. And the statue of the nymph, overseeing them all, her creamy marble skin streaked and weathered.

The wind whipped my hair around my face, the raindrops pelting my skin. Lightning flashed, and the thunder was so much closer now, only seconds after the spark of light. The earth seemed to growl its displeasure, the sound rumbling in my bones.

I wondered how it would feel to stand with my feet in the water of the Sound and let the storm rage around me. Was I strong enough to withstand the pull? Or would I fall into the depths and get swept away? Then I would not have to worry about Vince's true nature, or Lucas and Wright.

The next headstone was equally concealed, but the decoration was more ornate. And the next was weathered to a completely smooth surface. They sat in rows, tucked in amongst the brush and flowers, the walkways coming within inches of the stones. They'd been paved over, planted over. Visitors to the garden would walk over their bodies, six feet under, decaying and rotting into the lush earth, moistened by the Sound.

How many bodies surrounded me now? How many were underneath this earth? And how many had no markers, cursed to the endless obscurity of forever?

I touched each stone, laying my palm on the flat cool surfaces. I didn't know what made me do it; it wasn't a reverence for these dead, because I did not know them. These souls, buried next to this manor that hosted parties to ruin—did they ever make themselves known? Did they ever appear as apparitions and warn the humans that wandered into their domain?

I came upon a hedge, a wall of thorns that reached up above the height of a man. It was indistinguishable from the other four walls of the garden, the stone packed so tightly with vines, but I knew, after only a few moments—this hedge was where I'd been cornered. When that vampire had begged for my blood, offered to change me.

I reached up into the vines, feeling the cool wall beneath my fingertips, damp with the growing storm, the vines creaking in protest against the wind. Trailing my fingers along those vines, plucking a flower for my hair, the petals fluttering in the breeze. The hedge formed a corner—and around the corner was a door, overgrown with moss and gorse and rose bushes.

A shed of some sort? No—this was a graveyard.

A tomb.

I hadn't realized it in the dark that night, and the knowledge of it now sent the hairs on my neck upright. The vines moved like snakes in the wind, restless and slithering against the hidden exterior. The stone slab of a door, sealed shut with iron bars, much like that of the garden's gates. But the lock was broken, and I swore I saw deep indentations in the stone block, gashes stained a deep rust color, and a large crack traveling diagonally from the mechanism. Like a great force had tried to get in.

Or out.

The wind howled, moaned. Ghostly and frightening, whistling through leaves and tree branches, debris from the plants whipping in the air.

The moan grew like it came from within that tomb. Agonizing, rattling me deep in my bones, a sound of anguish.

I jolted as a hand grabbed my arm.

"Helena!"

Séra whirled me around.

"What are you doing?"

I opened my mouth to speak, but no words came out.

Had she heard it? Did she know what was within? The dead from long ago, or—

"You must get inside," she said, grabbing my hand and

pulling me toward the house. It stood tall against the riotous sky, the usually clean exterior looking stained black with the rain.

She wore a blue raincoat and hat, already soaked with water, and she pulled me away quickly, her grip strong.

"The sky is about to open up and you're outside," she said, more to herself than to me, shaking her head.

"I needed to clear my head," I lied.

Séra scoffed as the iron gate of the garden clanged shut behind us. "You'll get a chill—and if you're sick, who's going to keep Vince occupied?"

"He seems occupied enough as it is."

She glanced at me. "What do you mean?"

"He disappears. If he's not with me, he's doing... whatever it is that he does."

"You can always find me," she said as though it were obvious. We stepped under the covering of the veranda, just as the rain came down in sheets. My dress was soaked through, the slippers ruined.

"I don't know where *you* are half the time."

I didn't say how much I wished to invite Flora over. How much I wished to go to the city again—to get out of this house. It was grand and beautiful, but I was tiring of seeing the same walls, days on end. Of feeling like I was being watched, some specter spying on me for Vince—just as Séra had, just as Sinclair had.

"Then that's something we'll remedy," she said with a soft smile.

A servant appeared at the front door with two towels. Séra wrapped one around my shoulders, pushing my wet hair from my face.

Where were they before? Where had everyone gone? And what made them come back so suddenly?

"You're not my keeper, Séra."

She just shrugged, and I followed her back inside the house, into the foyer. I could hear the squall outside through the pelting of the roof, the creaking of the windows.

"I want you to like it here," she said simply. "Whatever I can do—"

"Where were you?"

She paused just before the ballroom, shucking off her raincoat into the hands of the dead-eyed, silent servant. "We just went out. Vince... had a call."

"And you left me here?"

"He didn't want to wake you."

I crossed my arms, ignoring the way my clothing clung to my skin, cold now with all the water that soaked through. "Where is he?"

It was too odd—their swift return, the sudden sense of life once more in the manor. As though I'd awoken in a dream-world and I was its sole inhabitant, until somehow, that veil had been lifted. And he hadn't found me, Séra had. The slight frown to her lips, the forced smiles...

"He's gone to his study. Working." She motioned to one of the many waiting servants, all standing in a line against the wall, hands clasped, like automatons waiting for instruction. "Let's get you a bath."

"I'm fine."

"I insist," she said, grabbing my hand once more. We started up the stairs, my slippers squeaking against the polished floor, a servant following, presumably to run the bath. She said nothing else as we made it to the hall of our bedroom. The servant went ahead of us, and as we approached the bedroom door, which stood ajar, the sound of running water coming from inside. "Would you like me to help?"

"You are not my maid anymore, Séra."

And I just wanted to be alone.

She wasn't giving me a straight answer. And I knew there was more to what she was telling me.

Who had called Vince and summoned him away for the morning? Who was so important?

Séra opened her mouth to retort, but her words were drowned out by loud laughter suddenly spilling down the hall. It echoed, jumping from polished surface to polished surface; a man's laughter, deep in its timbre and dark.

Séra's eyes widened, hands coming up to brace the doorway on either side of me. Caging me into the room.

"You're running out of time Vince!" It bounced off the walls, the gleeful lilt of his voice contrary to the unspoken threat.

"Go in the room," Séra whispered to me, moving closer as though to block my exit.

"Who is that?"

"A scoundrel," she hissed. "Go."

But then the figure of a man passed the end of the hall, and though he had no reason to travel down this corridor, he stopped in his tracks and seemed to sniff the air. He was dressed entirely in black, skin pale as the moonflowers outside. And then his head whipped toward me, eyes landing on me immediately, and he grinned a grin so unsettling, that even from dozens of feet away, my blood ran cold.

I recognized him.

I should have listened and escaped into the room. Whatever he wanted, that grin told me it was no good. My pulse quickened in my ears.

"There you are," he said, as though he were looking for me.

Marcel Brancato.

And in the blink of an eye he had traversed the hall, standing not two feet behind Séra.

How had I not noticed this weeks ago?

Séra whirled around, pushing me behind her with a protective arm. "*Leave.*"

He only chuckled at the display of her teeth.

Vince and Veronica turned the corner then, a wall of fury, and there was murder in my lover's eyes. "Your business here is through," he said, voice so low I hardly heard him, but not too low a vampire couldn't hear. Veronica stood completely still, her hands like claws at her sides.

"I said what I needed to say to you, Vering." The intruder simply rolled his eyes.

Vince's lip curled at the use of his old name. "And now you will go. She's of no consequence to you."

Another laugh. "You've been hiding a human, and haven't even offered to serve her?" Marcel's eyes flashed. He recognized me, too. "The lack of hospitality is appalling. Especially from you."

There was no way this was the same man—There was no way I'd dined with a vampire—

I hadn't seen him eat anything. Only throw back drinks.

Much like Séra had, like they were water—

Vince stalked forward, eyes trained on the vampire.

I didn't dare breathe, or move, even though both Séra and Vince now stood between me and Marcel Brancato.

"Relax," he said, raising his hands. "I'm not an animal." But he grinned at me again, showing off his teeth. "How does one get their hands on something as lovely as you? I've been trying," he said, pointedly, "but they always run away."

Vince wrenched his shoulder back. "Out."

Marcel held my eyes—and after a moment, shrugged Vince off, backing down the hall. Eyes trailing along my throat, my chest, to the fabric plastered to my legs, my hips—

"Veronica," Vince commanded.

Her brows pinched in a scowl as she led Marcel away. "Let's go."

He only laughed, and when they made it to the end of the hall, he turned, giving us one last farewell. He looked directly at me once more, smirking, but when he spoke, it wasn't to me.

"He'll be glad to hear you're doing so well—*Vince Thornton.*"

THIRTY-EIGHT

"Who was he?"

I decided not to let the bath go to waste. Every nerve in my body was alight, buzzing with the same energy a deer must feel in the face of its killer. Marcel had shaken me, even if he had not touched me, and my body responded by readying to run—however futile it would really be.

Sinking into the water, murky with lavender and citrus oils, steam rising and swirling, I inhaled deeply, relaxing every muscle, letting the heat seep into my skin.

Vince sat upon a stool, elbows propped on his thighs, hands falling between his knees. At my question, he breathed in deeply, straightening in the chair. His gaze turned to my body, obscured in the milky water.

My racing heart had yet to calm. And he knew it.

He'll be glad to hear you're doing so well.

"An old acquaintance."

"That much was obvious," I muttered, propping myself on my elbows. My knees rose like mountains in the water.

It could not entirely be a coincidence that I'd had drinks with him not long ago. Had he been a vampire this whole time? And—how had Dixon not picked up on it that night? How had Dixon not warned me? I couldn't believe he'd just sit by while I dined with a predator.

And there was no doubt that Marcel was a predator.

"His name is Marcel Brancato," Vince admitted, jaw clenched tightly. "He should not have seen you."

"And yet he did." I leant my head back against the rim of the tub. "What did he want?"

I knew one part of the answer—me.

Because I had turned him down that night, was this his retribution?

He had joked that it was a shame I wasn't served to him. But I knew the truth underneath. If he had gotten to me, and the others had been preoccupied, I'd be dead.

He wanted to drain me dry.

What if he had found me in the garden? What if it had been *his* strong grip pulling me away, not Séra's?

I shivered, despite the burn of the water.

I didn't tell Vince I knew him, that Brancato knew *me*. Something told me to keep my lips sealed. That if Vince knew, I'd never leave this suite again.

His hands came to rest on the edge of the tub. He still wore his shirt, sleeves rolled up, tie gone. He had run his hands through his hair so many times in the last hour it fell in his eyes, his pomade ruined. "He wasn't meant to see you. I will kill him."

Vince had been called away to the city. They were all

gone. What if Brancato came while I was alone—was Brancato the reason they'd gone at all?

The air of the bathroom was thick like fog, settling heavily onto me, onto Vince's form. His back bowed in his chair. "He... was Made by my Sire. Not long after I was."

He'll be glad to hear you're doing so well.

Andreas.

Marcel had brought a message from the Sire.

You're running out of time. For what? What was Vince running out of time for? What was he running *from*? He hadn't left because the war was over, hadn't returned to New York *just* to find me.

But would he stay for me? Was I enough?

The suds of the water lined my chin. "What did he want?" I asked again.

With a glance, I saw he wanted anything but to tell me, to have to expose whatever trouble he was in. I sat up, water sluicing off my chest, goosebumps pebbling my skin. There was so much I didn't know, so much being hidden from me, and I was tired of it. "Don't do that."

His brow twitched upward.

"I can handle whatever it is."

In a few short weeks, I had found out my lover was not dead, even though I'd wasted six years believing so, six years drinking, kissing men I didn't care about. I'd run away from Lucas and his iron fist, from Mother's expectations, from Wright Highsmith and his English money. I was making peace with the fact that there were monsters walking amongst us, bloodsucking creatures, and that Vince was one of them, that I was *in love* with him.

My fear was shrinking the bigger the world seemed to grow. But it was still there, holding onto my heart, tight.

He studied me, scanning my face. "He frightened you."

"I just—didn't expect it." I reached for his hand, dripping water on the tile.

I had not accepted him, accepted this strange new world, just to let him take it on all on his own.

"I will kill him," he repeated, anger curling his lip. "The fact that he knows of your existence has damned him. Half the vampires that walk in these halls don't deserve to look upon you."

I squeezed his fingers, bringing him back to me. "He didn't come just to antagonize you, surely."

"That's all he wants, is to antagonize me."

"Why?" I whispered.

I touched his cheek. *I accept all the dark parts of you.*

He took another breath, coming to some conclusion within himself, and covered my hand with his. "He is the heir of our Sire, and it has gone to his head."

"Your Sire has an heir?"

I was realizing just how much I still had yet to learn.

"When I was Made, the Sire's entire coven was decimated by the war. Many had wanted to join the fight for their land, as they saw it, to protect what was theirs. And many died, in the firefight, or in suffocating under dirt, or by gas. So the Sire made me." He peeked up at me through his lashes. "I was the first, Made to replenish his coven."

And Marcel was second.

If Vince was first, did that mean—

He swallowed, saying aloud what I was beginning to

suspect. "I was Made so that, should he die, one day, I would rule over the coven." He let go of my hand, letting it slide back into the water. He reached for my face instead, brushing a wave behind my ear. "I was gone so long, because I was not allowed to leave."

A numb anger spread through my heart. "Now Marcel is the heir."

And I had dined with him.

He nodded once again, his features hardening. "And now they know about you. About why I ran."

"Is it so bad?" I asked, moving to sit on my knees in the bath. I was face-to-face with him, my water dripping onto his clothes, my bare body reacting to the cool air. "That you left?"

His hands found my waist. "In my Sire's eyes, it was a crime to run away," was all he said.

"And Marcel—he knows where you are."

My stomach dropped. If Marcel knew, then *Andreas* did.

Marcel Brancato's appearance was an omen. He was the harbinger.

I stood, the cooling water splashing against the rim of the tub, over the edge, spreading on the tile. Vince reached for a towel, wrapping it around my body. The air was frigid with the ghost of our visitor, with the untold future hovering nearby, waiting to unspool.

You're running out of time.

And how much time did we have?

I set back my shoulders. Pulled the towel tight. "We should strategize. Talk with the others."

His eyes flashed. "I—"

"Do not exclude me," I said, letting the shallow fear I still felt harden my voice. "Do not shut me out."

His chest rose with a breath, and he leaned forward and kissed me. "As you wish."

THIRTY-NINE

"I have an idea."

I had time to think. It was two days after Branca-to's appearance, and I had been mulling over what to do, how to go about this.

Why had he shown up now, and what did it have to do with our meeting weeks ago?

It couldn't be a coincidence. I refused to believe it.

Not with the way he had looked at me, like he knew exactly what he was doing. I hadn't caught it that night weeks ago, but I saw it two days ago, when he stared me down, dropping his human mask.

My skin crawled. I was right to listen to my instincts and walk away from him. Who knows where I would be if I had taken up his offer for dinner?

Vince glanced up at me now, sat behind the files sprawled across the surface of his desk. It was just me and him in his study, the other three elsewhere in the house. "Go on."

"We should throw another party." I was on one of the couches, flipping through one of the many novels. A fire crackled in the hearth, though with the changing weather, we wouldn't need to light it much longer. "Lure him in."

His answer was immediate. "No."

"He'll return, we know it," I reasoned. "Or, if not him, someone else. Why not invite him?"

"I won't allow him to step foot on these grounds again."

I had thought about it over the past couple of days, putting things together in my mind. And then came the realization that I had never planned for anything in my life—it had all been decided for me. My schooling, the serendipity of meeting Adam—then stumbling upon Vince; the decision of my betrothal to Wright. All happenstance, or someone else's concern. Without Fate's intervention, my days had played out the same way, with late nights, skipped breakfasts, and apologies to my mother, before it began all over again, waiting for an interruption of the monotony.

Only I hadn't realized it. Never had I changed the course. Not until I ran away from it all, deciding I needed Vince more than anything else.

"Think about it," I said, placing the novel onto the tea table.

"I am thinking about it," he nearly growled. "No."

"Is it not better to know *when* he's coming? That way we can prepare."

Vince's eyes bore into me as he tapped the pen to his lips.

Outside, the sun was close to setting, sending ribbons of pink and orange across the sky. With every nightfall, we were one day closer to Brancato doing *something*. None of us knew what. But that mischievous smile had said it all, that he would return and wreak havoc in doing so.

"And when do you suggest we do this?"

"As soon as possible," I said. "Tomorrow. We throw the biggest party this house has ever seen. Invite everyone. And Brancato will come."

"We don't need invitations," Vince said, cocking his head. "It's never been done."

"Yes, but what if?" I stood, stepping closer to him, meeting his stare across his desk. "What if we invite the whole city? If they see *invitations* to the great house of Vince Thornton, they'll come in droves."

A pause. His jaw ticked. "Is that what we want? Human collateral?" His pen stopped its tapping. "There *will* be blood."

I leaned closer. "A distraction."

Marcel was starving.

If he brought others, they'd either spend their energy fighting their instincts, surrounded by so many humans and their fresh blood, or they'd expose themselves for monsters, wreaking havoc. None of the victims would forget his face—he'd be relegated to the shadows.

"Besides that," I added, "we know the house. He doesn't."

It was a veritable labyrinth, easy enough to get turned around down these halls, with its hundreds of rooms, some locked, some not. It was a testament to the servants' abilities to clear the entire house, to find all guests after these shindigs, as I'm sure many a partygoer got lost after the heavy drinking, passing out on one of the many guest beds in the house.

The past few days, I had scoured each hall, twisting every door handle I could find. I had made a map in my mind. And I couldn't get cornered.

I couldn't tell him the entirety of my plan; it wouldn't work if he knew. He'd never allow it.

He sat silently, eyes flicking over my face, considering as I spoke. "I will not risk such violence." He shook his head.

"There will be violence either way," I said, palms against the surface of his desk. "Better it is here, where we have the advantage. Ask the others if you need a second opinion."

I knew what he wanted to do—he wanted to handle this himself, wanted to fight Brancato one-on-one. But Sinclair, Séra, Veronica—they all would help. It was their lives at stake, too.

Brancato represented everything Vince had left behind. Sending his head back to Andreas would be a clear message.

"I don't want him anywhere near you."

"I will be with you the whole evening," I said, reaching for his fingers.

He sighed and leaned back in his chair. Tugging on my fingers, he brought me over to his side of the desk. He uncrossed his legs, pulling me into his lap.

We were face-to-face. Equal.

Those gray eyes studied me. Leaning forward, tracing his nose along my jaw, wrapping his arms around my waist, bringing me close. "You make me want to be violent," he murmured. "You make me want to hurt everyone that dares put a hand on you."

"Then do it."

A spark ignited in his eyes. "What a savage woman you are." Inhaling deep, he pulled away just enough to bring some clarity. "We will ask the others. But I cannot promise that I won't hide you away until this is through."

"This could very well go one of two ways," Séra said. "He will either conceal himself and sneak in, or he will walk right in as he did before."

Vince stood with his arm around me, as though if he let go, I'd vanish. "He will not hide."

"And then what?" Sinclair spoke around the ever-present cigarette between his lips. He leveled his gaze at Vince. "What would you have us do?"

Fingers tightened around my waist.

Marcel Brancato would not bring Vince back, just to lose his position as heir.

Vince's time was running out—Brancato's words had been clear. I feared what would happen to him, should Marcel, should *Andreas* successfully draw him back.

He shook his head as he stared at a point on the floor. His mind was running through all these thoughts, too.

"He'll make an offer I can't refuse," he murmured, unmoving. He didn't blink. "He is just the messenger. My Sire—"

He tensed.

The silence between the five of us was thick, the air clouded with anticipation. Uneasiness roiled in my belly and I couldn't help but feel I had some responsibility in bringing this upon us—upon him. Still as a statue, my lover seemed to stop breathing, for just a moment, or perhaps it was a figment of my imagination.

He cleared his throat. "Marcel will have my hands tied."

"Wait—*I* know!" Sera's face lit up, lips tightening into a savage grin. "A masquerade!"

Sinclair sighed.

"No, there's something to it," Veronica mused. She'd remained silent thus far. Gazing directly at Vince, she nodded. "He may walk onto the grounds unguarded, but if we can hide our faces..."

Then her eyes flicked to mine.

A slight uptick to the corner of her mouth—a conspiratorial smile.

Vince's arms seemed to bring me closer, my spine to his chest, so he could feel every beat of my heart against his. Encased as I was in his arms, I felt for just a moment some semblance of safety—some naive hope that all would turn out alright.

I simply couldn't let myself fathom the alternative.

"We'll distract him," Séra said. "Sinclair and I can draw him in one direction or another, wherever you want him. We'll all have eyes on him."

"And if there are others?" Sinclair shook his head. "We may very well be outnumbered."

Vince hesitated. "We do not know for sure if there will be others."

Veronica raised a brow, and if I did not know better, I would have thought she looked *thrilled*. "Best to prepare for the worst, yes?"

My fingers wound through Vince's. "He does not know

this house as we do," I said, squeezing his hand, leaning back into him.

"He's easy to fool," Veronica said. "And it'll all be over in just one night."

Frustration forced the words through his teeth. "We should be so lucky that this was all over in only one night."

Forty

S tanding at the precipice of what was to come, I had never before felt I could reach out and touch the future, a weight pressing at me from all sides.

Would Marcel even show?

The plan was in place

"What will you do?" Sitting on the bed, alone, while he stood at the window, staring down at the grounds. A rigidness to his spine, his jaw; a distant look in his eyes that told me he knew exactly how this played out.

It did nothing for my nerves.

"What I must," he said. "But at the end of this, he will be dead."

My problems with Lucas seemed minuscule in comparison.

I shuddered to imagine the violence that would make this true. Just what would I witness my vampire lover do? What cruelty would he be forced to commit to protect himself, to protect us?

"I'll help you. We all will." If the sheer number of vampires attending his parties was an indication, there were plenty of people loyal to Vince on our side. "We'll be prepared, and—"

"I do not want you there." Still facing the window, he shook his head.

I opened my mouth to speak, but he interrupted me, knowing what I'd say.

"It's too great a risk. You're—" the next word stalled in his throat, but I heard it anyway.

Human. I was a human girl. I couldn't outrun or fight a creature meant to prey on me.

"So, change me." I stood, making my way over to him.

That fire burned in those gray irises. Want, need, lust for me, for my blood again.

I pressed my hand to his chest, feeling the dull thud of his heartbeat, each thump so spread out from the others that it was undeniable he was living and dead all at once.

"Make me," I whispered, looking up at him.

"If only you understood what you were asking of me."

"I do."

"No." He was all steely resolve.

Disappointment crept in, but I did my best to hold it at bay. "Why not?"

His throat slid, likely remembering the taste of my blood, how he had almost done it that night in the sacristy. How I had been on the brink of death.

On the precipice of transformation.

He shook his head with much more conviction. "Now is not the time."

I stepped away. "When will it ever be time?"

Though he moved silently, I knew he followed. "I—" A pause. "The transformation is too drawn out. It will take days for you to think clearly, months to be able to control yourself around humans."

I could only think, then, we should have done it long before.

I sighed and turned toward him again, my back hitting the bed frame. He stood not two feet behind me.

"I do not want to Make you for any reason other than I cannot bear to be without you," he whispered, hand coming up to rest on my cheek. I leaned into his touch, savoring the feel of his cool skin, the solid presence of him before me. "It shouldn't be rushed. I want to take my time with you."

The phantom prick of sharp teeth into my flesh, the pain, the heart-racing fear that melted into a pleasure so heady I wanted nothing else—how did it feel to be so changed, when every part of you died, only to come back with supernatural vigor?

"I won't leave you," I insisted.

But he was shaking his head, a regretful frown to his brow. "I cannot decide if you're safer near me, or safer if I send you away." His thumb skittered across my cheekbone.

"With *you*." How could he think any differently? I looked into those dark pupils, seeing the torment peeking out there. "You must kill him. Before he gets to you first."

Silently, he gazed down at me, eyes tracing over every inch of my skin like a caress, memorizing each curve—like he didn't want to forget the way I looked in this moment, staring up at him with pleading eyes, knowing, *knowing* something was about to happen.

"Why did you not tell me?" I asked, voice feeling small—

not because I was afraid, but because speaking it aloud would cement the truth that Vince had been hiding this from me.

"That my Sire and my coven would insist upon my return?" A muscle feathered in his jaw. "Because selfishly I did not want to dwell on *him* ever again."

There was still so much I was missing, so many events in his life in those six years we were separated, that he had locked away inside him. Secrets he held close to his heart, pushed down until they were nothing more than wisps of demons that haunted him.

It sparked an anger in me—what had his Sire *done*? What was so terrible that Vince wouldn't speak of it? I saw it now, how the burden of those six years sat on his shoulders, how they weighed him down. How the torment dimmed his eyes, how the memories both tortured and *fueled* him.

"My hope was to return under the right circumstances. Though, it seems, I'm being forced to make that decision quicker than I intended." His hand was fisted in the hair hanging over his face. He clenched his jaw, glancing away from me. "I wanted to make something of myself here. I found you, and I wanted to start over. To feel—*human*."

I realized then another reason Adam never returned: there was no history of Vince here. If his Sire came sniffing, there would be no trace of Vince Thornton anywhere in the country. Not until he started throwing the parties a year ago.

"I can't let them take you," Vince said, his arms suddenly coming around my waist. His face came to my chest, pressing against the spot where my heart beat. "They can't have you. Can't harm you."

"I'll be fine," I said, winding my fingers through his auburn hair, though truly, I wasn't sure.

I still felt the ghost of Brancato's stare on my pulse.

"You can't be there," he repeated, his voice muffled by my slip, the warmth of his breath against my sternum. The contrast between his exhale and the cool feel of his skin was a jarring reminder of how different we were.

I was human.

He was a vampire.

His eyes flashed up to mine. He was wholly supplicant, on his knees between my legs, looking up at me like his thoughts never revolved around anyone else.

"Flora. Go to her," he pleaded, fingers tightened on the fabric at my sides.

"She's already going to be mad that I'm not inviting her to the biggest party you've ever thrown," I said.

His fingers curled tighter. "*Please.*"

It broke my resolve. I could not deny him, not when he asked so sweetly. He whispered the word over and over again, pressing his face once more to the soft skin below my breasts. Our need for each other was overwhelming; not only as lovers, but as *soulmates*. He was mine, and I was his. We'd borne the injuries of separation already. We would not do it again.

The thought of my harm, the thought of someone taking me away from him, of us separating, drove him mad. He pressed against me as if to make our bodies merge.

"Fine," I said, realizing my own hand had tightened in his hair.

His shoulders sagged.

If I was not there, he could focus on his task. If he knew

I was safe somewhere in the city, he would have nothing to distract him, no human girl to watch over.

"I'll call her." I smoothed down his unruly waves.

He turned his head and pressed a kiss to my wrist. "Thank you."

FORTY-ONE

The city was as cacophonous as ever.

My time at the manor had made the quiet famil-iar, comfortable. Now, the honking of horns, the screech of tires, the shouts of men selling wares, was all too loud, too overwhelming. I wondered at how I had never noticed before.

Sinclair, Séra, and I had made a day trip into Manhattan to post the flyers. The invitations to the Masquerade. Hastily ordered from a printer with a massive sum to have it ready this morning.

It would be the party of the century. Dancing girls, costumes, imported liquor—the expensive stuff—acrobats, a wax museum of hired entertainers, the whole manor done up in the likeness of the Garden of Eden. It was to last the whole weekend. Séra had quipped that maybe we could actually enjoy the festivities after our ordeal was done and over with.

Vince had been vehemently against the trip, as though if

I ever left the house, I'd never come back. There was a violence simmering in him, perhaps deadlier than the beast I'd yet seen. The glimpses of darkness that came through here and there—only, I knew, it wouldn't take much for him to snap, to unleash whatever it was he kept at bay.

It had taken some convincing, but eventually Vince agreed to let me out of his sight . Not when the vampire who hunted him knew of my existence, and not when the human world was searching for me, too. Lucas had yet to rescind his award of one million dollars for my return.

I wore a pair of tinted glasses and wrapped my hair in a scarf, for good measure.

We could have sent one of the servants, but Séra insisted on making it a day trip. I think she knew how stir-crazy I was feeling, even though I hadn't voiced it. She linked arms with me, holding Sinclair's hand on her other side as we made our way down the street.

My two vampire companions didn't burn in the sun. Didn't cower at the touch of iron or at the sight of the Christian crosses on churches we passed and around the necks of other pedestrians. The robust smell of garlic from a street vendor didn't phase them, though perhaps the scent was stronger, more pungent, given Sinclair's scrunched nose.

"We should put one on every block," Séra said, swinging their joined hands.

"We have enough to." Sinclair held the bundle of flyers in his free arm.

Admittedly, I paid less attention to the posting of the flyers. I watched the people on the street with a new set of eyes, inspecting each stranger through my glasses, wondering who was a vampire, hiding, and who was human? Was it obvious to Séra and Sinclair if we were to run into another inhuman creature? Or was it possible to blend in so completely that one could live wholly as a human, even if every cell in their body said differently?

And the humans—it felt strange to refer to them as such, but how else could I?—they were all the same, yet different. I saw now the twinge of grime at the hem of many girls' skirts; the worn cuffs of a man's coat; the stray mark of kohl at a woman's eye. I saw the tiredness pull down their eyelids, saw the sharp cheekbones hidden under rouge. Some with a glaze to their eyes, the telltale sign of an early drinker; some with blank, exhausted stares.

Perhaps I'd been ignorant to the strife of others before. My privilege gave me leave to spend away my days partying, dancing, living, while so many others—like Adam, so long ago—wasted away, slowly, beneath the surface. It was a fact I'd forgotten in our time apart.

No, not forgotten.

I knew. I knew what Adam went through. I knew how different his life was from mine, but I chose to ignore it, especially once he was taken from me. Preferred only to live at night, when only the shiny things caught the light.

Séra was pestering Sinclair for a treat, the sweet scent of cinnamon wafting down the block we walked. "I still love the taste of sugar," she argued, turning to me and winking. "Besides, Helena can enjoy it, too."

Sinclair grumbled and passed her a few coins.

As soon as they hit her palm, she was pulling me in the direction of the stand selling tarts, coated almonds, and pretzels. My mouth instantly turned watery, having forgotten how delectable some of the food on the street was.

"A cinnamon roll for me, please," she said to the vendor.

He looked at me as he began to wrap her pastry in paper.

"The same, please." I gave him a smile, but he didn't return it.

Séra dropped the coins into his palm—more than double the cost from the look of it, but the vendor didn't say anything, pocketing the change.

"Can you taste it?" I asked once we began to stroll away. Taking a bite, the sweetness spread across my tongue.

"Not like you can," she said, but she began to eat it anyway. "But I still have a soft spot for it." She linked her arm with mine again, and we began a slow stroll, in no hurry to join with Sinclair again. We could see him across the street, tacking a flyer to an electrical pole.

"You know, I had to eat human food when I worked at your house," she said.

It had never crossed my mind before. "I hope it wasn't too torturous."

She shrugged. "At first, it was unpleasant, but I found the more I did it, the more enjoyable it became." She took another bite of her cinnamon roll as though for proof. "If I ate nothing at the house, the cook would be suspicious."

As we neared Sinclair, he turned, spotting us amongst the crowd on the sidewalk. But then his eyes darkened. I could see even from as far as I was, and he started toward us, dropping a few flyers in his wake.

Séra turned and spotted what Sinclair had seen before I even knew what was going on.

"Not another step," she demanded, just as I was able to whirl around.

Dixon stood not five feet away from us. He stopped, rooting himself to the pavement, but his eyes were on me.

"Dixon?" His name tumbled dumbly from my lips.

"You should know better than to walk up on us like that," Séra hissed.

I felt Sinclair approach from behind, creating a barrier between me and the rest of the street. If something happened to me, Vince would have their heads, never mind that it was just Dixon.

He still didn't pay Sinclair any mind. "Why did you call Flora?" he asked me. Some shadow moved in his pupils. He was slightly ruffled, like he had run down the block to reach us, his jacket undone.

I sputtered for words. "I wanted to come over."

"Liar," he accused, but there was no venom in it. "What's going on?"

"This doesn't concern you," Séra said, stepping just slightly in front of me.

He turned to her then, his ire directed at her. "I think it does." His low voice dripped with warning, a flare to his nostrils, before he looked at me again. "Don't you dare bring any attention to her."

"What are you talking about?" I laughed, but it felt flat.

"Perhaps you've not paid any attention to the news lately, but mortals are going missing left and right. Why do I have a feeling it is because of Vince?"

My silence betrayed my confusion.

"That's something you'll have to take up with him," Sinclair said.

"Call off your *dogs*."

I stepped away from Séra and Sinclair, earning protests from both. "It's fine," I insisted. "Dixon won't hurt me."

I'd known him longer than the both of them, as it was. Never before had he done anything but stand guard for Flora and me while we enjoyed our evenings, driving us around, keeping us from trouble. But I knew to whom he was loyal, and this posturing just revealed his worry for Flora's safety.

Sinclair, after a moment, backed away, motioning for Séra to follow. She had dropped her pastry in the surprise of Dixon's appearance, the sugar now leaking onto the sidewalk.

"Thank you," Dixon said, swallowing and straightening his jacket as the two gave us a moment alone.

I waited until they were across the street once more— close enough to rush over if need be, but far enough to give us some semblance of privacy, likely still able to pick the conversation up amidst the noise of the street.

"What are you doing?" I turned to Dixon, hand on my hip.

"That's what I came to ask you," he seethed through his teeth, attempting to keep his voice low. "What is this about a huge party? And Flora can't come?"

"I thought you didn't want her at the manor, anyway."

"I don't." He ran his hands through his hair. "But you— Vince is planning something."

I grabbed his arm and pulled him toward a wall, throwing my pastry in a trash can. I couldn't tell him the truth while in the center of the crowd. Who knew who was listening?

"Marcel Brancato? Does that ring any bells?" I whispered, knowing he would hear me.

Dixon's eyes turned to slits. "If he's here, then he's the one killing mortals."

Mortals.

"How do you know?"

"He has a penchant for making a mess," he grumbled, and with one sentence, I had so many questions. "He's come to collect Vince, then?"

"You must know." I looked at him directly.

This vampire was not as disconnected from Vince's world as he'd like me to think. And if he knew Brancato...

Hesitation. "Andreas?"

When I nodded, he cursed under his breath. "So you're throwing a huge party to draw Brancato's attention?"

I crossed my arms. "Who are you, Lloyd Dixon?"

"You sound like my mother."

I gave him a look.

"You're involved; I know you are. Do all vampires just nose around in each other's business, or do you have some hand in this?"

His narrowed eyes showed his disgust at being associated with them—but another hesitation, and I knew it was true.

He pressed his lips together tightly. Debating what to reveal.

I threw my hands up in the air in exasperation. "You men! Telling your little half-truths! You know, keeping things from me, from Flora, is only going to put us in danger. We're mortals." I threw the word back at him. "We can't protect ourselves if we don't know what's after us."

His resolve broke. "I was sent here to watch Vince. By

my own... coven," he said through gritted teeth. "His Sire has caused a lot of problems for us."

Of course he had a coven, a den, whatever they were called, back in England. He was Born—his whole family must be vampires, then. "Your coven. Do you... are you the heir?"

He looked annoyed. "No, I am not. Which is why *I* was sent."

"A brother, then."

"Does it matter?" He looked around, as though worried passersby would hear. "I was sent because of Vince, and because of Andreas. He wants to establish a sort of royal hierarchy for our kind, of course, with himself at the top." Another pause. "Though my family claims their line runs even older."

Vampire politics. Something I hadn't considered.

"And he wants Vince back? Why, when Brancato is right there?"

Dixon shook his head. "It's not about either of them. It's the fact that Vince refused and defected. His Sire still claims ownership, but Vince has refused. And many of the vampires across the oceans are starting to take notice."

A weight settled in my stomach. Glancing across the street, I saw Sinclair leaning against a building, staring at us with his arms crossed. Séra had disappeared.

"Not many stand up to their Sires and survive," Dixon said from beside me.

"So, you must help us." I faced him again. "Go to the party. I'll be with Flora, at her house. We'll be safe there."

Dixon took a deep breath, one that he didn't need, and peered over at Sinclair with furrowed brows. Perhaps thinking about the company he'd have to keep tomorrow night. The Made vampire across the street smiled sharply.

"Please," I whispered, holding onto Dixon's arm. "It's going to come down to one or the other. Brancato can't win. He—they can't have him back."

"Have you ever seen vampires fight before, Helena?" Dixon said absently, still watching Sinclair, almost with curiosity.

I shook my head.

"Be glad you haven't."

FORTY-TWO

Grim finality loomed over the manor, skies turning streaked with clouds, gray and heavy. Exhaustion weighed on me and my companions. The entire ride was silent.

I had told Sinclair that Dixon promised to help, and when Séra appeared, insisting she'd never been far, they looked to each other, and something passed between them. Sinclair ushered us back into the car, parked a few blocks away, the driver waiting.

And when we returned, Vince was watching us come up the drive. His eyes met mine through the window, and he was there before I could step out, opening the door and offering a hand.

He whisked me away upstairs, where we fell into each other, and as he kissed me, I couldn't help but feel like he did this as though it were the last time.

His lips lingered on mine, savoring the feel of us together. Holding me close, he gazed at every inch of me, hands tracing every curve of my hips, my breasts. Giving me pleasure and memorizing every detail.

We did that all afternoon, and when I was sore and spent, he rolled off of me and ran his fingers through my hair, down my sides, lazily stroking and sending goosebumps across my flesh.

We lay facing each other, a sheen of sweat on my skin, his long hair mussed and ruined. Even then, he studied me, running a finger over my lips, caressing my cheek.

"I ran into Dixon today," I said quietly, afraid to disrupt the calm silence we'd settled into.

His fingers paused before resuming their ministrations, a muscle in his cheek flexing, but he said nothing.

"He's going to help."

Vince nodded.

"He told me about his coven. The conflict with... Andreas'." I almost said, "yours," but realized how much of a mistake that would be. It was not Vince's coven. He had left, for a reason, even if he didn't tell me the whole of it.

"I suppose another set of hands is a good idea," he acquiesced.

Vince pulled me closer, wrapping his arms around me, so our chests met. He buried his face in my neck, his nose drawing circles on my throat, placing kisses at that spot under my ear. And though we'd made love already, his touch sent excitement through my veins.

I buried a hand in his hair, holding him to me.

"You should feed," I whispered. It had been a few days since the last time, and he hadn't asked since then.

He shook his head against me, but didn't pull away,

breathing in deeply the scent of my flesh, right where my heartbeat pulsed against my skin.

I pressed him again. *"Please."*

With a groan, he gave in, his tongue lapping at my throat, before drawing the thin flesh into his mouth. I arched against him, tugging on his hair as his teeth pierced my skin.

There was no longer any fear when I had the maw of a monster at my neck. The line between pain and ecstasy was paper-thin, a nervousness so exciting. Pleasure taken and pleasure given.

He clung to me as he drank, his arousal growing hard between my thighs. I hitched a leg over his hip, wanting him closer, wanting him to take all of me, again and again, until there was nothing left.

I sighed as my vision grew fuzzy with the gratifying light-headedness of his drinking. And when he was satisfied, pulling away, his lips were dark with my blood, his pupils blown and dark. I tasted myself on his tongue, tightening my fingers in his hair.

He eased himself into me, my center ready for him, the muscles sore but wanting. He slid home with ease until our hips were flush. I ached with how much I wanted him, our bodies sliding together so perfectly. Laid out on the bed, I had no energy to do much else other than receive him, limp against silky sheets.

"You belong to me," he whispered, falling over me, spreading my legs wider.

A low moan erupted from my chest. In moments, I was panting, yearning for air, my climax barreling toward its peak before I could stop it. I came shuddering against him, my muscles clenching around him, and he groaned in approval, thrusting deeply, harshly.

He spilled inside of me moments later, cock twitching, hips snapped to mine, exhaling roughly in my ear. Murmured praise, my name at his lips, teasing my jaw with his tongue.

"Loving you has been the greatest torture," he breathed, "and my greatest feat." He sucked on the sensitive skin on my neck before groaning and grinding into me once more. My back arched off the bed.

"And you will have an eternity to do it," I sighed.

He hummed, and when he pulled away from me, leaving me empty, there was a look in his eyes that only later I realized was his goodbye.

FORTY-THREE

Within an hour, a bag was packed for me, sent to the driver waiting outside.

Sundown was coming, the bright blue of the afternoon fading into a watercolor of hues. In the time Vince and I spent upstairs, the servants had begun stringing up decorations, setting up a huge buffet-like feast in the center of the ballroom. Enough food to feed an army.

Entertainers shuffled in, the newcomers staring up in awe at the swirling demons and angels, the ones who'd been here before moving on without a glance. Even without any guests, the house still buzzed with energy; so many people milling about and working in anticipation of the thousands we expected this evening.

I let Vince usher me outside without a fight. Pressed my lips to his in a lingering kiss, not wanting to pull away. That beast was pacing, waiting to snap.

And when the driver pulled up in front of Flora's house, the sun nearly below the horizon, I told him to wait there.

His eyes widened in confusion for a moment, but he couldn't refuse, couldn't make his way back to the manor just yet.

Vince had said his servants were mine to command.

Flora opened the door before I had a chance to knock, golden light spilling onto the street. Dressed in her evening gown, a soft rosy dress, with her evening robe and slippers. The smell of dinner wafted onto the doorstep.

She gave me a skeptical look. "You know I am always open to you coming over," she said. "You will always be welcome here, but—are you sure you're okay?"

I stepped past the threshold, shooting one last glance at the driver to make sure he didn't leave.

"I'm perfectly fine."

Over the phone, I had told her everything she needed to know—that Vince was throwing a huge party, and though I knew she would want to come, seeing that *invitations* were posted everywhere, I needed her to stay home, where she was safe. That Vince thought maybe some dangerous people would show up at an open invite, and he didn't even want *me* there. So I needed to stay the night.

I set my overnight bag down after she shut the door.

Flora's eyes narrowed. "You look suspicious."

"Because I'm not staying."

The clink of cutlery, her parents dining, twinkled down the hall, the soft murmur of voices.

Flora, hands on her hips, raised a brow. But it took only a moment for a grin to pull at her lips.

"Will you help me get ready?"

"Is that a question?" She grabbed me, pulling me toward the stairs, up to her bedroom. The same childhood bedroom we gossiped over boys, the same bedroom we cried over things that now seemed so frivolous.

"Let's make you so stunning that he won't think twice about jumping on you," she said, a sparkle in her eyes.

We were never very good at listening to what our men told us to do.

How I managed to sneak one of the sequined evening dresses into my overnight bag without anyone noticing, I don't know. But as I donned the dress, the fabric a midnight black, the skirt barely reaching my thighs, exhilaration coursed through me.

Knowing what I was about to do. Knowing *who* was going to be there.

Flora whistled as I turned in front of the mirror.

"I think he'll forgive you," she said.

"I hope so," I grumbled. The dress fit like a glove, the beads scintillating in the lamplight of her room as I turned. It hardly covered my curves. "Maybe I need stockings."

"Less is better." She grinned. "We should've been wearing dresses like this the whole time."

"If my mother ever found a dress like this in my wardrobe, I'd be forbidden from ever leaving," I said, smoothing my hands down my front, feeling the ridges of the beads under my fingers.

"You were," she deadpanned, patting the seat in front of her vanity.

In a few moments, she was applying all sorts of makeup to my face, lining my eyes darker than she ever had before, accentuating the rich, dark color of my irises. Penciling in my brows. Setting my hair in waves.

"I still can't believe I can't go," Flora grumbled after she finished applying rouge to my lips. She took a step back to admire her handiwork, fingers at my chin, moving me this way and that.

"Dixon would kill me," I said.

She rolled her eyes. "Yes, he's been quite stuffy lately," she huffed, capping the tube of lipstick she'd used. She quirked her lips before grabbing some powder and a brush. "Maybe if I dress sexy enough, he'll forgive me."

"*I* wouldn't forgive *myself* if something happened to you," I said.

"If it's as dangerous as you say, then why not stay?"

"Because," I frowned. "It's my house now, too."

She sighed, shaking her head. "I can't believe I've been banned from my best friend's house."

I stood and wrapped my arms around her. "Just for tonight," I said. "Besides, you have a hand in this plot—if anyone asks, I'm here with *you*."

FORTY-FOUR

The drive back to the manor took longer than I was expecting, the traffic over the bridges doubled this evening. The sky above us sparkled with a thousand stars, flickering like electric bulbs about to go out, their brightness only increasing the further from the city we drove.

"Drop me off here," I said once we pulled into the drive.

I couldn't even count the amount of people on the lawn. Even this close to the gates, groups of partygoers crowded the long gravel drive, all adorned in costumes, their best dresses, faces obscured by elaborate masks. Some in costume, red queens and jesters and a few even in gowns harkening eras long ago. There were a few faces who'd already lost their masks, their cheeks red from the alcohol they'd consumed, eyes shining.

The driver looked displeased as he stopped the car, worry bunching in his brows. Perhaps the most emotion I'd ever seen from one of the servants—Made vampires—in Vince's employ. Though, I suppose he *was* going against direct orders Vince had given him.

Without a mask of my own, I felt naked on the lawn of the house. I couldn't deny the fear that was creeping up, that Marcel Brancato was here and would find me before I could even *see* him, or one of his goons, if he had any.

That was the frightening part—we just didn't know what to expect tonight. It's what had Vince so on edge. What had me glancing over my shoulder, over and over again.

I weaved my way through the crowd, heels crunching in the gravel. I felt their eyes—following me as they always did, but this time, it seemed I couldn't escape anyone's attention, being maskless, and almost as unclothed as the entertainers up in the house. My identity fully on show.

A few men tried to catch my eye, grinning, their eyes shadowed by their masks. Every single one of them could be with Marcel. Could be waiting for the right moment to—

"Hey."

The voice came from right beside me. I nearly jumped from my skin as a lithe hand grabbed my arm, whirling me around.

Veronica eyed my dress, frowning at the way the beads skimmed the tops of my thighs. "Not so subtle, huh?"

I rolled my eyes, wrenching my arm away. "I thought I was bait."

She sighed and motioned for me to follow. "You'll certainly catch his attention."

Him.

Not Vince.

We continued on, pushing through the crowd as we

neared the house. It stood bright against the pitch-dark sky, the stars hardly even visible once within the glow of the lights. The drive was packed, luxury cars of every brand parked in a line all the way to the gates. Servants were already making their rounds, even this far down the lawn, their trays filled with champagne glasses, stacked in perfect pyramids, not a drop spilled on the grass.

The only thing I could think, seeing all these people, was Vince's warning that *there will be blood*. "Is he here yet?" I whispered.

She glanced at me out of the corner of her eyes, a line of concentration between her brows. "Not yet."

She carried a handbag and pulled a black mask out from within, reaching up and tying the ribbon at the back of my head. It only obscured half my face, my painted lips still exposed to the air. Decorated like a Venetian mask, with a lacy applique over the velvety material.

"Where's Vince?"

"Inside. Brooding."

She was the only one—besides Flora, now—that knew I was here. Vince had been so against my presence tonight, but I knew, *I knew*, the best way to grab Marcel's attention, the best way to distract him, was to offer myself for the taking. Draw him into a corner, and let the others take care of him.

She didn't need much convincing when I told her my plan.

Tonight she was wearing a deep blue dress, cut off right above the knee. Not as flashy as mine, but stylishly devastating all the same. A deep V at her chest, her long limbs on full display. Her makeup looked like she'd just walked off a stage.

"Sinclair? Séra?"

Her eyes slid to me. "Partying."

There was a blood party this evening, if anything, so that Vince's Made vampires were close by—newly Made, and other vampires in the area here just to get a taste. Back up, should we need it.

"We're going through the front door?" We were approaching the colonnade, strings of lights leading to the gardens, almost like the stripes of a circus tent. Music spilled out onto the lawn from inside, the massive front doors propped open. Even the servers wore masks, simple, single-toned eye masks, that helped them blend in.

"*You* are going through the front door," she said, stopping at the bottom of the steps. "I'm staying out here."

"But—" I glanced at the doors, at the crowd within, knowing the Vince and the others were inside, and if they saw me before Brancato came—

"Don't be so scared." Veronica glanced me up and down once more. "It doesn't suit you."

I straightened my shoulders at that.

She gave me a nod, satisfied at what she saw in me. "We've got you," she said over her shoulder, a bit softer this time, as she turned to go. The first time I'd seen any softness from her.

And with her words, I steeled myself, and stepped foot once more into the manor. Ready to bait a vampire who lusted for my blood.

FORTY-FIVE

The party raging within was like nothing I'd seen before. The previous affairs had been rowdy displays of opulence, a peek into some mythical, palatial world. A chance for the common man to feel like a god. Tonight was a bacchanal.

As though stepping past the threshold once more into a veiled otherworld, a sort of haze settled around the foyer, a sweet smokiness that I couldn't decide was real or in my head.

Something about being unable to discern anyone's identities was frightening and thrilling. If I were just a simple partygoer, I'd revel in it, finding a man to pull into a corner somewhere, without taking off our masks, knowing that tomorrow his name would still be a mystery. And plenty of people were doing just that—alcoves full of small groups of huddling people, deep in conversation, some with only couples, mouths fused together, in compromising positions. Like something out of *A Midsummer Night's Dream*, with their elaborate costumes, a sense of wonder permeating the room.

The room was so full, I wasn't sure how I'd make it into the ballroom, or even further into the house.

There was no way that none of Lucas' men were here, either. Friends of his who would know my face could cash in for that million-dollar reward.

My only saving grace was *my* mask, but I wasn't sure that would hide me from Marcel. I'd dined with him, long enough he probably knew my scent. He seemed to that afternoon he'd come to the manor, stopping in his tracks.

His grin still sent shivers through me, nothing like the man I'd met that first night at the speakeasy.

But I needed that smile pointed at me tonight. Needed him to think he could have me, just long enough for Vince's rage to turn deadly.

He'd said he would kill for me—would that promise ring true tonight?

I shoved my way through the room, the heat of the bodies bringing a dampness under the mask at my eyes. That haze didn't help, making the room seem smaller than it was. The crowd closing in on me, the air becoming thick.

In the ballroom, deep emerald sheets hung from the ceiling, like the trunks of trees. Vines hung from the beams. A few girls twisted through them, their limbs tangled in the sheets, flipping through the air like they were flying. They beamed at the partygoers below them, wearing floral masks, soaring through as though they had wings.

Flora would be delighted.

When all of this was over, after we all had a chance to breathe, I would insist on throwing another party like this.

The decorators had turned the house into a faux forest, a mythical dreamscape that made me want to do nothing but waste the hours away, drunk with Vince under a willow tree.

Just like we used to.

A quick glance up at the balcony revealed no familiar faces, just the masks and costumes of strangers, downing champagne, spilling gin over the railing.

If he saw me before Marcel did, this whole thing would go up in flames.

But a part of me wanted Vince to find me, to turn that beast onto me. I wanted to forget all about the task at hand. I was betraying him—I had *lied* to him—and I was putting myself into danger, all to fuel his fury, entrap Marcel, and release his wrath onto our enemy.

I just needed to get upstairs, where I could pull Marcel into the room Veronica and I had talked about. He must be wandering around. Or he would, soon. And he needed to find me.

He would find me. He had been frenzied for a taste.

It wouldn't be that hard, it just needed to go according to plan.

I took a deep breath, letting the oxygen settle into my limbs, clearing out all the anxiety in my chest, before I shoved into the crowd of the dancefloor.

There were some revelers that danced, though most were staring at the entertainment, the girls in leotards defying gravity. The sheets ruffled like waves as they skimmed the crowd. The band began to play a popular song, and the crowd shifted, girls pulling their partners to the middle of the floor.

And in the shift, I saw a pair of dark eyes staring right at me.

No.

No.

Not yet—I hadn't even made it upstairs—He wasn't supposed to *be here yet*—

I shoved against bodies with more strength, ignoring shouts of indignation when I pushed a girl's drink into her chest.

I needed to get away from the crowd, to lure Marcel elsewhere—

"Miss Helena Quintrell," his cloying voice came from behind me, sweet saccharine and brandy.

I froze.

Fuck.

There was a lump in my throat as I took another breath to center myself. *Okay. It's fine. Just convince him to follow you.*

Did Veronica know he'd come in? Did the others? Were they hunting him down right at this moment?

So much could go wrong.

When I turned to face him, he looked exactly as I expected: impeccably dressed, a pin-stripe suit pressed and ironed, his loose collar a stark white against his skin, though he had discarded his tie somewhere. Dark hair gelled back, his deep irises shining as they took me in. I could feel them creeping down my legs, catching on the curve of my hips, up my chest. Gaze lingering on my throat. Unmasked.

Marcel was a beautiful man, and it was a wonder I hadn't fallen into his trap when I first met him.

I swallowed. "Marcel."

"Fancy seeing you here," he purred, staring at my neck, his bloodlust darkening his eyes.

"How did you know it was me?"

"I'd know you anywhere." We were inches apart.

My eyes narrowed. What was his plan tonight? He had to have one.

"Care to dance?" he asked, offering me his hand.

Everything within me recoiled, knowing *what* he was, what he wanted—from me, from Vince. Yet, at the same time, I forced myself to ignore the strength in his cheekbones, the charming way his hair fell around his ear. Like the girl within me saw him for face-value, his attractiveness—or maybe it was the fact that he was a predator, and I knew I was within his grasp. A certain primal part of me told me to get close, to let myself be taken.

Give up the fight and maybe I'd make it out alive.

Make him believe it. Bring him upstairs.

Without a word, I placed my hand in his. I couldn't corner him if I didn't play the part. Even if he made my skin crawl in more ways than one.

"Why the frown?" he asked, though he grinned as he pulled me closer, my breasts against his chest, his arm around my waist. I gasped at the sudden movement. "I haven't put you off, have I?"

"You're awfully comfortable—"

"Yes," he said, dark eyes intense as they skimmed my face, my neck, my collarbones. His nose coming so close to mine. "You inspire a comfort in me, Miss Helena. I quite like holding you to me. *Feeling* you."

My frown turned to a scowl, no matter how much I resisted or tried to act like he didn't disgust me.

He only laughed.

"Don't get too used to it," I said.

"Why? Because of your loyalty to Vince?" There was a delighted arch to his brow. His cool hand wrapped around my own, his grip strong. He pulled me into a sway, pressing our bodies closer, his chest hard against mine.

I truly was trapped by him now, his arm caging me against him. And it was so different from the way Vince held me, the way Vince pressed our bodies together. I glanced around the room, hoping to spot his familiar face somewhere, or Dixon's—*someone*.

"Worried he'll see you dancing with another?" His voice was low, lilting, not the least bit concerned.

Hoping he sees me with you.

"I noticed an interesting letter in the paper the other day," Marcel mused, whirling me around, moving us so quickly I couldn't stay steady on my feet. Solely dependent on him to keep me upright. His hand tightened at my hip.

My stomach was in knots. I grit my teeth. "And?"

"A million dollars." He leaned in closer, his breath hot against my ear. "That's a lot of money, *Helena Quintrell*." He said my last name like it was damning.

I looked him right in the eyes. "You don't need a million dollars."

"No?" He laughed again, the sound deceptively endearing. "How would you know? Have you been doing some research on me? Maybe I'm dirt poor. Maybe I was once a printer in another life."

A flicker of anger sparked, the emotions threatening to bubble up. Marcel knew what he was doing. He'd been doing *his* research.

And if he knew Lucas, too, I was done for.

Marcel sighed dramatically. "His poor parents. And they didn't even know he was alive."

My stomach dropped.

"Well, alive as could be."

I searched the crowd for Veronica, for *anyone*. One of them had to know I was here by now.

But the balcony above was all masked partygoers. The servers couldn't even weave through the crowd, staying to the outside of the dancefloor, watching with clear, emotionless expressions. None of them noticed me, either.

"Once I revealed the truth to them," he leaned in closer again, his lips brushing my ear, "they were devastated. How could their son rise to the top and leave them behind? How could he be *so rich* and leave them so poor?"

I swore I felt his tongue on my ear, sending chills down through my shoulders, down my spine. I shut my eyes against the sensation, against the brightness of the room, the racing of my heart.

"Don't worry, Helena," he whispered again, his hands tight on me.

His fangs were so close. He could bite me and no one could do anything about it.

"I relieved them of their problem," he said. "They don't have to worry anymore."

Bile rose in my throat.

Then, he really did press his lips to my neck. I cried out, the sound swallowed by the cacophony of the party. Shoving against him with all my strength, I tried to wrench myself away, but he didn't budge, his grip on me too strong.

He'd bite me and drain me.

He had looked at me with such bloodlust before. He would do it with glee.

"Relax," he breathed. "Your heart is beating a mile a minute." He traced his nose along my jaw, against my cheek. Such an intimate caress, one I'd felt over and over again from Vince—the way he'd press his face into my neck as though to cement himself to me.

"Have I ever harmed you?"

I clenched my jaw so hard I thought I'd hear a crack. "Not *yet.*"

"Have I been nothing but truthful to you?" he murmured, speaking against the flesh of my throat.

To anyone else, it just appeared like he was kissing me, kissing my neck. No one would be the wiser. No one likely even noticed, caught up in their own dancing, the other women too preoccupied with the men holding them, the men too preoccupied with the girls in their arms.

None of them knew they were rubbing shoulders with a vampire.

He could pull himself away from me and turn on any one of them in a split second.

There were probably other vampires in the crowd. Some of *his* allies.

If I ran, would I even be able to lose him? Or would a stranger dig their nails into my arm just for him to catch me again?

"You don't know me." I forced myself to speak.

"But I want to." His leg came between mine, my bare thighs against his clothed ones, his arm around me, crushing me to him. "You're right, I don't need a million dollars. I think I'll just keep you for myself."

"*Let go.*" The words came out of me in hardly more than a whisper.

"Why, so you can go running back to your boyfriend?"

"You don't want me."

"Playing hard to get isn't going to go in your favor." His voice darkened. "What does he do for you, anyway? He came back to America years ago, and it took him this long to get you back? Has he told you the truth? Has he told you everything?"

"Let *go*," I insisted, pushing against him, however futile.

"Didn't you know that he's been paying Lucas off?" Marcel said in my ear.

I froze.

I felt the exhale of a chuckle on my throat. His hands tightening on me, one hand curling into my hair.

"Didn't you know *Vince* is the one that told Lucas to marry you off?"

Something in my chest broke. "You're lying."

Marcel pulled away, just enough for me to see the glint in his eye, the grin plastered on his face. "Why would I lie to you, my dear? *I* am not a liar."

He brushed some hair out of my face, pulling the mask off. He threw it to the floor, where it was immediately crushed under feet. The people around us moved about as though we weren't even there—never bumping into us, giving us a sort of privacy in their midst.

"Why would he do that?" My hands shook against Marcel's chest.

"Didn't you know he's been threatening your family all along?" he continued, sneering, enjoying this.

I shook my head. It couldn't be true.

How would he know?

He's lying, he's just trying to get you to run away with him—

I didn't want to be here anymore. I couldn't breathe, my lungs feeling shallow.

Movement above. A shock of auburn hair at the balcony. I almost cried out in relief, the sob pulled from me involuntarily at the sight of him.

Vince stood there, like he did my first night here, when he found me—*he found me*—amongst a crowd and zeroed in like he only had eyes for me.

Only this time, cold fury hardened his face. Hands gripping the banister so tight I thought I saw them splinter. He wore no mask, either—for once standing out against his partygoers, instead of blending in.

He watched Marcel cling to me, hands wandering. A crack to his visage, and whatever he kept locked up within himself, nearly came spilling out, teeth bared.

There's always collateral.

My cold companion chuckled, pressing his face to mine, gripping my jaw so we both gazed up at the second level, at the enraged vampire standing there.

"Look at that. We've been caught."

The rest had to be nearby. Séra, Dixon—Veronica would stop Marcel if we got outside—

But Veronica was supposed to let someone know Marcel was here. She was supposed to be guarding entry from the front door, waiting to see him creep up. And she hadn't. He could've come in another way, but why do that just to join the fray in the main rooms?

Unless he didn't mean to face Vince here. He planned on getting out.

"Ah, he's angry." Marcel spoke with the same tone from the afternoon he came to taunt Vince.

It had been a matter of seconds, but felt like forever. Vince stared as though he couldn't believe what he saw. Icy gray eyes taking in the scene—his *human* lover in the hands of one of his enemies—before he took in the rest of the room. I saw it in his eyes: he wanted to just jump down from the second story, to get to us quicker.

I wished I could shout loud enough for him to hear me, to wait, to not do anything too rash—

His teeth were out, glinting bright white against his skin, almost bristling like an animal.

He looked at me, to *me*, for a moment, the message clear, before he turned and ran.

"No!"

"We only have so long now," Marcel said in my ear. He began to move us, whirling me around but keeping an arm around my waist. It didn't take long for me to realize we were heading back to the front door.

I dug my heels into the floor. "Wait!"

It did nothing against his inhuman strength, moving me like I was a rag doll and weighed nothing.

My heels only skidded along the floor, leaving scuffs that would be gone by sunrise. The people dancing around us, the human crowd, parted for Marcel and me, none of them looking at us. Like we weren't even there.

None of them were looking.

No one noticed my struggle.

"Wait!" I shouted again, digging my fingers into the arm around my waist.

This was going so, *horribly* wrong.

Vince couldn't take him on, one-to-one, I couldn't bear to see it—

If Vince died—

Marcel laughed, glancing behind his shoulder, eyes focusing on something I couldn't see. His fangs were on full display, those sharp teeth that had been seconds from puncturing my flesh.

When he looked at me again, his pupils were pinpricks. Crazed, like the madman he was.

"Do you not like being in my arms?" he asked. He didn't move any quicker, almost as though he was unbothered by the chase. Oozing a confidence that made me nervous, a darkness souring my tongue. "You're not trying very hard."

How had the evening turned this way?

It was supposed to be simple—I would lead him into a suite, and Vince and the others would be there, and Vince would take care of it. Marcel was supposed to be *dead*. But with every step closer to the front door, my heart picked up pace, rattling in my chest, telling me to *get out of here*.

"Interesting how no one else comes to your rescue," Marcel said, but the way he said it made my blood freeze in my veins.

What had he done?

"Let go of me!" I growled, unable to even touch my feet to the ground.

"And Lloyd Dixon is here, too," Marcel went on, dragging me past the threshold into the foyer. The devils above watched on, grinning at the devil who had his arms around me. All the while, the rest of the party went on like nothing was happening. Bursts of laughter all around me, lovers embracing, drunken carousing, with little care for the girl being dragged away against her will.

"Where's his gal, that beautiful blonde?"

My head snapped up at that, staring daggers into Marcel. "If you touch her—"

"I don't need to."

He had pulled me all the way to the front door. Vince was still somewhere inside, no one else coming to my rescue.

I searched the crowd, pleading with every god in my head that Vince would appear.

I had walked right into a fucking trap.

"I don't need to hurt your little friend, because you're going to come with me without a fight." Marcel looked at me in seriousness, the deadly side of him seeping through his gaze. Eyes flickering to my neck once more, the tip of his tongue tracing a route along his lips. A threat. "If you come with me, Vince and your friend will be safe. I'll leave them alone."

I wanted to scream. To bash my fists against his face.

"You won't be able to get me out of this house," I said, hoping he saw how much I hated him. How much *I* wanted to kill him. A heat lined my eyes, watery anger threatening to spill. "You're outnumbered."

Marcel grinned one last time. It was almost a sad, curious smile, like he expected more from me. "That's where you're wrong."

And we were invisible to the crowd.

We were at the front door, the heat of the manor escaping in a breeze to the outside. As people walked out, just as many, if not more, walked in. Only dozens of minutes ago I'd been standing right here, ready to take this *creature* on, and somehow, everything had gone so wrong.

"Ah, there he is!"

Like Marcel was greeting a friend.

But it was Dixon who stood before us, blocking the exit to the outside.

I shouted his name, the sound swallowed up by the crowd.

His glare was tangible, his loathing for the vampire clear. "Marcel." His lip curled, his own fang daring to peek out of his lips. But he didn't move. Rooted to the spot.

Marcel paused in his steps. His fingers gripped my hips. "What will it be, Dixon?"

"Do something!" The tears threatened to spill over.

His eyes slid to me, and he faltered for a moment—just long enough for me to see that hesitation. But he didn't move. Rooted to the spot.

He was holding himself back.

"*Dixon!*"

I had to be going crazy. *Why wasn't he doing anything?*

And then all my breath, all my fight, left me as he stepped to the side.

"Dixon, I will *never* forgive you," I cried, wet tracks staining my cheeks. Beating against Marcel's body, my fists smashing into his hold on me.

Dixon's eyes flashed, his resolve cracking. His hands were in fists at his sides.

"How *could* you?"

"Oh, hush now." Marcel pushed me to keep moving.

Not a person turned their head.

"I had no choice." Dixon's nostrils flared. "He threatened Flora." And he watched as Marcel marched me right past him. Doing nothing to stop the vampire from taking me away.

No, no, no, no, no—

A shout came from the crowd behind us.

"*Brancato!*"

Vince emerged with all the fury of a vengeful god, shoving bodies out of his way as he stormed toward us.

I didn't recognize him. His eyes had turned so dark, they were almost wholly black. His veins had darkened, deep indigo webs at his neck, his hands. I blinked—surely my eyes were playing tricks. The frenzy of the evening, I was seeing things, surely—

"Your fight is with *me*, not her, Marcel." Hands fisted at his sides as he stalked closer.

This was the beast that looked out at me through those eyes.

This was the beast that came back for me.

This was the beast I loved.

I reached for him, hand outstretched over Marcel's shoulder. "Vince!"

We were outside, on the front step, moving further and further away—

In a flurry of movement, Dixon was suddenly on top of Vince, wrestling him to the ground.

I screamed, watching Vince's body hit the floor with a sickening *thud*.

He bared his teeth, all that rage directed at the one man. He punched and clawed and there was blood everywhere, spatter flying away from the fight, landing on other guests, who cried out at the fight.

But Dixon was a Born vampire and had about twenty years on Vince.

In moments he had Vince in a headlock, arm wrapped tight around my lover's neck from behind. Vince kicked at the ground, clawed hands tearing at Dixon's arms.

So much blood.

"How could you?" I sobbed, even though Dixon couldn't hear me, my vision growing blurry.

Marcel pulled me away, turning, so he blocked the view with his body. He rolled his eyes at my tears as he led me away. I wanted to collapse, to fall to the ground and let it swallow me whole, but he kept me upright, dragging me on.

"You'll learn that love is dangerous," he said with grim finality. "It forces your hand."

FORTY-SIX

Marcel hauled me away from the house, ignoring my cries, my curses.

No one around us batted an eye as he dragged me down to the lawn, around the gravel drive leading up to the house. The gravel gave me something to dig my heels into. I kicked out my legs, no longer caring if anyone saw up my skirt.

I had no idea what Dixon would do to Vince.

I had to get Marcel's hands off of me, had to get back to Dixon and Vince, to stop their fight—

"Cut it out," he hissed, adjusting his grip, hoisting me higher so I couldn't reach the ground anymore. The good humor he had earlier was gone. His face morphed back into the serious, self-important man I knew before. Deadly contempt in his eyes, that flash of lust that zeroed in on my throat.

"What did you do?" I pleaded, squirming, trying to twist in his arms, to make him lose his balance. The words coming again and again in succession, begging for the truth. *What did you do, what did you do, what did you do?*

Whatever he had said inside—it had to be a lie. Lies to make me stop in my tracks, to doubt Vince.

None of it made sense.

My heart raced, my breathing coming in quick, shallow gasps.

Where was Marcel taking me?

He was going to hide me away, and no one will be able to find me.

What is he going to do to me?

"Nothing that no one shouldn't have seen coming." He glared at me, lip curled, before he stooped down and threw me onto his shoulder.

The world turned upside down. Another scream was ripped from me.

Slumped along the veranda around the house, in her deep blue dress, was Veronica. Her head hung back, throat exposed, eyes half-shut. Looking just like all the other drunk men asleep on the lawn by the end of the evening.

"What did you do to her?!"

I scrambled to get to her, beating my fists at his back, but it was like punching a brick wall.

"Had my new friend Dixon help," Marcel said, like it was nothing. "Convinced him to slip some poison into the blood supply earlier this evening."

Oh my god.

Was she dead?

A sob sputtered forth from me. "Take me back!" My anger pushed through the tears ruining my makeup, throwing as much power as I could into my fists.

If I let him take me somewhere, I'd never come back.

He'd drain my blood and kill me—for what? For his own enjoyment? Revenge?

And if Veronica was dead, did that mean—

"What do you want?" I insisted, his shoulder blocking enough air from filling my lungs. An ache began in my skull, a pounding at the base of my neck.

I couldn't see his face, couldn't see where he was taking me. But he turned his head, and his lips were brushing my thighs, his exhalations warm in the cool night air, and I almost screamed again. One arm was wrapped around my knees, keeping me still.

He made my skin crawl.

"I've told you what I want," he said, voice deep. A loud inhalation. "*You.*"

"You want my blood?" I cried. "Just take it!"

I wanted this *over* with. We never should've done this. I shouldn't have come. It was almost like Marcel knew I was on my way; he knew just what to do to ruin the night.

I felt him shake his head. "I don't want just your blood, sweet Helena." Though his hot breath on my flesh said otherwise.

And then, a gate creaked on its hinges, a loud groan into the night. He walked within, and in a moment I knew where we were.

But why was he taking me into the garden?

To bury me amongst the headstones?

For a brief second, I hoped whatever he planned stopped here. At least someone would be able to find me eventually.

A few guests milled about, smoking cigarettes and speaking in hushed tones. None glanced our way. From where I was hanging, the moonflowers bloomed above me, the sky an ocean below.

I wanted to sink.

I wanted to let go.

I needed to get back to Vince.

"Where are we going?" Trying to right myself, to stop the rush of blood to my head while I hung, I pushed against his back. The strength in my arms faltered, a dizziness from hanging, breathing too quickly.

But Marcel didn't answer.

His footsteps scuffed along the stone path, taking me deeper and deeper into the flora of the graveyard. The headstones watched as I was carried helplessly amongst them.

I cried out to a few of the other people—shouting to get their attention, but they shied away, turning to their drinks, their cigarettes. They couldn't even look at me, couldn't even bring themselves to bear witness to my anguish.

Veronica might be dead, Vince was being beaten by Dixon, and who knew what happened to Séra and Sinclair?

I growled in frustration, wiping the tears at my eyes, not caring how streaked my face became. "If you don't put me down, I'm going to scream." My voice wavered.

"Please do it, dear," he said, fingers tightening on the back of my knee. "No one will hear it but me. It'd be music to my ears."

"Just—put me down!"

I needed to get back. Needed to get back to Vince.

As he walked, the partygoers became sparse, until eventually I couldn't see anyone, just the huge sycamore trees and the night flowers bobbing in the breeze, going on as if nothing was amiss this night.

But I had been taken by a vampire—Vince's enemy—and I had no idea what he wanted with me.

The path was familiar. I'd walked this way a few times now.

He came to a stop right before a vine- and moss-covered wall. Bending over to set me down, once my feet touched the ground, a dizzying rush of air filled my lungs—and suddenly I was against the wall, cornered by a fanged predator.

Marcel's eyes shone in the moonlight.

He stared at me for a moment, and I couldn't stop the tremble to my hands, fisting them against his chest. He leaned close, one hand on either side of my head. A glance down to my lips, the smudged rouge there.

"Would you really give yourself up for him?"

"What?" I was breathless, trying to calm my racing heart while keeping him at bay.

His dark hair shined with gel, the white of his collared shirt luminous under the moon. "Would you *really* give yourself up for him?" He inspected me, like the answers were there in my eyes. "Would you really sacrifice yourself for Vince? After everything he's done?"

I shook my head, willing fresh tears away. "I don't know what you're talking about."

Marcel hummed. Waited a moment longer. Then moved back, just an inch. "Pity."

Leaning back into the wall, I tried to put as much space between us as possible. The leaves on either side of my head crunched as he tightened his hands, crushing the vines. He pushed off, and suddenly I could breathe again, now that there were a few feet between us.

I glanced to where we came from, that path clear. Maybe if I just—

"Don't think about running," he said, gazing at me through half-lidded eyes, his pupils dilated.

I lifted my chin. "And what if I did?"

He smirked, eyes tracing down to the flimsy skirt barely brushing against the tops of my thighs. "Unless you want me to chase you."

My cheeks turned aflame at the notion.

I wished he would just get it over with. Press me against the wall and drain me. I'd only been back in Vince's life for a few weeks. He had all the time in the world to move on, to find someone else to love, and I could be just the girl he thought of fondly from his youth.

Marcel pulled open a stone door, the lock busted and hanging as though it'd been forced open not too long ago.

The mausoleum.

The color of rust streaked the stone, a deep red stain that soaked through. In the moonlight, I couldn't tell if the dark liquid had spilled on the ground as well—and I didn't want to know what dark liquid that was.

"Come on," Marcel said, holding the door open.

He watched me, eyes narrowing, and I knew if I turned and ran, he'd bring me to the ground just as Dixon had Vince.

And he really wouldn't hold back this time.

It was a truth I felt in my bones.

All my thoughts turned to just hours ago—my time with Vince. Whatever coursed between us was palpable; I felt it every time he was within me, a heat rushing through my veins. We were made for each other, but maybe we were truly star-crossed. I told him I'd go to Flora's. I lied to him. And the relief he'd felt at those words...

It was an utter betrayal.

It was my fault this all happened.

Maybe if I hadn't insisted on being useful, on being bait, Marcel would be dead by now.

I glared at him, vowing if I didn't end up dead at the end of this, Marcel would.

He raised a brow and motioned toward the door. "Now."

But once I was on the threshold, I saw it wasn't a tomb —it was a staircase leading down. There were no lights here, just a pit of darkness, the first step or two illuminated by the soft light of the night.

Everything within me told me to turn and bolt, to try my best to get away.

Marcel's hungry stare burned into my back, his body just behind mine.

"What is this?" A musty smell wafted up. Images of half-decayed bodies hanging out of their coffins shot through my mind. Vampire creatures so crazed for blood, they no longer looked human. Vines growing from the earth to wrap around me and drag me down.

"You'll see soon enough." Marcel moved closer. "Go."

My throat ached with all the emotions bottled up inside me.

A cobweb was strewn across the step. The whole interior was dusty, dead mice in a corner. The walls on either side appeared to hold shelves, but no caskets, no name plates. Like this tomb was abandoned. It'd been created as a facade for whatever lay beneath.

I took a tentative step and heard Marcel sigh behind me.

I should've told Flora how much she meant to me, how I always felt we were like sisters. And I should've told my mother exactly what I thought of her, should've told her everything I'd been doing these past few years, just to see her expression.

But most of all, I should've said the words to Vince more often: *I love you.*

Marcel crowded me in, his body a moving wall behind me, as he forced me down the stairs.

The air was damp, warm. I coughed, the humidity thickening the air until it became hard to breathe.

We were walking into straight darkness and I couldn't see anything. I felt for the walls on either side.

A voice echoed up from the darkness. Indeterminable.

Someone waiting below.

But it was nothing like the moan I'd heard when I was in the garden last.

This time—

I gasped. Stopped in my tracks.

Icy fear rushed down my spine.

"No."

Turning, I tried to find Marcel in the darkness, reaching for him. My eyes widened against the perpetual blackness in front of me.

"No, *please.*"

"Please, what?" He grabbed my arms, turning me back around.

"I can't—You can't make me go down there. *Please,*" I begged.

He purred in the inky darkness. "I do like hearing that word come out of your mouth."

More tears built up in my lashes, but this time I let them fall. "I'll do anything."

"Anything?" His fingers brushed my chin, a phantom's touch. The ghost of his thumb along my cheek.

The voice below didn't stop, a low murmur that echoed up the stone stairway. Every muffled word a stab to my heart.

There was possession in Marcel's touch, a familiarity. Like he'd gotten what he wanted all those weeks ago. I let him. Let him run his finger along my lips, let him curl his hand into my hair. Pulling me closer to him, while hot tears streamed down from my eyes.

First Vince, now...

His hand tightened in my hair, forcing my head back. I stifled a cry.

In the darkness, I knew he was smiling.

"Too bad I have an agreement," he muttered, his lips almost brushing mine, the warmth from his mouth barely a centimeter away.

And he turned me around so quickly I thought I'd fall.

"*Go.*"

As we neared the bottom, a soft orange glow emerged from the darkness. An entryway into a room, where there was some sort of light.

And as we neared the bottom, I steeled myself against what was to come. Letting the anger settle into me. Reminding myself why I left. I thought about all of it—the betrothal to Wright Highsmith, Lucas forcing Adam to die, the way Lucas thought he could control me.

Didn't you know Vince is the one that told Lucas to marry you off?

It had to be a lie. I couldn't wrap my head around it, couldn't fathom *why* he would do that.

It didn't matter, not in this moment.

I reached the bottom of the steps, Marcel at my back. The orange lamplight washed over my feet.

The voice—no, there were *two* voices—hushed.

And as I stepped into the room, my heart a steady rhythm in my chest, I gazed upon my brother, sitting, waiting.

Lucas turned to me, and those eyes, so much like mine, yet so much darker, glistened.

"Hello, Helena."

Acknowledgments

First and foremost, this book would not have happened without the support of my partner, Trey, to whom this book is dedicated. You have always believed in me, even when I didn't believe in myself. Thank you for letting me bounce ideas off of you, thank you for pushing me to finish, thank you for giving me the space to put all my energy into this project, and thank you for being so, so understanding—I love you more than anything.

Thank you to my cover artist, Dayna Watson, for collaborating with me and making my book beautiful. I seriously catch myself staring at the cover all the time!

Thank you to Maggie, Ava, Minna, and many others who've supported my writing journey, many of whom watched me finish my first novel in seventh grade.

And thank you to everyone who has given my debut a chance 🖤

About the Author

Shaye Madison writes dark and stormy romances, and when she isn't lurking around bookstores and drinking iced chais, she's conjuring up gothic fantasy worlds she (sometimes) wished she lived in. Based in North Carolina, she lives with her partner and their cat, Phoebe. Red Masquerade is her debut novel.

instagram.com/shaye_madison

threads.com/@shaye_madison

www.ingramcontent.com/pod-product-compliance
Lightning Source LLC
Chambersburg PA
CBHW031836310726
48972CB00005B/1308